Raised in  s bestselling au   n New Orleans, where she now lives with her husband and two sons. She has won several awards for her fiction in the US and her books have been turned into graphic novels and a daytime drama in Japan.

For more information about Erica visit her website www.ericaspindler.com, follow her on Twitter (@Erica Spindler) or look her up on Facebook: (www.facebook.com/EricaSpindler).

Also by Erica Spindler

The Final
Seven

Erica Spindler

sphere

SPHERE

First published in the United States in 2016 by St Martin's Press
First published in Great Britain in 2016 by Sphere
This paperback edition published in 2016 by Sphere

1 3 5 7 9 10 8 6 4 2

A CIP catalogue record for this book
is available from the British Library.

ISBN 978-0-7515-6293-4

Typeset in Sabon LT Std by Palimpsest Book Production Limited,
Falkirk, Stirlingshire
Printed and bound in Great Britain by Clays Ltd, St Ives plc

Sphere
An imprint of
Little, Brown Book Group
Carmelite House
50 Victoria Embankment
London
EC4Y 0DZ

An Hachette UK Company
www.hachette.co.uk

www.littlebrown.co.uk

For the many angels in my life

ACKNOWLEDGEMENTS

Thanks to the many folks who had a part in bringing *The Final Seven* to life. This series was a long time coming, and a great number of people spent time with me and my Lightkeepers: assistants, agents, family and friends.

A special shout out to assistants Misty Dixon and Peg Campos; writing gal pals Alex Kava and J.T. Ellison; beta readers Deb Carlin, J.T. Ellison, and Kathy Kirby. Thanks also to my agent Scott Miller and all the folks at Trident Digital Media & Publishing – what an awesome team! And finally, gratitude, appreciation and unending love to my husband and sons, my personal Lightkeepers.

Prologue

Angel Gomez hurried across the Tulane University campus. She shouldn't have let Fran talk her into this. *A rockin' party*, her friend had promised. *Not to be missed*.

Instead, Fran had slipped off with a sketchy-looking dude, leaving Angel alone with a bunch of drunken fraternity types. Their antics had annoyed her and she'd been bored out of her mind.

Then her side had begun to hurt. Not an ache; a burning sensation – on her left side, directly over her latest tattoo. She'd scurried for the bathroom to check it in the mirror.

Nothing. No sign that anything was wrong with it. Why did she even try to fit in? She never had and

1

never would. Even the nuns had said so. She was too much of a weirdo.

Her side still burned and she brought a hand to the spot. Fran's desertion had left her with no ride home. Angel stopped a moment to get her bearings.

She figured she could catch the St Charles Avenue Streetcar at Broadway and ride it all the way downtown. From there she could duck into the Quarter and home.

Angel crossed from Tulane University's campus onto Newcomb College's. The quad was deserted. Dark, except for the dim glow of the lamplights.

But she wasn't alone.

The hair at the back of her neck prickled. She glanced quickly over her shoulder. She swept her gaze over the area, the line of trees and shrubbery that bordered its edges. Nothing. Just the dark silhouette of the statue at the center of the quad, the spotlight on it casting a long, oddly shaped shadow.

Like a B-movie monster, she thought staring at it, half expecting it to rise up, take on three-dimensional form.

Get a grip, Angel, she scolded herself. A couple of the frat boys had followed her, hoping to scare her. *Immature assholes.*

She increased her pace anyway, moving closer toward the edge of the yard and the buildings that circled it. A sudden breeze stirred the trees and Angel shuddered, gooseflesh racing up her arms. A chill wind in July? Impossible. Yet here she was, feeling cold clear to the bone.

2

She must be getting sick, she thought, bringing a hand to her head. The pain from earlier, the chill now. The flu? Angel hoped not. She didn't have the time or money to—

She caught a movement from the corner of her eyes. She stopped and turned. 'Who's there?' she called. 'It's not funny. You're just being stupid.'

The foliage rustled in response. The tree limbs above her groaned. The pain in her side intensified.

Whimpering, she glanced back at the statue once more, its shadow.

Longer. Deeper. Stretching toward her. Reaching . . .

She brought a hand to her head. She didn't feel right, she realized. Light-headed. Tingly, as if she had been sucked into a bubble of static electricity. Save for her tattoo. The symbol she'd dreamed in pieces: a heart being eaten from within by fire, surrounded by seven constellations. She'd had it tattooed onto her left side. To join the others.

Angel blinked, working to clear her mind. This wasn't the flu. She'd been drugged. At the party. Something in her cola. The frat pack had thought it a hoot that she didn't booze. But she hadn't set it down, had she? Left it unattended?

When she went to the bathroom, she remembered. To look at her tat.

Another movement from the corners of her eyes. A stirring. A sound with it.

Run!

She responded to the voice in her head. Zig-zagging. Heart thundering. A black cloud passed overhead. A

3

bird, she thought. Prehistoric. Giant wings, a creaking sound, like new, stiff leather.

No matter which direction she went, it followed. Hanging above her, a bird of prey.

That way! Right.

She turned sharply, stumbled across a planting bed. Looking up, she saw a parking lot. Its safety light called to her.

Sobbing with relief, she raced for the light. Almost within its reassuring circle, it went out.

'No!' she cried. 'Help, someone! Please!'

At the far corner of the lot, a car door flew open, light spilling from its interior. A man stepped out. 'Here,' he called, waving her over.

Angel darted toward him. As she passed under it, the safety light flickered, then came back to life. She saw the man was young, twenty-something, fair-haired.

Her knees went weak with relief. 'Someone's following me!' she cried as she reached him.

'Where?'

'The line of trees,' she said. 'I didn't see him, but I heard him!'

He reached into his car and retrieved a flashlight. He aimed it toward the trees, then directed the beam across the quad.

'I don't see anything. You wait here, I'll go—'

'No!' She grabbed his arm, terrified for them both. 'Please. I just want to get out of here. I want to go home!'

'Ok.' He went around and opened the passenger side door. 'Climb in.'

She did. A moment later, he was behind the wheel.

And at that moment, she wondered if she was making a terrible mistake.

Angel hugged herself. 'Just give me a lift to the streetcar stop on Broadway. I've got it from there.'

He looked at her. He had the strangest eyes. Oddly bright. Compelling in a way she hadn't experienced before.

'I'll do better than that, I'll drive you home.'

'No, really. I'll take the streetcar.'

'It's nearly three A.M. I'm driving you.'

He shifted into reverse and backed out of the spot. She noticed the safety light had gone out again.

Angel clasped her hands in her lap. 'Look, my mind's probably playing tricks on me, it does that a lot. My friend ditched me for a guy and I—'

He stopped the car. His bright gaze pinned her once more. 'I'm driving you home.'

Getting into a car with a stranger then giving him her address was about as stupid as it got.

But something in his gaze seemed to reach inside her.

You can trust me.

Trust me, Angel.

His voice in her head. Clearly. The same voice that had told her to run, which way to go.

She blinked. This was nuts. She'd been drugged and was hallucinating. Or was sick with fever.

It's going to be all right, Angel. You're safe with me.

Is this really happening? she thought.

Yes, Angel, it is.

She pressed her lips together. *Who are you?*

I'm Eli. One of your brothers.

5

1

Detective 'Micki' Dee Dare had gotten the call just as she'd been about to step into the shower. The brass wanted her downtown, ASAP. She'd been forced to resort to what her snake-bit family called a whore's bath, then pull her unruly mass of dishwater blond hair back into a quick ponytail.

Her family. What a joke. Mama, Grandma Roberta, and Aunt Jo – all three crazy. Not certifiable. No, just deep, southern-fried nuts. Baked by the sun and awash in sweet tea and sloe gin.

And hulking Uncle Beau. Silent as he crept down the hall, given away by the smell of cheap cigars and Kentucky bourbon. The combination still had the ability to turn her stomach.

It was no wonder she was such a frickin' mess.

7

'Sorry, Hank,' she muttered, her friend's deep drawl filling her head: *You're no mess, girl. You're a work in progress, just like the rest of us.*

Hank, taken from her by a bad ticker. She'd always found his death cruelly ironic. That big, kind heart, the thing that had made him the only wholly decent person she'd ever met, was the same thing that killed him.

Micki drove her '71 Nova 396 V into the Broad Street lot reserved for NOPD. The wheels had been Hank's – a broken-down hulk he'd hauled home from a junk yard with the dream of restoring it to its former glory.

She had fulfilled that dream for him. And as she had, weirdly, she'd rebuilt her own life as well, with his deep, steady voice guiding her, encouraging her. It was because of him she'd become a cop.

The Nova was more than a means of transportation; it was her pride and joy. Her baby. She freaking loved this car.

Micki parked and climbed out. Her commander had sounded choked. Really off. She hoped to hell she wasn't walking into PID ambush. The Public Integrity Division investigated claims of abuse against NOPD officers, not that she had anything to hide, but shit happened every day.

Inside headquarters, she took the lobby elevator to the third floor. Major Nichols said he'd be waiting for her in Captain Patti O'Shay's office. She reached the office; the receptionist directed her to the war room down the hall. Feeling more than a bit queasy over the unusual turn of events, she headed that way.

Micki reached the room and stepped inside. Something was definitely up. Too many suits in the room. Some of them looking at her strangely. Very strangely.

She immediately found her superior officer. 'Major Nichols, I apologize for not getting here sooner.'

'Actually, you're right on time. You know Captain O'Shay?'

'Of course.' She nodded in the woman's direction. 'Captain.'

He ran through the introductions: Krohn, the Deputy Chief; Richards, community relations point man; and Roberts, FBI Special Agent in Charge of the New Orleans office.

The agent nodded. 'Excellent to meet you, Detective.'

Okay, nobody from PID. But the Bureau? WTF?

A sinking sensation settled in the pit of her stomach. 'You, too, Agent Roberts.'

Nichols motioned the chair across from his, though he didn't meet her eyes. 'Take a seat, Micki. Chief Howard should be here any moment.'

She did. Nobody spoke. A strange energy crackled in the air, and every so often she'd catch one of them looking speculatively at her.

What the hell was about to happen?

Chief Howard arrived, striding into the room – polished, confident and oddly exuberant. 'Where's Detective Dare?'

'Chief Howard,' she responded, standing.

He smiled broadly. 'There you are. Perfect.' He crossed to her, hand out. 'This is a big day for you. We're thrilled. Absolutely ecstatic.'

She took his hand. 'Thank you, Chief.'

Instead of the brief handshake she expected, he pumped her hand, then clasped it between both of his. He looked her dead in the eyes. 'I want you to know, we're expecting great things.'

'Yes, Chief. I just wish I knew for what.'

He laughed loudly, released her hand, and motioned the others. 'Take a seat, people.'

As expected, Chief Howard took the head chair. He looked directly at her. 'Major Nichols only learned of this assignment a couple hours ago, though we've known of the possibility for several weeks. Law enforcement is changing, Detective Dare. Starting today. And you're going to be a part of it.'

He paused a moment as if waiting for a response, so she gave him the BS he expected. 'Happy for the opportunity, Chief. I won't let you down.'

He leaned forward with unconcealed glee. 'Here's the deal, Detective. The government has officially acknowledged the existence of a sixth sense. In conjunction with the FBI, they've initiated an experimental program called Sixers. In essence, this program—'

'Excuse me, Chief. Did you say a sixth sense? As in, I can read your mind or move stuff just by thinking about it?'

'Yes, Detective, that's exactly what I'm talking about.'

She had expected him to laugh. Had expected everyone else to join in. She had been prepared to be the butt of a joke for clarity's sake.

She hadn't been prepared for this. She did her best not to look comically thunderstruck.

'As I was saying,' he continued, 'the Bureau has assembled a team of these Sixers, evaluated their—'

Chief Howard stopped, as if uncertain what to call their qualifications. Gifts? Talents? Super-powers?

'—abilities,' he finished, after a moment, 'then trained them at a specialized police academy. The first crop of recruits has graduated—'

'It isn't my birthday,' she interrupted, moving her gaze from him to her commander. 'Y'all know that, right?'

'Excuse me, Detective?'

'I mean, I don't know who put you up to this – or how they managed to get you involved, Chief Howard, but—'

'This isn't a gag.'

He looked dead serious – they all did – but no way this *wasn't* a gag. Sixth sense? Specialized police academies? It had to be bullshit.

'It's one of those TV shows, isn't it? That's how they got you involved. I know they're probably makin' a big donation to the department and I hate to ruin all that, but the gig's up.'

She stood and turned in a slow circle, looking for the video cameras. 'Stop rolling, y'all. C'mon out. You can bring in the next sucker.'

She expected a smiling show host and camera crew to magically appear. Maybe even theme music to sound or confetti to fall.

Something other than this toilet-paper-stuck-to-the-bottom-of-your-shoe awkwardness.

11

Major Nichols broke the silence. 'You'd better sit back down, Micki. This is the real deal.'

Stunned, she sank back to her seat. 'My apologies, Chief,' she said. 'But I've got to be honest, y'all are starting to freak me out.'

He chuckled. 'I reacted the same way. In fact, it took a bit longer for them to convince me my wife wasn't behind it.' He leaned forward, hands folded on the table in front of him. 'This is some pretty far-out stuff, but it's happening. The first crop of recruits has graduated. An even dozen.'

He paused as if for dramatic effect. She wanted to tell him to get on with it, but figured that'd go over as well as a fart in church.

'The NOPD has been selected as one of the inaugural PDs to receive a recruit. He's being assigned to the Eighth. Congratulations, Detective Dare, you have a new partner.'

Micki stared at him. *No way he meant . . . he couldn't be saying—*

'You'll be meeting him shortly. Detective Zach Harris.'

As what he was saying sank in, she shot to her feet. 'With all due respect, Chief, hell no. Absolutely not.'

'It's done, Detective.'

She looked at the major for help, but saw none would be coming. She was on her own here. 'Again, with all due respect, Chief Howard, find someone else.'

'You're their choice, Detective Dare. Not mine. I suggest you consider it an honor. I do.'

'An honor,' she repeated. 'I don't see how—'

'You have the opportunity to make history here,' Howard said. 'As do we all. You'll not jeopardize that.'

Nichols spoke up. 'Sixers are being paired with tough, experienced cops. Part of your responsibility will be to keep your Sixer safe from harm. The government's spent too much time and money training him to have him killed by some street thug or gangbanger.'

Retorts jumped to her tongue, ones about being a glorified babysitter. The look in Major Nichols' eyes told her to keep them to herself.

'What kind of cop is this guy?' she asked. 'What's his service record?'

'He has no service record, Detective.'

'I don't understand. If he has the rank of—'

Then she did. 'He graduated from his hocus-pocus academy with the rank of Detective. That's what you're saying, isn't it?'

She saw from their expressions that she'd guessed correctly. It pissed her off. Big time. She, like every other sworn officer in the room, had worked for her rank, paying her dues by putting her life on the line every stinking day.

'Son of a bitch. Does he even know how to use a firearm?'

Chief Howard ignored her question. 'The Sixers program is top secret. No one other than those personally involved are to know anything about it. Beyond this room, Detective Harris is just like every other officer on the force.'

It took a moment for the ramifications of that to

sink in. When they had, she shook her head. 'How do I explain him?'

'You don't, Detective. Your partner moved up and we paired you with Harris.'

'Let me get this straight. Carmine's promoted. But instead of replacing him with someone from within, you've imported this Harris dude.'

'Correct.'

She shook her head. 'There're going to be some mighty pissed-off folks. Off the top of my head, I can name a half dozen deserving candidates in the Eighth alone.'

'That's not your concern.'

But it was because she was part of the team. 'Since the truth's not an option, what's the official story? And it better be good, or my partner's going to have a great big bullseye on his back.'

Captain O'Shay spoke up. 'I can help you with that, Detective. He has connections to the force.'

Micki looked her way. Patti O'Shay had broken down a lot of NOPD walls, making it easier for the next generation of women cops. Like her. There were those who had whined 'nepotism', pointing to O'Shay's familial ties to the force, including that of her husband, Sammy. The naysayers, in Micki's opinion, suffered from sour grapes. Patti O'Shay had earned her rank, every bit of it.

'What connections?' Micki asked.

'Me.'

'I don't understand.'

'Sammy had a younger sister, Erin. At seventeen, she

ran off with her boyfriend. At eighteen she had a child, a boy.'

'Zach Harris?'

'That's the story we're using. She put him up for adoption.' O'Shay passed Micki a file folder. 'Unknowingly, he followed in the family footsteps and became a cop.'

'Nice scenario so far. How did you find him?'

'He found us. Searching for his roots.'

'And his mother?'

'He hasn't located her yet.'

Micki flipped open the file. The best lies contained elements of truth. The more elemental those truths, the more believable the lie. Truth: Sammy O'Shay, like his wife, had been a captain. During Hurricane Katrina, he'd been killed in the line of duty. Also true: he'd had one brother, Sean, who'd retired the force shortly after. He and his wife had moved to Florida.

And, obviously, the third truth had to do with the sister. Micki nodded. 'Sammy really did have a sister named Erin who ran away at seventeen.'

Captain O'Shay nodded. 'She was wild, always getting in trouble. When she ran off, she was pregnant. Or so she said.'

'Sammy never tried to find her?'

'He and Sean both did. Without luck.'

'What do you really know about her child?'

'Nothing. We don't even know if she actually gave birth.'

'And the adoption angle, that's part of the fabrication?'

'Not entirely. Detective Harris was, himself, adopted.

15

All he knows about his birth mother is she was young and from the south.'

Micki let that sink in a moment. 'And Carmine's promotion – you pulled strings.'

'Yes.' Captain O'Shay paused. 'So you see, I'll be the one with a bullseye on my back.'

But Harris would, too, Micki knew. Without a doubt. And depending on her level of involvement, so would she.

'With all due respect, Chief Howard, this blows.'

A hint of a smile touched his lips. 'Welcome to the Sixers program, Detective Dare. We'll give you an hour to familiarize yourself with your role. The real party starts after that.'

'The real party?'

'When your Sixer arrives.' He stood. 'Congratulations. The future begins now.'

2

Micki stopped Major Nichols on his way out. 'Could I have a word in private?'

She imagined that in his heyday, Frank Nichols cut a formidable figure. He topped six feet three inches and had the shoulders of a professional football player. Although more paunch than punch now, his physical presence still demanded respect.

To hell with all that, she was fighting mad. And when Micki Dee Dare got mad, smart folks took heed.

'This is total bullshit!' she exploded when the door snapped shut. 'Did you really think I'd go for this?'

'I suggest you back down, Detective Dare. Now.'

She held her ground a moment, then took a step back, her gaze never wavering from his. 'Undercover in my own department? No. Absolutely not.'

17

'You've got your orders, Detective.'

His mildly amused tone infuriated her. 'I'm not the only one being jerked around here. You're talking about my family. The Eighth's my kin.'

'I'm on your side, Mick, but my hands are tied. This is bigger than you, me, or even this department. They want you, they get you.'

'Dammit! Why me?'

'I don't know for certain. As I understand it, they reviewed the service records of every detective in the Eighth.'

'What are my options?'

'I think you know.'

Go along with it or suffer the consequences. Demotion. The worst details, the shit sandwich brigade. Micki stood a moment, absorbing the truth of that, quivering with indignation and fury. At the Fed's arrogance. Chief Howard's disloyalty. At her own helplessness.

She wore none of those well, and for a moment thought of quitting – handing Nichols her gun and badge, then giving the lot of them the bird on her way out.

But where would she go? This was it; it was what she did. Who she was.

'What about Carmine?' she asked.

'Don't worry too much about Detective Angelo, he's Cold Case squad now. He got his dream job.'

'Fucking wonderful.' She rolled her shoulders. 'Lucky me, Sideshow Mick.'

'That's the way it is.'

'I still don't get it. Why me? It doesn't make sense.'

He lowered his voice. 'I think the bigger question here is, why New Orleans?'

'I don't follow.'

'If Sixers fails, they blame it on us. Not on their *brilliant* idea. Face it, to a lot of the country the NOPD is still the face of Katrina. The Danziger Five. The chaos outside the Convention Center and the wild rumors from inside the Superdome. To a lot of folks, New Orleans is a drunken, dirty, amoral city with one of the highest crime rates in the country. A place that's a whole lot of fun to visit but they sure as hell wouldn't want to live here.'

She nodded, understanding. 'The rest of the country expects us to screw up anyway.'

'That's my thinking. The Bureau's covering all bases but keeping expectations low.'

That ticked her off. New Orleans may be flawed, but it was her home; the NOPD might not be her blood, but it was the only family she had.

'I'm not a sideshow after all,' she said. 'I'm a sacrificial lamb.'

'Not necessarily. Yes, they won't hesitate to throw you under the bus, but they genuinely want this to work. For whatever reasons, they decided you're their best bet for success.'

Micki let her breath out in a huff. All right, then. She would do her best to make this whole blasted Sixer thing shine so bright it'd glow in the frickin' dark.

She caught him trying not to smile and scowled. 'You knew I'd respond this way.'

'Yup. And I suspect from reading your file, they knew it, too.'

She hated being predictable almost as much she hated being helpless. 'For the record, I'm not happy.'

'Noted. I'll see you back at the Eighth.'

Her cell phone, holstered to her belt, vibrated. Her friend Jacqui, she saw. She answered it but before she could say hello, Nichols stopped and turned back. 'It's not a total loss, Micki. Saw a picture of your new partner. He's easy on the eyes. Real easy.'

'Great,' she muttered. 'A pretty boy with *powers*. God help me.'

'Micki? You there?'

The call. Jacqui. 'Sorry,' she said, sounding as frustrated as she was.

'Bad time?'

'There've been some developments here. Is everything okay?'

'Everything's fine.'

Micki frowned. Four years ago she'd caught the then-seventeen-year-old, very pregnant Jacqui breaking into her neighbor's house in search of food. The girl had reminded her of herself at the same age – alone, hungry, and desperate.

Hank had been the one who caught Micki. He had been her guardian angel.

Micki had surprised herself. Instead of busting the teenager, she'd offered her a meal and, eventually, a place to stay.

'You're sure? What about Alexander? He's not—' Micki began.

'Zander's wonderful. Really.'

'Then why'd you call?'

Jacqui made an exasperated sound. 'I don't know. To say hello maybe? To hear your voice? Besides, I thought I'd catch you driving in. Obviously not.'

Micki laughed, the sound more sheepish than amused. 'Sorry. Like I said, developments. I promise, I'll call you back as soon as things settle down.'

Even as the words passed her lips, Micki admitted she had no clue when *that* would happen. She didn't need a psychic to tell her that, for the short term at least, her life was going to be anything but settled.

3

Zach Harris stood at his twenty-fifth-floor hotel room window. Below him lay Canal Street, with its streetcars and imported palm trees; beyond Canal, the beautiful decay of the French Quarter. The Mississippi River hugged the city's southern border, creating the crescent shape for which it had been named; from his perch, he could see a steamboat docked at the Toulouse Street wharf.

New York hustled and Los Angeles pranced, but New Orleans, Zach had learned, swayed.

A love affair had begun.

He smiled to himself. He was good at pissing folks off, and changing his reservations to arrive two days ahead of the FBI schedule had done that in spades. Parker, his Sixer point man, had been furious when he'd realized what Zach had done.

Which was too damn bad. Zach wasn't here for Parker's agenda. He was here for his own.

Parker had discovered him in a club. His offer had intrigued: become a part of an elite group of crime fighters, ones the likes of which the world has never seen outside the realm of fiction. A superhero of sorts. With a shot at fame and everything that goes along with it.

What guy didn't have *that* on his bucket list?

Besides, if he didn't dig it, he'd move on.

His signature move.

But this gig wouldn't be as easy to maneuver his way out of. He'd realized that the moment he stepped out of the New Orleans airport and into the humid night. A hum had settled into his head. A low vibration, like a radio between stations. The closer to downtown he'd gotten, the louder and more insistent the hum had become.

The city, talking to him.

He'd experienced this kind of chatter before. But not to this extent. It'd disoriented him, knocked him off balance. He'd felt drunk. Not a happy inebriated – not at first – but room spinning, unable to walk a straight line, head in the commode drunk.

Instead of trying to stifle it or hopping on the next flight back to the west coast, he'd faced it head on.

Hair of the dog, baby. Soak it up. Roar back.

And in the process, he'd fallen in love with the city. A freaking magical place, full of shadows and whispers, celebrations and despair.

And others like him. Many of them. More than he'd

23

ever sensed before. Zach turned away from the window. Did they know what they were, he wondered. Had they learned how to use their gifts? Or chosen to bury them?

Parker's arrived.

A moment after the realization, his cell phone pinged, signaling the arrival of a text.

In lobby. We're behind schedule.

Typical Parker. Few words. All business. Something about the guy made Zach want to mess with his head. Considering the thin ice he was already skating on, he'd resist the urge. For the moment.

Zach grabbed his jacket and headed down to the lobby. He joined Parker at the hotel entrance and together they walked out to a waiting SUV. Shiny. Black. The agent behind the wheel wore dark sunglasses nearly identical to Parker's. Zach chuckled and climbed into the vehicle.

'Something funny?' Parker asked.

'This vehicle. Your shades. His.' He motioned the driver. 'It's all such a cliché.'

Parker removed the sunglasses, pinned him with his icy gaze. 'Is this a game to you, Harris?'

He settled into the SUV's back seat. 'Define game.'

'After that stunt, I should pull you.'

'Do it.'

For a split second, he thought Parker might. Instead, the other man leaned forward. 'You son of a bitch, get this now. We make the rules. Not you.

We say get on a plane on the seventh at two P.M., that's when you get on the fucking plane. Not before. Not after.'

Zach knew he should acquiesce. Back down, go with the flow. But that voice couldn't compete with the part of him that had kept him on the edge all his life. 'Let's get *this* straight, Parker. You don't own me. This program doesn't own me. And right now, you need me more than I need you. That may change, but for now, get off my back.'

'Others are watching. Evaluating. You *and* me.' He paused. 'I've put my ass on the line for you.'

He got that. Zach nodded. 'Okay. Since it's your ass, I'll work at being a bit more considerate.'

No smile in response. No acknowledgement of the concession. Parker handed him a manila envelope. 'Everything you need is in there.'

Zach removed the contents of the envelope, then thumbed through the papers, stopping on a photograph of a blond woman in a police uniform. She had looked directly at the camera lens; the tilt of her chin suggested either arrogance or a chip on her shoulder; the serious set of mouth, that she meant business. He cocked his head. If she'd relax that beautiful mouth, she'd look a bit like a blond Angelina Jolie.

He tapped the photo and glanced at Parker. 'My new partner, I presume?'

'Detective Michaela Dare. Goes by Micki or Mick. Also Double-D or Mad Dog.'

'Mad Dog?'

'She has a temper and isn't afraid to use it.'

Zach laughed. 'Attractive woman.'

'She's along to protect you, not as entertainment.'

'You're no fun at all.' Zach tapped the photo again. 'Why her?'

'Hardcore cop. Ferocious. Loyal.' He paused. 'She's had to fight for it.'

'It?'

'Everything.'

Zach digested that. Compared it to his own life – everything had been handed to him on a silver platter.

Everything but one.

'Tell me more about her,' Zach said.

'She can't be corrupted.'

'Everyone's corruptible.'

'Not her.'

Zach gazed at her picture. Those straightforward brown eyes telegraphed honesty. The loyalty Parker had mentioned.

'Why?'

'She lives the job. Little social life, no romantic interest. Alienated from her few relatives. NOPD's her family. She decides you're good for the family, she'll protect you to the point of death.'

'Sacrifice herself for me.'

'Yes.'

The static in his head spiked. Zach closed the file. 'That doesn't sound too heroic on my part.'

'Leave the heroics to her. She can't do what you do.'

'And what if she doesn't think I'm good for the "family"?'

26

'That wouldn't be in the best interests of either of you.'

'Is that a threat?'

The rare hint a of a smile touched Parker's mouth. 'Not at all, Detective. Just keeping it real.'

4

Easy on the eyes didn't begin to cover it, Micki realized, as her new partner entered the conference room. Neither did pretty boy.

Zach Harris was knock-down gorgeous. Brown hair, streaked by the sun, with just the right amount of wave. The bluest eyes she'd ever seen. Brilliant, million-dollar smile.

Like that actor, Bradley Cooper. Better-looking, even. Although how that was possible she couldn't fathom.

Why couldn't he have been a troll?

He was accompanied by a dark-haired man in a suit. Put together, real slick. Carried himself like he had a steel rod for a spine. Or a corn cob up his butt.

FBI or military. She was guessing the former.

28

As she watched, Harris made a beeline for Captain O'Shay. 'Aunt Patti,' he said warmly, then hugged her. 'I'm so happy to finally meet you.'

Unbelievably good actor, Micki thought, noting O'Shay looked surprised as well. Effing brilliant.

If he could maintain that level of artifice and keep his story straight, this assignment might be less of a clusterfuck than she'd expected.

Harris turned. Looked straight at her. She saw his amusement and squared her shoulders. He could play this bullshit Sixer game all he wanted, no way she was playing along.

She smiled confidently and crossed to him, hand out.

He took it. Something about his fingers curving around hers felt too close. Ditto the way his gaze held hers. Startlingly intimate. But not in a sexual way. As if they really *knew* each other. Every secret. Their pasts, present fears, and future dreams.

As if he could reach into her soul.

For the love of God, Micki. Get a grip!

'Michaela,' he said softly. 'Good to finally meet you.'

Irritated, she freed her hand. 'Don't call me that again. In front of the guys, it'll blow your cover. And between you and me, I might have to hurt you.'

He laughed softly. 'I like you, Detective Dare. This is going to be fun.'

'What do you think we're doing here, Sixer? You think this is a game?'

'Of course not. This is serious, serious business.' Those spectacularly blue eyes crinkled at the corners.

'At your service, Detective. Ready to help catch the bad guys.'

'You've been misinformed. I don't need any help with that.'

He smiled again, real easy. Colored contacts, she decided. It had to be. Vain and cheesy.

'Some folks feel differently about that.'

He knew she was pissed and he was enjoying it. Son of a bitch was playing her. Pushing her buttons on purpose. Studying her reactions.

An angry retort jumped to her lips; she didn't get the chance to utter it.

'People,' Chief Howard called out, 'take a seat.'

They crossed to the table. Harris held out a chair for her.

'That crap stops now,' she said through gritted teeth. 'Got it?'

'Whatever you say, sweetheart.' He took the seat for himself, leaving her standing. The last one standing.

'Detective?'

Dammit. She nodded at the Chief and slid into the closest available seat, clear on the other side of the table.

The Chief began. 'Detective Harris, we're excited to have you on board. Agent Parker,' he continued, turning to the dark-haired man who had arrived with him, 'Welcome.'

Micki's lips twitched. *Corn cob, check.*

'I'll be brief. We all know our roles. This initiative is top secret, leaking any information to the press will lead to immediate dismissal. Detective Dare, you blow cover, you're out.'

Her get-out-of-jail-free card.

The agent's eyes settled on hers. She noted his were as brilliant as Harris's, only green. What was with these guys and colored lenses?

'Agent Parker, the floor is yours.'

'Good morning,' he began, his gaze never wavering from Micki's. 'Welcome to the Sixers program. Each one of you plays a very important part in this initiative. But none more important than yours, Detective Dare.'

He paused a moment, as if to let the weight of that sink in. He needn't have bothered. She was screwed and she knew it.

'The Bureau has a lot invested in this program. Protect your asset at all costs. From all quarters. The success of this project could determine the future of law enforcement.'

She held his gaze. 'From all quarters. What does that mean?'

'I think you know.'

'Spell it out, Agent Parker. I'm a southern girl. I believe in God, country, and dealin' from the top of the deck.'

'You back him up, no matter what the circumstance.'

'He screws up, I take the hit?'

'Yes.'

'Or the bullet?'

'Hopefully it won't come to that.'

'It comes to that every day, Agent Parker. May I ask you a question?'

'Of course.'

'Why so secretive?'

'Another question I believe you already know the answer to. The general public isn't ready for this. The media attention would make it impossible for our operatives to perform and for us to evaluate those performances.'

'Plus,' she said softly, 'if the initiative fails, no one's the wiser.'

'Damage control is costly and embarrassing.'

'Why PDs, Agent Parker? Why not keep the *assets* within the Bureau?'

He didn't blink. She realized he hadn't since their gazes locked. 'We've had Sixers working within the Bureau for several years. It's time we get them on the street and evaluate their effectiveness combating everyday crimes.'

'Sounds like you're looking to put me—' she motioned around the table '—to put us, out of work.'

He laughed, the sound silky. Too silky. *Sweet-talkin' men are serpents*, Grandma Roberta used to say. *Like the one in the garden, temptin' Eve.*

Micki should know, she'd given in to more than her share of them.

'Hardly, Detective. Harris is here to assist you.'

'So Harris here, using his "superpowers", finds us our perp, and we use legitimate science to nail him.'

'Excellent assessment, Detective. Law enforcement for the twenty-first century and beyond.' He moved his gaze around the table, then brought it back to hers. 'Each Sixer has different strengths and weaknesses. We plug them in accordingly.'

'Such as?'

'We prefer to keep that information as need-to-know. You'll be able to observe them in the field soon enough.'

She swiveled to face her new partner. 'What am I thinking?'

'Detective Harris doesn't read minds,' Parker said softly. 'He perceives events, future and past. Picks up the echoes of acts and feelings. Snatches of thoughts, past and present.'

'Pictures, sometimes,' Zach offered. 'Mostly like faded snapshots, though occasionally vivid. It's unpredictable.'

'Unpredictable,' she repeated. 'Now, *that'll* help me sleep at night.'

Agent Parker cocked an eyebrow. 'You're in a dangerous, unpredictable profession, Detective Dare. What does help you sleep at night?'

Parker folded his hands on the table in front of him. Something about the move translated amusement – and arrogance – to her. And it pissed her off.

She unclipped her service weapon from its holster and laid it on the table. 'Glock. .40 caliber, semi-automatic. A full magazine with a bullet chambered. Having a partner I can trust. One I've worked beside, depended on, and with the same training as mine. One who I know, without a doubt, has my back.'

Major Nichols cleared his throat – it sounded to her as if he was trying to hide a chuckle – but Chief Howard was anything but pleased. 'That's enough, Detective Dare.'

'Actually,' Harris said, 'I appreciate her honesty. And I don't blame her for being less than thrilled with this arrangement. She doesn't know me or what I can do.' He swiveled to face her. 'So, I'm going to be just as honest with her.' He reached across the table. 'Your hand, Detective Dare.'

She hesitated a moment, then laid her hand in his. He closed his fingers around hers. She experienced the slightest tingling sensation, as if something had passed between them.

His expression didn't change. 'You're pissed about this whole thing. You think this initiative is bullshit and you're furious you drew the short straw—'

She cut him off, dismissive. 'I think I've made that more than obvious.'

'—even though I am eye candy.' The corners of his lips lifted. 'You wish I looked like a troll.'

'This is ridiculous!'

She moved to snatch her hand away; he stopped her by grasping it more tightly. 'And I don't suggest you use that get-out-of-jail-free card.' He lowered his voice. 'It wouldn't work out so well for you. These guys don't play.'

He released her hand. For a heartbeat, she felt weak. As if the contact had sucked up all her energy.

The room went silent. She felt all eyes on her. If they thought she was going to go all giddy or effusive, they had the wrong girl. She squared her shoulders. 'Seriously? That's what you've got?'

Harris laughed. 'I like you, Mick. We'll get along just fine.'

Chief Howard stood. 'Detective Dare, you head to the Eighth. You and Detective Angelo will have a

34

chance to say your goodbyes and you and Detective Harris will officially "meet".'

'And if I'm asked, what do I know about him?'

'Almost nothing. He was transferred in from outside. He has a familial connection within the force. Follow his lead. Are we good?'

Follow *his* lead? No frickin' way. But she couldn't say that. She nodded. 'Yes, sir. Absolutely.'

They filed out of the war room. Harris caught up with her in the hall.

'For future reference, Mick, yes, I am.'

She drew her eyebrows together, annoyed. 'You are what?'

'Good in bed.'

He turned to walk away; she stopped him. 'If that was another attempt at your bullshit mind-reading, you're way off base. The way you perform in bed hasn't even crossed my mind.'

'I know.' He smiled, slow and sexy. 'But it will.'

5

Zach had known the minute he caught Dare's hand why Parker and company had chosen her to partner him – at least part of the why. Simply, she wouldn't let him in. Not easily, anyway. With some people, he could slip in, take a quick tour, and really *know* them – hopes and hurts, dreams and disappointments. Not Michaela Dare. She had erected fortress-like walls around herself, especially her soft spots.

And she wouldn't buy into his bullshit. Which would help keep him alive.

He was his own worst enemy. Had been from the moment he'd discovered he was different from other people and had learned how to use his special abilities. Step one: uncover people's secrets. Step two: exploit them. Not to hurt or destroy, but to manipulate and leverage – to advance his own agenda.

He just couldn't help himself. Why fight traffic if you knew a short cut? It just didn't make sense to him.

Zach reached the 8th District Station. He tipped his head back and gazed up at the iconic French Quarter building. Black wrought iron fence, tall French doors, white columns, salmon-colored stucco.

Home, sweet home. For now.

He climbed the steps; entered the building. The desk officer looked his way. Skin the color of coffee, dark eyes steely. He held her gaze, smiling slightly as he approached.

'Good morning, Officer.'

No smile. Nothing. 'Detective Zach Harris. Reporting for duty.'

'Identification.'

He handed it over. She inspected it, then handed it back. His fingers closed over it. *She'd dealt with it all and wouldn't take any crap off anyone. Taser first, ask questions later.*

And she'd had a horrendous morning already.

'Major Nichols is expecting you. Investigative Unit Office. Through the doorway to your right, take the stairs. You'll see it.'

'Thanks.' He held her gaze, smiled again. 'Have a beautiful day.'

'You, too,' she said, then frowned slightly, as if she'd surprised herself.

Zach headed the way she had directed, found the

doorway, stepped through. Like Alice down the rabbit hole, a bizarre scene greeted him. Where the entry and main floor public areas had been faded but charming, this was derelict. Peeling paint; years of it. Lead based, no doubt. Mold on the crumbling stucco walls. Dirty.

He'd thought being a superhero would mean nicer digs than these.

So much for glamour.

Zach reached the second floor. No security. None. Nothing. After Quantico, this blew his mind. White door with the NOPD logo and a sign that read EIGHTH DISTRICT, INVESTIGATIVE UNIT OFFICE. And below that: AUTHORIZED PERSONNEL ONLY.

Wow, that'd make the bad guys think twice.

He stepped inside. Activity. Noise. And energy – light and dark, a chaotic, swirling mess.

New environment.

Own it.

His gaze landed on the receptionist. No badge or gun. Civil service. Thirty-something, he'd guess. Attractive in an overblown, teased-up sort of way.

He sauntered over. 'Detective Zach Harris. I'm looking for Major Nichols.'

She eyeballed him. 'You're the new guy.'

'That's me.'

'You're pretty, I'll give you that.'

'Thanks.'

'Bunch of folks are pretty pissed about this.'

He cocked an eyebrow. 'This?'

'You. Being here.'

'Yeah. Well—' He lifted a shoulder. '—they'll just have to get over it.'

She laughed, the sound a cross between a bark and a cackle. 'You're partnering with Mad Dog.'

'Heard that, too. Any advice?'

She studied him appraisingly. 'Don't get on her bad side. Mad Dog don't take prisoners.'

'Good to know.'

'I'm Sue.' She held out her hand. 'And single, just in case you're looking.'

Zach took it. *A lot of pain. Hunger for affection.* 'I'll keep that in mind, Sue.'

'You do that.' She buzzed the major. 'Detective Harris is here. Yes, sir.' She ended the call and stood. 'He needs a minute. C'mon, gorgeous. Let's go find your new best friend.'

Zach followed her past a row of uncomfortable-looking chairs and into the maze of desks and bodies manning them.

'Mick,' she called. 'Your new partner. And he's super-yummy.'

The room went quiet. Folks peered up from monitors and out of cubicles. All gazes landed on him.

Not the introduction he had hoped for. But it'd do.

'Hey,' he said. 'Good to be here.'

Mick stood, looking grouchy. 'That's right, everybody,' she said, 'this is the guy who's replacing Carmine. Detective Zach Harris.'

The others who weren't on the phone or with someone stood and came over. A flurry of names. Mac. Killian. Rooster. Red. J.B. and Buster.

With the introductions came handshakes. Too many, and too fast to get any kind of a read on them. A sensory onslaught.

'Where're you from?' J.B. asked.

'California. Hollywood PD.'

'Hollywood?' J.B. repeated, eyebrows lifting. 'So, you took care of all the beautiful people? Wiped their fancy asses, so to speak.'

'So to speak,' Zach agreed. 'Tough job, all those tight buns.'

'Welcome to N'Awlins, Hollywood. Get ready to get your hands dirty. We deal with some real shit down here.'

'Bring it, dude. I'm ready.'

A grin spread across J.B.'s pockmarked face. 'You sure of that?'

'I look forward to it.'

'Dare,' Major Nichols called from his doorway, 'Harris. My office. Now.'

They started that way. 'Just so you're aware,' Micki muttered, 'J.B. can be a relentless asshole.'

'I got that.'

'Good. 'Cause it ain't gonna be easy.'

They reached the commander's office and stepped inside.

'Close the door,' he said. 'Take a seat.' They did and he moved his gaze between them, settling on Micki. 'Everything good so far?'

'Typical J.B. It's about to get stupid.'

'I have a nickname already,' Zach said. 'I figure that's a good sign.'

Micki rolled her eyes. 'Hollywood.'

Nichols' eyes crinkled at the corners. 'Let's cut J.B. off at the knees, shall we?'

Zach smiled. 'You give the word, I'll bring the chainsaw.'

He chuckled. 'Best way to get J.B. and his pals off your back is to earn their respect. Got a homicide. Corner of Royal and St Peter. Rouse's grocery. Around back, by the garbage bins.'

'Are you kidding me?' Micki popped to her feet. 'A homicide? Right out of the gate?'

'Why not?'

'Obvious reasons, Major!'

'Detective, what's the first thing you do when you get a new gun? You see how well it shoots.'

'But—'

'Discussion's over. Keep me posted.'

'No worries, partner,' Zach said as they exited the office. 'I promise not to puke.'

6

So much for promises, Micki thought, listening while Zach retched. He hadn't even gotten a look at the vic yet, just a good, gut-roiling whiff. At least he'd made it outside the perimeter. Nothing screwed up a crime scene worse than a steaming pile of vomit.

It was going to be a long frickin' day.

'Man, he's really sick,' said the first officer, handing her the log. 'I still remember my first time.'

'We all do, Strawberry.' She signed both of them in and handed it back. 'One way or another.'

Harris shuffled back over, looking embarrassed. 'Sorry about that.'

'It's cool.' She handed him a stick of peppermint gum. 'Most everybody does it, one time or another.'

He unwrapped the gum. 'Most everybody but you, I'm guessing.'

'Good guess, Hollywood.' Weakness wasn't an option, not for a blond with a big rack and southern twang. Not anymore, it wasn't. 'Ready?'

He nodded and they made their way back under the crime tape. She noticed the closer to the vic he got, the faster he chewed the gum.

'Does it always smell this bad?' he asked.

'Not always. You've got yourself a primo-stinko set-up here. Dead body. Loaded dumpsters. All of it cooking in the miserably hot July sun. Your stomach empty now?'

'I'm thinking yes.'

'Good. This ain't gonna be pretty.'

It wasn't. The vic sat in a crumpled heap, head resting against the side of the dumpster. Someone had put a bullet in his brain. It'd made a big mess.

She crossed to the body, studying it while she fitted on her latex gloves. She noticed that Zach had stopped several feet behind her.

'Meet Martin Ritchie,' she said. 'Also known as Marty the Smarty. Not so smart now.'

'Poor guy. What's his story?'

'Besides that he's dead?'

'Yeah.'

'He dealt drugs, pimped girls, and was an all-around piece of human refuse. This little weasel doesn't deserve your pity.'

'They all deserve our pity.'

Micki snorted. 'Let's revisit that comment in six months.'

'Six months the going rate on compassion?'

She looked over her shoulder at him. His gaze was fixed on Marty; his skin pasty white. 'Pretty much. What do you think happened here?'

He met her eyes. 'Beyond the obvious?'

'Yup.'

He took a moment, seeming to drink in the scene, his attention darting from one thing to another. The color, she noted, had come back to his cheeks, and he started toward her.

'Drug dealer, pimp, all around weasel,' he said. 'Plenty of reasons for him to be in this situation. If one of those got him killed, my money's on the drugs. Fits the statistics.'

The Bureau, it appeared, had made him do homework.

He squatted beside her. 'Shot looks clean. Bullet entered his skull here—' He indicated the wound on Marty's left temple. '—then exited back here. And down he went. Our UNSUB's a good shot.'

'Where was the shooter?'

He drew his eyebrows together. 'No gunpowder residue or tattooing, so farther away than three feet.'

Better than she'd hoped for. He got an A for listening in class.

'Check for his cell,' she said and stood, circling around the body to get a better look at the dumpster.

'No cell in any pocket,' he said after a moment.

'It may be under him. Leave it for the techs.' Micki

found what she was looking for – blood and brain matter splattered across the top of the bin.

'He was standing here,' she said, 'waiting for his connection. One way in, one way out.' She turned in that direction. 'Connection arrives, climbs out of vehicle, aims and shoots. There's no time for Marty here to lift his hands, let alone run for it. Down he goes.'

'Where's Marty's car?'

'Good question, Hollywood. My guess is he lived here in the Quarter. It's easier to get around on foot, even if it is hotter than hell.'

Micki backed away from the garbage bin. 'Shooter was most likely here,' she said, stopping at the beginning of the drive. 'Far enough in not to be seen from the street, but an easy reverse out.'

She glanced at Zach. He was staring at the mess that had been Marty, his expression strangely removed.

She snapped her fingers. 'Hollywood, you getting all this?'

He nodded, and she swiveled to survey the concrete pad: cigarette butts, rotten produce, stacked cardboard boxes. And winking up at her from the pavement, an expelled bullet casing.

She crossed to it, then stooped to get a closer look. Stubby. Brass. 'Forty-five-caliber shell,' she said. 'My guess is the gun was unregistered, maybe stolen. It's looking more and more like you called it. Props, Hollywood.'

She heard Zach's quickly drawn breath and looked his way. He had his hand curved around Marty's; he appeared to be prying something out of it.

'Whoa, Hollywood! Gloves, dude.'

The crime scene techs arrived. She'd worked with all of them before, but none more than Ben and she crossed to him. 'Welcome to my party.'

'Your party stinks.'

She laughed. 'Tell me about it. Vic was a small-time drug dealer. Thinking it probably got him killed. Bullet casing,' she said, pointing it out. 'Bullet exited the skull. With a little luck we'll retrieve that, too.'

They started toward the body. 'No sign of his cell phone yet. Be on the lookout for it—'

Micki stopped, realizing that Zach was gone. She looked around, frowning. 'Yo,' she called, 'anybody see where my partner went?'

The only female on the tech team answered, pointing toward the sidewalk behind her. 'The hot one? He went that way.'

Micki finished up with Ben and hurried in the direction the tech had indicated. She reached the sidewalk and stopped, scanning right then left. She caught sight of him two blocks down.

What the hell was he doing?

Micki started after him at a run. She didn't know which was worse: leaving a scene before it was processed or letting Boy Wonder out of her sight. Either way, Major Nichols would have her head.

'Hollywood!' she shouted when she thought he could hear. 'Wait!'

He stopped and turned. She reached him, sweating and out of breath. 'What the hell, dude? Where do you think you're going?'

'I can't talk right now.'

'You can't— The crime scene's that way.' She jerked her thumb in the direction they'd come. 'We're not done there.'

'I'm following a lead.'

'What lead?'

'I don't know. I've got to go.'

She grabbed his arm, stopping him. 'We're in charge of a murder investigation. The very first thing we do is secure and process the scene. We can't just . . . wander off.'

'You go back. I have to follow this.'

'Follow *what*?' she exclaimed, exasperated.

He opened his hand. A hotel room key. One of those cards with the magnetic strip.

The French Quarter Inn.

'It was in his hand.'

'And you took it?' She brought a hand to her eyes. 'You can't do that.'

'I had to.'

He's crazy. Off his fuckin' nut. 'It's worthless now. Contaminated. FBI didn't teach you anything about evidence and chain of custody?'

'Of course. But in this case, that's inconsequential.'

It took her a moment to swallow that one. 'You're dangerous, you know that?'

'We'll find what we're looking for at the French Quarter Inn. That's where I'm going.'

He started off. She hurried after him. 'Find what? The killer?'

'I don't know. Something.'

Something? Seriously?

The Bureau didn't have to worry about some gang-banger taking him out, she was going to do it herself.

She grabbed his arm, stopping him. 'Police work's not just about following hunches. The investigative process is meticulous, logical.'

He seemed not to hear her, and she went on. 'You may be a high-powered channel to Freaksville, but we'll need evidence to get a conviction. And if you expect me to save your ass, you need to play by my rules.'

'You finished?'

She sucked in a sharp breath. 'No.'

'Too bad. Because I really need you to shut up now.'

7

Monday, July 8
10:45 A.M.

Zach led the way. If he was like everyone else, he would say he was following his gut. Or a hunch. But this was more like being led. By turning off one part of his brain and turning on another.

He'd picked up the energy when he'd touched Marty's hand. It'd grown stronger as he'd pried the man's hand open. The energy, the memory, clung to the room key. Wordlessly speaking to him. Calling him to follow.

It was dark. Powerful. Like nothing he'd experienced before.

What would they find at the end of this journey? Or should he call it a trail? For that's what this was. Not epic. More like psychic breadcrumbs.

Leading to . . . something. It sounded crazy, even to him.

Micki was right. He'd broken the rules of investigation. Left the scene. Disobeyed his senior officer's command. Contaminated evidence. But he hadn't become a Sixer to follow the bullshit rules of those with only five senses.

The street dead-ended. And so did the energy. Gone. Nothing but static.

Zach stopped. He looked left, then right, confused.

'FYI, dude,' said Micki, not masking her irritation. 'Not a nice neighborhood.'

'I lost it.'

'Excuse me?'

'It's gone.'

Her expression was incredulous. 'What do you mean? You can't just "lose" it.'

He understood her frustration. He felt it himself. He was as deep into uncharted territory as she was.

'Try again. Otherwise we're heading back to the scene.'

He closed his eyes. Focused on his hand, the room key in it. The energy. Pulling it forth, as much by memory as sheer force of will. It gathered, swirled, raced up his arm. With the force of an ice pick to his skull, the static spiked. His eyes and hand popped open and the key dropped to the ground.

To the right.

'Harris? Holy Christ! Are you okay?'

He looked blankly at her. 'Fine.'

'That wasn't cool.'

'What?'

'I thought you were having a frickin' seizure or something. Your eyes rolled back in your head.'

That'd never happened before. At least he didn't think it had. Surely he would've freaked out somebody before now.

'Just trying to add a little levity to the moment.'

'Well, it didn't work.' She frowned at him. 'Don't do it again.'

'I'll do my best, boss. This way.'

They found the French Quarter Inn up a block on the right. More like the French Quarter Shithole, he thought, taking in the hotel's dilapidated facade: faux wrought iron, water-stained stucco, peeling paint.

He'd bet tourists who booked the FQI expected charming, three-star accommodations. Instead, they found this roach motel.

They entered. It felt damp, smelled musty. The kid behind the desk immediately pegged them as cops. He looked nervous.

'I'll handle this,' Zach said.

No way she was going to argue with that one. 'Have at him, partner.'

The kid's name was Vince. Judging by his pimples and pallor he didn't spend a lot of time outdoors. Video games and junk food, the twin curses of young America.

'Hey, Vince,' Zach said. He held up his badge. 'I'm Detective Harris. This is my partner, Detective Dare.'

He looked from one to the other. He stopped on Zach. 'What's up?'

'You know a dude named Martin Ritchie?'

He shook his head. 'I don't think so.'

'Marty the Smarty?'

'Never heard of him.'

Zach leaned on the counter. 'Look at me, Vince.'

The kid did. Zach held his gaze. It was a little trick he'd discovered in junior high. One that had lifted his grade point average in Algebra and gotten him a 'yes' out of Marisa Peabody.

'I think you do know him.' He lowered his voice. 'I think you know him well.'

The kid nodded. 'I do know him.'

'He's registered here at the Inn.'

The kid's Adam's apple bobbled. 'Yes. He rents by the week.'

'But he's not here right now, is he?' The kid shook his head and Zach went on. 'Did you see him leave?'

'I saw him leave,' he repeated.

'When was that?'

'Earlier.' Vince paused as if in thought. 'The beginning of my shift.'

Micki stepped in. 'What time was that? That you came on?'

Vince looked at her and the connection was lost. Zach kept his cool. Sometimes, the loss proved terminal, but it wouldn't this time. Not with this kid.

'I need to call my manager. I don't think he'd like me talking to you.'

'Vince,' Zach said. 'Look at me. That's right, you're talking to me, not her.'

Zach knew that wasn't going to settle well with Mick, but that was too bad.

'Actually, Vince, your manager's happy you're talking to us. He wants you to help us in any way you can.'

'He does?'

'Yes. He likes you, Vince. Thinks you're doing a fine job.'

The kid smiled. 'Really? That's good.'

'It's very good. What time did you come on last night?'

'Nine.'

'And that's when you last saw Martin Ritchie, leaving the hotel?'

'Yes.' He nodded as if for emphasis.

'Was he alone?'

'Yup.'

'What room is he staying in?'

'I can't tell you that. It's a rule. Besides, Marty wouldn't like it.'

'Here's the deal,' Zach said. 'Marty's not going to care. Because he's dead. Somebody shot him last night.'

'Somebody shot him?' the kid repeated. 'No shit? That really blows.'

'Yes, it does.' Zach held out the key card. 'Do me a favor. Tell me what room that key belongs to.'

He took it, ran it through the key reader, then handed it back. 'Room 412.'

'And that's Marty's room?'

The blood drained from his already pasty face. 'I can't tell you that.'

'But you already have.' Zach slipped the key into his pocket. 'Which way's the elevator?'

He pointed and Mick headed in that direction.

Zach smiled at the kid. 'That'll do it, Vince. You've been very helpful. Which you'll remember, by the way. And feel really good about. Have a great day.'

'You do the same, Detective!' Vince called as Zach hurried for the elevator.

8

Monday, July 8
11:07 A.M.

Micki held the elevator door for Zach. What she'd just witnessed had been damn creepy. It'd also been frickin' brilliant. The way Zach had held the kid's gaze had been mesmerizing. And when he'd talked to him, something in his tone had changed. She couldn't put her finger on what the difference had been – softer but deeper, warmer yet firmer – but the hair on her arms had stood straight up. It was like Zach had exerted some crazy mind control over the hapless desk clerk.

When Zach joined her, she punched the button for the fourth floor. The doors slid shut; the car lurched, then started to creep upwards.

'What the hell was that?' she asked.

'What?'

She felt him look at her but kept her gaze on the illuminated floor numbers. 'That hocus-pocus bullshit you just hit that kid with.'

'A technique I developed a few years ago.'

'Why?'

'Because I could.'

She wasn't amused. 'Your buddy Parker said your special abilities were "need-to-know". I need to know. Now.'

The elevator shuddered to a stop. They stepped off and turned right in unison.

'I was thirteen when I learned I could get the answer I wanted from people. It just took a little . . . finesse.'

'And what answers were you looking for?'

'The same one everyone looks for: a "yes".'

They reached 412 and stopped. She still didn't look at him. 'To what?'

'Anything. A dance. A date. An A instead of a C. Whatever.'

Micki processed what that meant. Who that made him. 'That was a lot of power in the hands of a stupid kid.'

'It was,' he agreed. 'It still is.'

He battled it, she realized. The realization wasn't all that comforting.

'You can look at me, you know.'

'My no-good, son of a bitch uncle used to have this saying: you can't keep a bird dog from hunting.' Micki looked at him then, eyes narrowed in challenge. 'I catch you trying to use that voodoo on me, I'll mess you up. You get me?'

'I get you.' He smiled. 'By the way, it doesn't always work. Some folks are too strong-willed. I suspect you fall into that category.'

'Don't test that theory.'

'I won't.'

She gazed at him a moment, uncertain if she believed him, then motioned the door. 'You gonna use that key, or what?'

A moment later, they were inside. Martin Ritchie had not been what you'd call organized. The place was a pigsty.

They made their way further into the room, a suite concept: bedroom and bath, a small living room, bar area with mini-fridge and microwave.

Micki decided the place gave pigsties a bad name. Fast-food wrappers and cartons littered every surface. A Popeye's Fried Chicken box with the remnants of the meal still in it, a pizza box growing something fuzzy and green, near-empty beer bottles Ritchie had used as an ashtray. Disgusting.

She looked at Harris. 'If I was going to sell drugs for a living, I'd do it to afford the good life. Not to live like . . . *this*. Just sayin'.'

'No joke. Bedroom or bathroom?'

She made a face. 'Give me another choice.'

'Sorry, I'm clean out.'

She chose the bedroom. Her search of it turned up nothing of investigative value: no drugs, weapons, little black book of names. Nothing.

Zach poked his head out of the bathroom. 'Take a look at this, Mick.'

'What the hell,' she said, stepping into the room. It was spotless. Even the towel hanging over the shower rod was perfectly folded.

'Marty used it as his office. Check it out.' He opened the cabinet under the sink. A small safe: scale, adding machine, plastic bag, the whole shebang.

Her cell phone went off. 'Dare,' she answered.

'Where the hell are you?'

Hollister. Coroner's detective. 'Hello to you, too. A few blocks away. The vic's residence.'

'That's unusual, detective.'

She glanced at her partner. He was staring intently at the safe. 'You have no idea. Start your thing, we'll be there ASAP.'

She re-holstered her phone. 'That was the coroner's man. He's waiting at the scene.'

She squatted down beside Zach. The safe had a classic combination lock. She reached for it.

'Don't touch that!'

She looked at him, startled. 'What's up? Marty wasn't the brightest bulb, I doubt it's booby-trapped. It might not even be locked.'

'It is. Locked.'

'All-righty then.' She sat back on her heels. 'What's your plan?'

'To open it.' At her frown, he added, 'Combination locks have a memory.'

'A memory?'

'And I have really sensitive fingertips.' He held them up and wiggled them. 'It's like magic.'

She cocked an eyebrow. 'Even *with* gloves on?'

'Crap. Right, gloves.' He dug them out of his jacket pocket, fitted them on, then flexed his fingers. 'I hope these babies still work.'

'You didn't explore this during your training?'

'Can't train for everything.'

Micki bit back the retort that jumped to her lips, and watched as he placed the fingers of his right hand lightly on the wheel. He closed his eyes and sat unmoving for long enough that she wanted to push his hand away and give the wheel a spin herself. Finally, eyes still closed, he slowly turned the wheel to the right, one full revolution, then another. He stopped, then spun it smoothly to the left for a full revolution, then again to the right.

The tumbler clicked and the safe door popped open.

'Un-fucking-believable!'

He grinned. 'Anybody ever mention you have a potty mouth?'

'Yeah. I'm working on it.'

'I hadn't noticed.'

'Fudge you, Harris. See?'

She peered into the safe. The contents were pretty much what she expected. Drugs. Cash. Gun. The holy trinity of small-time dealers.

What she hadn't expected was the stack of credit cards, driver's licenses, and a Louisiana ID card – issued to one Angel Gomez.

9

By the time Micki and Zach reported back to the Eighth, most of the guys were packing up for the day, talking about cold beer and a game of pool at Shannon's Tavern. CSI had processed the scene, collected evidence from the French Quarter Inn, and acquired video surveillance footage from the Rouse's grocery and other businesses surrounding it. Marty had been bagged and tagged and was now at the morgue, awaiting his turn on an autopsy table. She and Zach had canvassed the neighborhood, interviewed potential witnesses, and begun tracking down Ritchie's known associates.

She was hot, sweaty, and tired; she would give her right breast implant for an ice-cold beer and a cheeseburger. The left one, too, come to think about it.

But that wasn't going to happen. Crime scene techs had delivered copies of surveillance videos for analysis. It was gonna be a long frickin' night.

'Hollywood,' she said, pushing away from her desk, 'making a vending run. Want anything?'

He didn't respond. He had the New Orleans White Pages open on the desk in front of him and was scrolling through.

'Yo, Harris.' She snapped her fingers. 'Vending machine. Want something?'

He looked up. 'They have anything that's not crap?'

She arched her eyebrows. 'Seriously?'

'Bottle of water. Thanks.'

Micki got them both an H2O, and a pack of cheese sandwich crackers for herself.

Just as she was about to stuff the first cracker into her mouth, Major Nichols stuck his head out of his office.

'Dare and Harris. Now.'

'Saved by the bell,' Zach said, hopping to his feet. He plucked the cracker out of her fingers and tossed it in the trash.

'I can't believe you just did that. That's my dinner.'

'That stuff's poison.'

She shook her head. 'God help me, you're a health nut?'

'I prefer health advocate.'

'Just when I didn't think you could get anymore annoying, Harris, here you go and surprise me.'

He grinned. 'It's only because I care.'

They reached the Major's office before she could

express herself verbally, so she settled for flipping him the bird behind her back.

Micki heard him chuckle a moment before Nichols snapped, 'Close the door. Sit.'

Somebody's in a mood. 'Cracker, Major?'

She held out the pack. He refused, so she plopped onto the chair and stuck one in her mouth and crunched loudly.

He stared at her a moment. 'Have I interrupted snack time, Detective?'

She washed the cracker down with a gulp of water. 'Actually, dinner. But that's okay.'

He opened his mouth, shut it, then said, 'Update me on Ritchie.'

'Single gunshot wound to the head,' she said. 'Recovered the shell and casing from the scene. .45 caliber. Crime scene techs collected his phone and we're awaiting a list of calls made and received. Canvassed the neighborhood, nobody heard anything.'

'Thoughts?'

'Drug related. The Rouse's had several security cameras, one pointed at the alley leading around back to the dumpsters, another at the rear entrance. Angle takes in the area where we calculate the shooter stood. Harris and I have a date with footage tonight.'

'Anything else?'

'I anticipate a suspect by morning. And if all the stars align, an arrest by noon.'

Major Nichols steepled his fingers, then began rhythmically tapping them together.

Micki had seen him do that before. Steeple equaled stack – as in he was about to blow his.

Damn. He'd heard about her and Zach's roach-motel-side-trip.

'There's something I need clarification on.' His steely gaze settled on her. 'You took charge of the Ritchie scene, did you not, Detective Dare?'

'Yes, sir.'

'When in charge of a scene, what are your duties?'

Here we go. 'I think I know what this is about, Major. If you'll just let me—'

'Your duties, Detective?'

'Assure the scene is safe and that the perimeter isn't breached.'

'And you take those duties seriously?'

'Very. I can explain—'

'So, when I get a report that you and Harris left the scene unattended for forty-five minutes, I should assume that report is false?'

She'd love to throw Hollywood Houdini under the friggin' bus but, whether she liked it or not, they were partners.

'The scene was secure,' she said. 'First officer at the perimeter, CSI processing.'

'So you did leave the scene?'

'Yes, sir.'

His face turned an alarming shade of red. 'I might expect this inexcusable bullshit from some rookie, but not you Detective Dare.'

'I'm that rookie,' Zach said. 'It's my fault. She was following me.'

Nichols turned to Zach. 'And where the hell were you off to?'

'Following a lead.'

'A suspect?'

'No, sir. A feeling.'

Nichols' expression could've been funny. One of those OMG, LOL moments. The next million-view sensation on YouTube. Could've been if Micki wasn't afraid her superior officer was about to bust a blood vessel in his brain.

'A *feeling*?'

'More like an energy.'

Nichols began to sputter. Micki fought back the urge to laugh.

'Are you playing with me, Detective Harris?'

'No, sir. Chasing the intangible is what I do. That's why I'm here, getting the big bucks.'

He said the last lightly. With only a touch of arrogance. Neither would go down easy with Nichols. When the other shoe landed, Micki thought, it'd be squarely on her ass.

'We have procedures, Detective Harris. Surely, the boys at Quantico explained them to you?'

'Yes, sir. But I had no choice.'

'And why's that?'

'The energy is transitory. If I'd waited, it could've evaporated.'

Major Nichols massaged the bridge of his nose. 'Okay, I'll bite. And where did this . . . energy lead you?'

'Ritchie's residence. The French Quarter Inn.'

Micki spoke up. 'We found drugs. Distribution paraphernalia. Also stolen credit cards and driver's licenses. It's all been collected into evidence.'

'But not the shooter? Or a lead to the shooter?'

'That's not clear yet,' Zach said. 'I'm still working on it.'

For long moments, Major Nichols said nothing. Micki sensed he was trying to keep from going off like a bomb.

'Let me make this clear, Harris. I appreciate your special *abilities*. I'm on board with this whole Sixer thing. But you're here to assist *us*, not the other way around. And our job is to solve crimes and put the criminals responsible in jail. Mick here is lead detective. You follow her lead; you do what she says. Understand?'

'Sure. Got it.'

The major glared at him. 'Good. Get the hell out.'

He shifted his attention to her. 'You stay.'

The moment the door clicked shut behind Zach, he turned on her. 'I've no doubt you have a unique perspective on this,' he said. 'It'd make my day to hear it.'

'You want perspective?' She popped to her feet. 'The man's a freaking nightmare! How do they expect him to help solve crimes? He's chasing down feelings. Energy, for God's sake. What is that?' She crossed to Nichols' desk and glared down at him. 'I've been handed an impossible task – do my job *and* babysit the magic man. Yeah, I should have stayed at the scene. By leaving, I jeopardized its integrity. But I was also charged with protecting the FBI's new "secret" weapon. Am I right?'

'You are.'

'Exactly.' She rapped her fists on the desk, then straightened. 'He refused to see reason, so I made a judgment call. And if you don't like it, pull me off this detail. In fact, please pull me off. I'm begging you.'

'Sorry, Detective, not happening. Just do your damnedest to keep him focused. And don't screw up.' He indicated the door. 'Now, get the hell out of here and make sure he's not off getting himself in trouble.'

10

Monday, July 8
5:35 P.M.

Zach sat at his desk, studying the identification card he'd lifted from Martin Ritchie's place. Sleight of hand: another of his abilities not-so-otherworldly, but extremely convenient.

He'd tucked it into a zip-style plastic evidence bag. This card, this rectangle of plastic-coated Teslin, was what had drawn him from the crime scene. The psychic energy that had clung to the hotel key had been nothing compared to what clung to this. He'd felt it the moment he entered the hotel room.

Zach drew his eyebrows together. But what was *it*?

Black as midnight. Quietly thunderous. He'd felt the reverberations clear to his bones. With it had come an overwhelming feeling of dread.

He didn't want to feel it again.

Angel Gomez. The birthdate on the card – this past Saturday – put her at eighteen. She looked younger than that. And, oddly, older as well.

Long dark hair, warm-toned skin. Features she hadn't seemed to have grown into yet. Not Hispanic. Middle European. Gypsy, he thought.

What was it about her eyes, he wondered. He narrowed his, studying the photo. Something about them unsettled him. They were dark.

But they weren't.

How could that be?

Mick, coming from behind.

He nudged the card under the open phone book.

She stopped behind him, glanced over his shoulder. 'What's up?' she asked.

'Not much. I got the list of names from the credit cards and IDs in Marty's safe. Started following up on those.'

'I appreciate the initiative, Hollywood, but none of those folks killed Ritchie.'

'How do you know?'

'Because it doesn't make sense that they would have. Look, Marty lifted those cards without the owners' knowledge. So—'

'How?'

'I don't know for sure. Most probably pickpocketed them. There're other ways, but—'

'What other ways?'

She made a sound of frustration. 'That doesn't

matter. What does is, he acquired them anonymously. It happens every day in New Orleans and in cities all over the world. So it's highly unlikely one of these people murdered Ritchie.'

'But it's possible?'

'Anything's possible.'

'So humor me, Mick. What other ways, besides pick-pocketing?'

'Okay.' She settled on the corner of his desk. 'A guy like Ritchie, he probably has a network of contacts throughout the Quarter. Bartenders and waiters, valets, bellmen, maybe even hotel maids. They prey on tour-ists. He gives them a few bucks for each card or driver's license they lift.'

Zach nodded. 'And he makes a few more bucks selling the information.'

'Exactly.'

Zach got all that. But how had Ritchie acquired the Angel Gomez ID?

'Clock's ticking, dude.' She hopped off the desk. 'Can we move on?'

'Sure.'

She made a sound of surprise. 'Seriously? You're going along with me on this?'

'You're lead on this case. Major Nicholas was pretty clear on that.'

She eyed him suspiciously. 'Why do I have a hard time believing your sudden agreeableness?'

'Trust issues?'

He saw her fight not to smile. 'F-you, partner. Just

for that, I'll have to subject you to an evening of studying grainy video footage.'

He didn't have time for that. He needed to talk to Parker.

'Get set up. I'll be right there. Got to grab some eats.'

'Vending's on first floor.'

'Anything better, real close by?'

'Cafe Beignet's right next door. Pastries and stuff. And a sandwich shop, Monster Po'boy, just across the street.' She glanced at her watch. 'They might be closed.'

'Mind if I check?'

'Go for it. By the way, that search, you don't need a phone book. That's why we've got computer databases.'

He frowned, thoughts already on Angel Gomez, the nasty-ass energy that clung to her ID card, and what Parker would have to say about it. 'What?'

'Your search. The names.'

'Oh. Right.' He stood and grabbed his sport coat. 'I guess I'll need to learn how to log on.'

She laughed. 'I guess you will. Thanks, by the way.'

He looked at her. 'For what?'

'Taking the heat. With Nichols.'

'It was mine to take.'

She stood studying him as if he was a strange new form of life. Which he supposed he was.

After a moment, she nodded. 'Cool.' She started off, then stopped. Looked back. 'If Monster's is open, bring me a turkey and swiss. Dressed.'

'Dressed?' he repeated.

'Lettuce, tomato, mayonnaise.'

The moment Zach exited the Eighth, he dialed Parker. 'It's me. We have to meet.'

11

Parker had given Zach an address on Frenchman Street, in an area adjacent to the Quarter called the Marigny. He had also directed him to a vehicle in the police lot – a white Ford Taurus with more than a few dents. The key had been under the driver's side wheel well. Curiously, the Taurus' GPS had been set for the Frenchman Street address.

The street's vibe was eclectic and cool, a collection of restaurants, bars and shops with what looked like apartments and lofts located above them. Like so much of New Orleans, it was old, crumbling, and beautifully unique; more akin to a European city than an American one. It couldn't be more different than Hollywood.

The sound of a band warming up greeted him as he stepped out of the Taurus. Number 610 was located above a vintage bookstore. He found the entrance to the right of the bookshop and rang 2-B.

'Buzzing you in,' Parker responded.

He caught the strains of Vivaldi a moment before he reached the apartment door. Parker was nuts for classical music, and the Baroque composer was a favorite.

'It's open,' Parker called a moment before Zach knocked.

Bookishly hip. Open concept. Comfortably worn with a modern edge.

'It doesn't look like you,' he said to Parker, who sat on a stool at the kitchen eating counter.

'But does it look like you?'

Zach looked around once more and nodded. 'Yeah, it does.'

'Good. Because you'll be calling it home for now.' He reached into his pocket, pulled out a keyring and tossed it to Zach.

'We checked you out of the hotel and moved your things here. I took the liberty of adding a few personal touches.'

Zach crossed to the sideboard. Framed photos of him and his parents, his group of high school friends at the beach. He arched his eyebrows at the next: his graduation from the police academy, his proud parents at his side? He picked it up and turned to Parker. 'And this one?'

'Photoshop. You'll find other "homey" items through-out. I suggest you familiarize yourself with them.'

Next, Zach perused the built-in bookcases, scanning

73

the titles. His favorite genre, Science Fiction and Fantasy, was well-represented; many of them he'd read. Books on crime and criminal profiling, surfing and classic American cars. He looked over his shoulder. 'The only thing missing is the Bible I got for eighth grade confirmation.'

'Your bedside table.'

'You dudes are creepy, you know that?'

A hint of a smile formed on Parker's mouth, then was gone. 'In addition, in the entertainment center you'll find the complete Harry Potter, Lord of the Rings, and Die Hard movie collections on DVD.'

Zach grinned. 'Bruce Willis, greatest action hero ever.'

'By the way, the Taurus is also yours.'

'And here I'd hoped for a Aston Martin or BMW.'

'You're not 007.'

'A guy can dream,' he said lightly, fitting the Ford's key onto the ring. 'I don't have much time; we have to talk.'

'You pulled a homicide investigation.'

It wasn't a question. He answered anyway. 'Yes. A low-level bad guy named Martin Ritchie. Appears to be a drug-related killing.'

'That's not of interest to us.'

'I didn't think it would be. There was an energy attached to him. One like I've never encountered before. It led me back to Ritchie's hotel room.'

He had Parker's full attention. He took a pen and spiral notebook from his pocket. 'Hotel? Address?'

'The French Quarter Inn. 1120 N. Rampart. Room

412. There, I found this.' He drew the plastic bag from his jacket pocket and handed it over to Parker.

'This was the source of the energy?'

'No. But the energy surrounded it.' He paused. 'I need to find her, I think she's in danger.'

'She could be dead already.'

'She's not.'

'Knowing that's beyond your abilities.'

'She's alive,' Zach said again. He didn't know why he was certain of that, but he was.

Frowning, Parker took the card out of the bag and, holding it by the edges, he turned it over in his hands, then held it to the light. 'It's legit.'

'What does it mean?'

'Nothing. It's not important.'

'Not important? That girl's life—'

'Is not your concern. Your job is to aid the police in the capture of criminals.'

'What if I could prevent crime? Stop it before it happened?'

'You can't,' he said simply. 'Don't you think we've tried?'

Parker had found Zach because they were brothers. Not in blood, but in their true natures. Parker was a Sixer, too. The original, recruited and trained by the FBI twenty-plus years ago. Twenty-plus years of seeing what could and couldn't be done. Of heady successes and epic failures.

He had come to know Zach's abilities as well as Zach knew them himself. Better even.

Parker dropped the bag and ID onto the bar. 'We

have a finite amount of time to prove ourselves. If we don't, the Sixers initiative will be terminated. I'll run Angel Gomez through our databanks. If the card turns out to be a fake, the name probably is, too. In that case, we may get a hit with face recognition software.'

'How long until you have an answer for me?'

'Morning.'

Zach nodded. 'That'll do.'

'Tell me about the energy,' Parker said. 'Describe it.'

'Dark. Very strong.' Zach paused, searching for the description of what he'd experienced. Then it hit him.

He met Parker's eyes. 'Not passive.'

'Explain.'

'What I usually pick up is static. Like a frozen moment. Or the fleeting sense that something's happened. This energy was . . . dynamic. Definitely aggressive.'

Parker grew very still. 'Aggressive, you say?'

He nodded. 'What does it mean?'

'Let's see if it'll transmit.'

Parker crossed to stand directly in front of him. He held up his left hand, fingers splayed. Zach fitted his right against it, making certain the heels and fingertips connected. He closed his eyes – if he didn't, the process affected his equilibrium.

The first time they'd attempted the process, Zach had blacked out. The next, he'd thrown up. Through trial and error, he'd learned how to comfortably control the flow of sensory information between them.

Relax. Breathe deeply. Open a pathway. He was a conduit. Parker, a receptacle. It was some weird shit.

Weird enough that no one else in his graduating class could connect this way.

The tingling at the base of his skull told Zach the connection had been made and was a strong one. The tingle spread, until it engulfed his whole body. His pulse points warmed, as if the blood now racing through his veins had become molten. Heat exploded at the points their hands met, searing them together.

Zach felt Parker shudder. It rippled over him in a wave. One wave after another. The burning sensation became intense.

Breathe, Zach. Don't fight it. Let it go.

The burning became intolerable. 'I've got to break it,' Zach said.

'One . . . more—' Parker sprang backward, severing the connection. He grabbed the counter for support; he'd gone white.

'You okay, P?'

'Of course. I'm fine.' The normally unflappable agent dragged a hand through his hair. Zach saw that it shook. 'I see what you meant about the energy. Damn.'

Zach rubbed his still-burning hand against his thigh. 'I don't think it liked our sharing that way.'

'Don't give it human characteristics, Harris. It's just a kinetic memory. A strong one.'

Parker's color had returned; his tone once again brusque and businesslike.

'Ever experienced anything like it before?' Zach asked.

'No.'

'But you have an idea what it is.'

It wasn't a question, but Parker shook his head in response anyway. 'None.'

It felt to Zach like a lie. 'You hiding something from me, P?'

'Why would I?'

'You're FBI, dude. That's why.'

'You are, too, Harris. I suggest you don't forget it.'

'I'm here, aren't I?' Zach glanced at his watch and saw that nearly an hour had passed since he left the Eighth. 'I've got to get back.'

Parker nodded and together they exited the apartment. Zach locked the door behind them and they made their way down the narrow flight of stairs to the foyer.

They stepped out into the humid night. 'I'll hear from you in the morning, then? About Gomez?'

'Yes.'

'Good. Talk to you then.' Zach started for his car. When he reached it, he looked over his shoulder.

Parker was nowhere in sight.

12

On a scale of one to ten, Micki's headache came in at
a solid ten – a sanity-stealing combination of sledge-
hammer and screw vice. It hadn't been brought on by
hours of staring at the minutia of videotaped images, or
too much caffeine or junk food. This one was all Harris.

Almost two freaking hours. Where the hell was he?

*'Sure. Whatever you say. Major Nichols made it clear
you're lead on this case.'*

'I'm just going to grab a sandwich. Be right back.'

Hocus pocus poser.

And she was the jackass who had fallen for it.

She supposed she should be worried about him. After
all, he was her 'asset' to protect. Ironic, but if he had
been Carmine – or any of the other guys – she'd be
concerned for his safety. But they were real cops.

He wasn't. He was on Hollywood fiddle-fucking-around time.

Besides, if he got himself kidnapped or shot, it wouldn't be her fault. He'd been going across the street for a sandwich, for God's sake. Surely, babysitting him didn't mean every moment of the day or night? Did she have to follow him into the crapper? Watch him while he slept?

She dropped her head into her hands and massaged her aching temples. Why'd she have to pull the lucky straw? She'd worked hard to get where she was. This wasn't a game to her; it wasn't some out-of-this-world experiment.

It was her life. Her career.

Dammit. Thirty more minutes and she'd call out the cavalry.

Micki refocused on the monitor. Reviewing security camera footage was one of the most tedious parts of the investigative process. Tech folks couldn't do it because they didn't know what to look for. So it fell on the detectives, hours piecing frames together, establishing a timeline from the various time-stamped tapes, manipulating and comparing blurry images.

Even without another pair of eyes, tonight had been productive. In just two hours she had a face – albeit a grainy one – a vehicle, and a partial plate.

Take that, you mothers. Mess with Mad Dog Dare, you're gonna get bit.

Her phone pinged the arrival of a text.

I've got him.

She didn't recognize the number and frowned.

who is this

Hollywood.

Micki rolled her eyes. He really did like that nickname. She'd have to come up with something new. Like Annoying Bastard.

where r u

Bourbon

Bourbon Street. Of course he was.

get back here

Ritchie's killer is here. Before she could respond, another text arrived. No joke.

how do u know

I just do.

And that was supposed to reassure her? Micki jumped to her feet. Hollywood could do anything, crazy bastard. He had a gun, for God's sake. A shield and handcuffs. He was a danger to himself and civilians.

She pictured him arresting some poor sucker from

Topeka. The charges of police brutality and lawsuit that would follow. The truth about him leaking out.

And who'd be the one taking the hit for it? Not him. Oh, no. It'd be his hardworking partner.

She dialed his cell.

He answered. 'It was so cool – I bumped into him on my way to get sandwiches. Telegraphed the murder, clear as a bell.'

'Where are you?'

'The Bourbon Street Hustle. It's a club.'

'A strip club. Dude, really?'

'Not my choice. I followed the suspect inside.'

'Have you been drinking?'

'I don't drink.'

Figured. She'd thought maybe they'd have *that* in common. Made worse by the fact that she'd be doing a whole lot more of it now, because of him.

'Do not approach the UNSUB until I get there.'

'No worries, I'm being totally stealth here.'

She grabbed her jacket. 'I'm on my way.'

'Wait. What if he tries to leave?'

'Follow him, but do *not* make contact. Understand? You might have the wrong guy. And even if he is our guy, without back-up, you're putting yourself in harm's way.'

'He's our guy, no doubt. Oh, crap, I've got to go.'

He hung up and her heart lurched to her throat. Maniac could do anything. What, did he think bullets would bounce off of him?

She reached the Nova in record time. Called for assistance.

82

The Bourbon Street Hustle was located at 410 Bourbon. Fellow Eighth District Detective Stacy Killian had pulled an undercover drug task force gig there a few years back – a bartender dealing meth. Ended up becoming much more, typical Big Easy dust-up.

Micki reached Bourbon Street and turned onto it. Except for police and emergency vehicles, Bourbon was pedestrian only, six P.M. to six A.M. The cruiser had already arrived; it sat in front of the club, cherry lights spinning. She eased her way through the throngs of partiers, stopping behind the cruiser.

She climbed out. The patrolman headed her way. Joey Petron, she saw. Good guy, solid cop.

'Hang here,' she told him. 'Homicide suspect is inside the club. My partner has a bead on him.'

'You got it, Detective.'

Micki made her way into the club. The Hustle was just the type of establishment someone who did business with Marty the Smarty would frequent. Sleazy with a capital 'S'.

But she wasn't getting her hopes up. No way Harris could get this lucky.

She held up her shield for the bouncer; he rolled his eyes and motioned her inside. It took a moment for her eyes to adjust. When they did, she saw the Hustle's owners had tried to spiff it up a bit – mood lighting, potted palms – but a sticky floor pretty much said it all.

Welcome to the Big Crazy. No cover, one drink minimum.

Micki looked at the stage. The dancer shedding what

looked like a Catholic schoolgirl's uniform was forty if she was a day. *Seriously?* She wished she could bust somebody just for the suggestion that it was appropriate – let alone *sexy* – but the law only stretched so far.

She caught sight of Harris. He met her eyes, then nodded toward a big dude at the bar. Shaved head. Tattoo of a dragon on his neck. Piercings.

Micki studied him a moment, recalling the grainy image from the surveillance footage. The suspect in the footage had been wearing a ball cap. And not any ball cap: University of Florida Gators. Here in Tigerland, totally uncool.

She drew her eyebrows together. Was this the guy? Maybe. Would she have recognized him on the street, after only viewing the footage? No. But after a little crime lab image enhancement? She thought so.

Harris might be just that lucky.

Harris looked at her. She inclined her head slightly to let him know they were a go. The trick now was to approach the suspect with finesse, avoiding any kind of commotion. The last thing they wanted was a scene in a crowded tourist spot.

She started toward the suspect. Nonchalantly, she unbuttoned the first three buttons of her shirt, then tugged the elastic pony from her hair. The waves tumbled to her shoulders and, as if it was the most natural thing in the world, she fluffed them.

Plan A: Distract Mr Wonderful and, while he's staring at her tits, Hollywood cuffs him.

She tried to signal Harris. Unfortunately, he seemed

to have forgotten she was lead here. Like a nightmare unfolding in front of her eyes, she watched him pull out his shield and start for the target.

She darted forward. The perp caught sight of Harris. She saw him slide his hand into his jacket, going for his weapon. Harris was too green to even notice.

'Get your hands up, Baldy,' she shouted. 'Police!'

He jerked her way. She didn't know if she was close enough to take him down. She better be, she decided, and dove.

Pain shot through her side as she connected with the barstool. Glass shattered, folks screamed. She knocked Baldy backwards, sending them both crashing to the floor.

The landing knocked the breath out of her. It felt like she might have broken a rib. She supposed she should be thankful she hadn't just taken a .45 caliber slug, but she was too damn pissed off.

The stars cleared, she realized she was on top of the perp, breasts in his face.

'Nice jugs, pig.'

He was bleeding. She liked that. 'Shut the fuck up.'

Micki twisted him onto his side and wrenched one arm behind his back. 'You have the right to remain silent—' She snapped a cuff on his wrist. 'Anything you say or do will be held against you in a court of law—' She flipped him the rest of the way over, snapped on the other cuff. 'You have the right to an attorney . . . if you cannot afford an attorney, one will be provided for you—'

Backup arrived. Officer Petron, from outside. A

couple more of the guys. Cameras flashed. Micki suddenly realized what they were seeing. Harris, his weapon drawn, trained on the suspect. The picture of cool competence. She on the other hand, was on her knees, straddling Baldy, breasts spilling out of her half unbuttoned shirt, hair a dirty-blond rat's nest.

She looked like a crazy person.

She hopped off him and yanked him to his feet. 'Do you understand these rights as I have just read them to you?'

'What're you pigs bothering me for?' he whined as another bar patron snapped a photo. 'I'm just a regular Joe, out for a good time in the Quarter.'

'The murder of Martin Ritchie,' she ground out. *And Lord help me if you're not our guy.*

13

The squad room was unnaturally quiet when Micki and Zach arrived the next morning. Micki saw several heads turn her way, and she frowned. She was tired, cranky, and sported a bruise the size of a grapefruit on her right side. She was not in the mood to be screwed with.

They'd already met at headquarters and debriefed the inner circle. To describe Chief Howard as over the moon would be an understatement. Agent Parker had even cracked a smile.

Ballistics were a match; enhanced video imaging placed Baldy at the scene, and the partial plate number from the surveillance tapes corresponded to the tag registered to one Benito Dumb-fuck Alvarez. They had him dead to rights.

Not *they*, Micki thought. Harris. He'd come off

87

looking like Superman. But her? She'd looked like one of those female wrestlers from TV. All she'd been missing was a pair of Spandex short-shorts.

She'd even seen the proof. Oh, yeah, adding insult to injury, one of the club's employees had videoed the whole thing with his smart phone.

And posted it to YouTube.

However, even her sideshow antics – the chief's description – hadn't been enough to burst his bubble. The department's PR director had promised to handle it, and that had been good enough for him.

'Great job, you two,' J.B. said, standing. He started to clap. His sidekick Buster joined him. 'Record time closing that one. Almost like magic.'

Mick's heart skipped a beat. How the hell had those two clowns found out Zach's true identity?

'We'd love to hear how you pulled that off. Right, Buster?'

'Right, J.B. Every scintillating twist and turn.'

She opened her mouth to respond, but Zach stepped in, slick as oil in the Gulf. 'Good old-fashioned police work,' he said and took a bow. 'Hollywood style.'

Killian whistled her approval. A couple others chuckled appreciatively.

J.B. looked irritated and shifted his attention to her. 'What about you, Mad Dog? What style were you going for?' As he spoke, he turned his computer monitor toward her. A second later, there she was: lunging at the perp, connecting with him, the two of them crashing to the floor. 'WWF Smackdown? You've got the talent, that's for sure.'

By talent, he no doubt meant her breasts, spilling out of her shirt. Her thought was confirmed as Buster added, 'Big Shot Benito Alvarez taken out by Double-D, a pair of 'em.'

A round of laughter rippled over the squad room. Stacy Killian called out, 'You look good, girl. Own it.'

'I'll do that, thanks.' She'd like to 'smackdown' both the idiots, but kept her cool. 'You finished being stupid, J.B.? 'Cause I've got a list this mornin' and no sense of humor.'

'I don't know. I'm thinking we need one more look at you and your new boyfriend, Benito.'

Zach stepped in. 'She saved my ass, okay? So screw off.'

The room went morgue-at-midnight quiet. Micki looked at Zach, furious. Other women, weak women, needed saving. Not her. She opened her mouth to tell him so when Major Nichols stuck his head out of his office.

'Dare, Harris, now.'

She fell in step with Harris, stopping him at Nichols' door. 'Don't *ever* do that again,' she hissed. 'You embarrassed me.'

He looked confused. 'I was sticking up for my partner. Since when did that become a crime?'

'Since always. You made me look weak. I can take care of myself. I don't need you or anyone else stepping in to save the day, my honor, or whatever the hell you thought you were saving. Got that?'

'Got it,' he said tightly.

The major waved them in. 'I don't have all day.'

When they were seated, he folded his hands on the desk and looked from one to the other. 'Great work. Both of you.'

'Thank you, Major,' they responded in unison.

'Absolutely what we hoped for, in terms of your participation, Harris. And you,' he said, fixing his gaze on Micki, 'how're you doing?'

She'd prepared herself for something completely different. 'My side hurts, but other than that, I'm no worse for wear.'

'Glad to hear it.' He cleared his throat. 'Bad news. Your take-down video's gone viral.'

'J.B. and Buster have already made me aware.' She glanced at Zach. 'I can handle them, and anyone else who has a problem with it. Without help.'

If Nichols sensed the tension between her and Harris, he didn't acknowledge it. 'What was your primary assignment, Detective Dare?'

'Cover Harris's butt. At all costs.'

A hint of a smile touched the major's mouth. 'At all costs. This situation seems to fit that description. Congratulations.' He turned to Zach. 'Next time you might not be so lucky.'

'I have complete faith in Detective Dare.'

'Then show it! Dare leads, you follow. You do your mumbo-jumbo Sixer thing and let her do her cop thing.'

'Yes, sir. But—'

'You're not a cop. You read me?'

'Badge and gun say otherwise,' Zach quipped. 'Just saying.'

Nichols launched to his feet, face the color of a

freshly boiled crab. 'You compromised the arrest and put yourself and your partner in the line of fire. Unacceptable.'

'I get it, Major.'

But Nichols wasn't finished. 'Dare knows how to do her job. If you had done *yours* and stood back, she would have quietly snapped the cuffs on Alvarez. End of fucking story!'

Zach looked unfazed by Major Nichols' tongue-lashing. 'Understood, Major. From hero to zero, got it.' He slid his cell phone from his pocket and glanced at the screen. 'If you'll excuse me, I need to take this call.'

Without waiting for permission, he stood and left the office.

The major watched him go, expression so perplexed, Micki had to fight back a laugh. The truth was, he was stuck with Harris, just as she was. He could shout, threaten, or beg, but Harris could do whatever the hell he wanted to.

14

Zach waited for Mick outside Major Nichols' office. Parker had run Angel Gomez's social through the computer. She was clean – not even a parking ticket – and worked at a Central Business District diner named Teddy's Po'boys.

Next stop, Teddy's. With or without Mick.

He'd rather with. They were partners. And as Nichols had so elegantly pointed out, she was better at this cop thing than he was.

Bringing her along meant coming clean about Angel Gomez. She was gonna be pissed.

She emerged from the major's office, saw him, and stopped. She frowned slightly. 'What's up?'

'What do you mean?'

'Cat. Canary. Swallowed.'

She had him there. 'Ever heard of a CBD joint called Teddy's?'

'Po'boys, right? Never been. Why?'

'Got a lead. We need to pay them a visit.'

'A lead, Hollywood?' She fell into step with him. 'We don't have a case.'

'We might. I'll explain on the way.'

Neither spoke again until they were in the Taurus, A/C blasting. She angled in her seat to face him. 'You better start talking, Harris. Because if you don't, I'm gonna lose it.'

'I didn't tell you everything. About the Ritchie scene.'

She started to sputter-cuss. A tricky combination of inarticulation and flaming language; artful really. Zach fought not to laugh.

'Finished?' he asked after a moment.

'Not nearly.'

He went on anyway. 'The IDs we got out of Ritchie's safe, one of them was special.'

That got her attention. 'How so?'

He eased out of the parking spot. 'You know that energy I followed from the Ritchie scene? It was all over that ID.'

'But none of the others.'

'Right.'

'I don't know what that means.'

'Neither do I, not really.'

'Of course you don't.'

He ignored the sarcasm. 'What I do know, for certain, is I need to find Angel Gomez.'

'The ID holder.'

'Yes. I think she's in trouble.'

'And that call you took in Major Nichols' office?'

'Parker. He ran her social.'

Her eyes narrowed slightly. 'And came up with Teddy's. Her employer?'

'Yes.'

She released a tight-sounding breath. 'You took this to Parker first. Why?'

'We were a little busy.'

'You didn't trust me.'

'I didn't think you'd get it.'

'But you do now? Please.'

'We've come a long way in less than twenty-four hours.'

'This is so flippin' fucked, dude. On so many levels. I can't even— Never mind.'

'I get it.' He turned onto St. Charles, then grinned at her. 'But what're you gonna do? You're stuck with me.'

'You're so right about that,' she muttered, then pointed. 'Teddy's is on the left. Park by the hydrant.'

He did, and moments later they stepped into the restaurant. The bell over the door jingled and a big man in a white apron called out a greeting. They'd missed the breakfast crowd and beaten the lunch rush. The few customers in the establishment looked like tourists.

They crossed to the counter. 'Morning,' Zach said, smiling at the man. 'How are you today?'

'Doing well.' He plucked two menus from a stack. 'Counter, table, or to go?'

'None of the above.' Zach smiled again. 'NOPD. Detective Harris. My partner, Detective Dare.'

He glanced at both their shields, then nodded. 'What can I do for you, Detectives?'

'You the manager?'

'Owner. Named after me.' He smiled and patted his rotund belly. 'Walking advertisement.'

Zach returned the smile. 'Smells great in here. Can't wait to try your food.'

'I appreciate that. What's up?'

'Looking for one of your employees. Angel Gomez.'

'Angel? She in some sort of trouble?'

'Not that we know of. But we're concerned for her welfare. Her ID was in the possession of a murdered drug dealer.'

The crash of plates shattering came from behind them. Zach swung around. A slim, overly made-up blond stood frozen, staring at them, eyes wide and face pale. On the floor around her lay an entire tray of food, drinks, and tableware.

Bingo.

'Fran,' the owner exclaimed, coming around the counter, 'wake up!'

Zach crossed to her and started helping pick up the broken tableware. He caught her hand as she reached for a particularly jagged piece of glass. 'Let me get that.'

Afraid. For Angel. Guilt. Regret.

He released her hand and deposited the piece of glass on the tray. 'Wouldn't want you to cut yourself,' he said softly, sending her a sympathetic smile.

She flushed. 'Thanks.'

They finished getting the mess back on the tray; Zach picked it up and carried it to the kitchen. On his way back, he noticed a hallway with a time clock and bank of lockers. He deposited the tray by the sink, then returned to the dining room. The owner had just finished mopping up the mess.

'Sorry about that,' he said, sounding winded. 'You were asking about Angel. Haven't seen her since last week. Last day she worked was Friday. We're closed Sunday, she didn't come in Monday.'

'Did you try to reach her?'

'Fran tried the place she stays. They hadn't seen her. So I hired somebody else.'

'What about her family?'

'Didn't have any that I know of. You should talk to Fran. They're friends.'

'You didn't report her missing?'

'To the police?' He shook his head. 'Nope. My employees come and go. And when they quit, it's either by walking out during a rush or not showing up. That's the business. And Angel . . .' He paused, as if collecting his thoughts. 'Sweet girl. But a flake. Always seemed to be somewhere else. In her head, ya know?'

'Would you mind if we talked to Fran now?' Micki asked.

'No problem.' He waved the waitress over. 'Detectives here want to ask you a few questions about Angel.'

'Okay,' she said, looking anxious.

'You overheard we're looking for Angel.'

'Yes.' She wiped her hands on her apron. Zach noticed they shook.

'And that we found her ID on a dead drug dealer.' When she nodded, he went on. 'We want to make certain she's all right. Ever heard the name Martin Ritchie?'

She thought a moment, then shook her head.

'When's the last time you saw Angel?'

'That last Friday she worked. We went to a party that night. Uptown, Tulane's campus.'

'Tell me about that night.'

'There's not much to tell. We went to the party, I met someone and when I came back, she was gone.'

'Did you ask where she went?'

She nodded. 'Nobody knew. A couple people saw her leave.'

He glanced at Mick; she liked this as little as he did.

'I wasn't really worried.'

'Why not?'

'Angel's like that. One of those different-drummer people. I thought maybe she was mad at me. I talked her into going, then left her. That wasn't cool. Especially since it was her birthday.'

'Her birthday?'

She nodded, expression pinched with regret. 'I feel real bad about it.'

The regret he'd picked up on. 'Teddy said you tried her place?'

'She rents by the week. A place on Tulane. I called; they hadn't seen her. They weren't very nice.'

'What about a car?' Mick asked. 'Or a cell phone?'

'She was saving for a car. And she didn't have a cell.' The waitress lifted a shoulder. 'Like I said, different drummer.'

'Was she going to school?'

Fran shook her head.

'What about family?'

'Don't think so. She never mentioned anyone.'

'She have a locker or anything like that here?'

'Yeah, but . . . there's nothing in it.'

'Mind if we take a look anyway?'

'If Teddy's okay with it.'

He was, and moments later, Zach stared into the empty twelve-by-thirty locker.

Nothing. Not even a hum. He ran his hand around the inside, then over the door. Still nothing.

He turned back to Fran. He smiled. 'By the way, the place Angel stayed, what's the name?'

'Tulane Courtyard Lodge,' she said.

'Thanks, Fran.' He wrote down his contact information and handed it to her. 'If you hear from Angel, would you call me?'

15

Tuesday, July 9
11:00 A.M.

Teddy insisted on sending them on their way with a breakfast sandwich and a half dozen take-out menus. The man knew how to market, that was for sure.

They sat in the Taurus. Micki unwrapped her sandwich and took a big bite. She made a sound of pleasure, then took another. 'The man's a culinary genius,' she said around her mouthful. 'I think I'm in love.'

Zach unwrapped his, lifted the bread. 'You know why it tastes so good? Eggs, bacon *and* cheese. Not a sprout in sight.'

'The holy trinity of breakfast sandwiches. This ain't California, partner. But I promise, it's gonna be delicious.'

He took a bite and agreed it was. For several moments, they ate in silence.

Micki broke it. 'How are you at taking constructive criticism?'

'That's a trick question, isn't it?'

She laughed. 'Not at all. You want me to make a suggestion, I will. You don't, I won't.'

'Hit me, baby.'

'Back there? You didn't have to do that.'

'What?'

'Smile. Be all helpful. They don't need to like you, you're the law.'

'Just bringing a bit of charm to the job.'

'You don't need charm, Hollywood. You've got the badge. And the gun. Which gets you the respect. And if not that, fear'll work.'

He wrapped up what was left of his sandwich and stuffed it in the take-out bag. 'Never heard you attract more bees with honey than vinegar?'

'I'm not interested in bees. It's bad guys I'm after.'

He laughed, shifted into gear, and eased away from the curb. 'That's my Micki.'

'Excuse me? *My* Micki?'

'Think about it, we're a classic combo. Good cop, bad cop. Easy-going charmer and badass skull-crusher.'

'I resent that.'

He looked at her, surprised. 'Really?'

'How come you get to be the charming good guy?'

'Because I am.'

'You're so arrogant.'

'Wait, I'm confused. You don't want to be the badass?'

'It's not that I don't like being a tough cop – I do.

100

It's your faith in your own charm that aggravates the hell out of me.'

He shrugged. 'I know who I am.'

'Aggravating.' She stuffed the last of her sandwich into the bag. 'What's your agenda, Hollywood?'

'My immediate agenda's the Tulane Courtyard Lodge.'

'That's not what I'm asking. What are you in *this* for?'

'The Sixers? To use my gifts for good. Make a difference in the world.'

This time it was she who laughed. 'We both know *that's* bullshit. There's not an altruistic bone in your body; it's all about you and what all that charm'll get you.'

'How about you, Mad Dog? Why're you in it?'

She answered as glibly as he had. 'Bust some skulls.'

'Like I said.'

She indicated the intersection ahead. 'That's Tulane Avenue. Take a right at the light.'

He did, and within a couple minutes they'd found the lodge – in actuality, a tired motel on a tired stretch of central city – parked, and started for the building's entrance.

'I've got this,' he said, glancing at her. 'If that's cool?'

'Asking permission? Wow, be still my frickin' heart.'

If sarcasm was marshmallow, he'd be sticky and drippy right now. Unfortunately, he seemed to enjoy it.

'Wouldn't Major Nichols be proud?'

'Whatever.' She swung the door open and motioned him through. 'It's all yours.'

The front desk lay ahead to their left. The guy manning the desk was young and scruffy-looking.

Zach smiled. 'Hey, dude. How're you today?'

'Chillin'.' He swept his gaze over them. 'What's up?'

'Detective Harris. My partner, Detective Dare. We're looking for one of your guests. Angel Gomez.'

He rubbed his stubbled chin. 'She in some sort of trouble?'

'Is there a reason she should be?'

'You're looking for her.' He lifted a shoulder. 'That's reason enough for me.'

'I understand she rents one of your rooms.'

'Did. She checked out.'

'Checked out?'

Micki heard the surprise in Zach's voice. He had not been expecting that. But neither had she.

'Yeah. Came in, got her stuff and paid her bill.'

'You saw her. In person?'

'Yeah.' He frowned. 'Shouldn't I have?'

'We talked to one of her friends. She called and was told a different story. Said you hadn't seen her.'

'Yeah, chick talked to me. At the time, I hadn't seen Angel. A couple hours later, here she comes and checks out. I told her that her friend was looking for her.'

'Was she alone?'

'As far as I could tell.'

Micki stepped in. 'Was she behaving strangely?'

He shifted his gaze to her. 'Depends on your definition of strange. We're talking about Angel here.'

'Did she seem agitated or uncomfortable? Or like she was under some sort of duress?'

He narrowed his eyes in thought. 'Now that you mention it, she did seem a little nervous. She kept glancing over her shoulder. Like she was watching for someone.'

Bingo, Micki thought, flicking a look at Zach. He was frowning.

'Any idea where she was going?'

'None. Didn't ask, didn't care.'

'Could we take a look around her room?' Zach asked.

'It's already rented to somebody else. Sorry.'

'Thanks for your time.' Micki slid one of her cards across the desk. 'If she comes back in, give us a call.'

He looked at the card, then at Zach. 'How about you, you have a card, too?'

'I'm new, no card yet.'

'Detective Harris, right?'

'Right. Zach.' He held out his hand. 'And thanks, dude. I appreciate your help.'

The clerk looked surprised at the offer of a hand-shake but took his hand. 'No problem. If she comes back I'll let you know, Detective Harris.'

Micki watched Zach's hand curve around the kid's, then shifted her gaze to her partner's face. Intent. Totally focused. And the clerk? He didn't have a clue he was being mind-fucked.

'Appreciate it,' Zach said, letting go.

As they stepped outside moments later, he looked at her and grinned. 'I told you I was the popular one.'

She rolled her eyes. 'You were just using your mojo on him.'

'Whatever you need to tell yourself.'

It was the second time in as many days that she'd been completely ignored by a witness.

And he was having a good time rubbing it in.

'You weren't using it?'

He unlocked the car and they both climbed in. 'If by mojo you mean boyish charm, then yes, I was.'

'You annoy the hell out of me.'

He started up the car. 'It's the mojo.'

'No,' she corrected, 'it's frickin' *you*.'

He flashed her a grin. 'You're cute when you're annoyed.'

Puppies were cute. So were little girls in ruffles and bows. Not skull-crushing, bad-guy busting detectives with nicknames like Mad Dog. Still, it took everything she had not to laugh.

She changed the subject. 'Was he telling the truth? About Gomez?'

'Yeah, he was.'

She heard something in his voice she didn't like. 'It's time to move on, Hollywood. She's alive and well.'

'Looking over her shoulder, he said.'

'We all do sometimes. Right?'

'Right.' He glanced at her and smiled. 'Letting go. Moving on.'

Why did she have the feeling he was totally scamming her?

Probably because he was.

16

The young woman sitting across from him looked anxious. She alternated between clasping and unclasping her hands in her lap and rubbing her palms on her shorts.

Zach looked her in the eyes. Pretty girl. Early twenties. Judging by her backpack, she was a student. He smiled reassuringly. 'How can I help you, Ms Camden?'

'It's my roommate,' she began. 'Gwen. I don't know where she is and I . . . I think something bad's happened to her.'

'She's missing?'

'Yes. At least I . . . I think so.'

'You *think* so? Why?'

'This is going to sound silly.'

'Try me.'

'She didn't eat her birthday cake.'

Birthday cake? Zach glanced across the squad room at J.B. If the man was punking him, he'd be watching, waiting for the Gotcha! moment. Instead, J.B. seemed oblivious, intently studying his computer monitor.

He returned his gaze to Nora Camden's. 'Okay, Nora, that needs an explanation.'

'I know.' She twisted her fingers together. 'But it's not *just* the cake. That's only . . . it's what I keep coming back to. Because Gwen's such a chocoholic. It's just so—' She stopped, eyes welling with tears. '—out of character for her.'

'I get that,' he said softly. 'Why don't you start at the beginning. It'll make more sense to both of us. I promise.'

She nodded, took a deep breath, let it out slowly, then began. 'It was her birthday this weekend. Saturday. But my brother was getting married in Napoleonville, so I couldn't stay for it. I felt bad leaving . . . not only 'cause it was her birthday, but she and her boyfriend had just broken up.

'She promised she would be okay. Some friends were taking her to the Quarter Saturday. I figured she'd sleep all day Sunday and I'd be home Monday.'

'Yesterday?'

'Yes.'

'And did you, get home yesterday?'

She nodded. 'In the afternoon. She wasn't there, but I didn't think anything of it. I figured she was at school.'

'School?'

106

'UNO. She's an art major. She's always out there working. In the studio.'

'Gotcha.'

'I woke up this morning and she hadn't come home. That's when I sort of freaked out.'

From the corner of his eye, he saw Micki enter the squad room. He waved her over.

'Nora, this is my partner, Detective Dare. Nora's in today about her roommate.'

'Nice to meet you,' Mick said and pulled up a chair.

'You said you freaked out, but only sort of. Why was that?'

'I thought maybe she'd gotten back with her boyfriend or crashed with a friend.'

'She wouldn't have called you?'

She shook her head. 'We don't get into each other's business that much. But then . . .' Tears filled her eyes again. 'I started to notice things.'

Micki took over. 'What kind of things?'

'For one, her birthday cake. She hadn't even touched it. I got it for her on Friday. Her favorite: double chocolate. She was going to save it for Saturday. Have a piece for breakfast.'

'Anything weird or out of place when you got home? Anything that would indicate a struggle?'

'If anything it looked . . . too clean.' As if suddenly chilled, she rubbed her arms. 'Just the way I left it. Gwen's messy.'

'Let's talk about the boyfriend. The breakup – who did the breaking?'

'He did.'

'Tell me about him.'

'Creep and loser. Why she was so crazy about him, I don't have a clue.'

'He a student?'

'Uh-uh. Bartender. At Cayenne's.' She paused. 'I found out they ran into him Saturday night.'

'Found out. How?'

'I called our friends, looking for her.'

'What happened?' Zach asked softly.

'Gwen was loaded. Insisted on going into Cayenne's. She made a scene. Crawled all over some guy, asked Darren how he liked it.'

'Darren?'

'That's his name. Darren Lacoste.'

'How'd he react?'

'Had her thrown out. On her birthday.'

'That's cold,' Zach murmured.

'It fits, though. The guy's a complete dick. Sorry, but it's true. Arrogant. Controlling. Thinks he's all that and a bag of chips.'

'Your friends, when was the last time they saw her?'

'They dropped her off at our apartment around three A.M. Like I said, she was totally baked, but they made certain she got into the apartment.'

'And they haven't spoken to her since.'

'No.'

'Did you speak to her over the weekend?'

She shook her head. 'I texted her happy birthday and posted on her Facebook wall.'

'She didn't respond?'

She shook her head. 'But I didn't expect her to.'

Zach looked at Mick. 'I think we should take a look at the apartment.'

She agreed, and twenty minutes later Nora unlocked the apartment door and ushered them inside. Halfway across the threshold, Zach froze. The same energy that'd clung to Angel Gomez's ID rippled along his nerve endings.

Why here? he wondered, thoughts racing. What did this scene have to do with Angel Gomez?

'Zach?'

Mick was frowning at him. He fought to center himself, clear away the chaotic thoughts. Stepping fully into the apartment, he closed the door behind them.

Nora Camden cleared her throat. 'This is the living room. Kitchen's that way.' She pointed toward a doorway to their left. 'There're two bedrooms and two bathrooms. Mine's the one in back. Hers is right off the hall.'

'Thanks, Nora,' Micki said softly. 'Is this the way the place looked when you got home yesterday?'

'Pretty much.'

'Mind if we take a look?'

She crossed her arms over her chest. 'Go for it.'

They started in the kitchen. A few dishes in the sink. Half full coffee pot.

'The birthday cake's in the fridge.'

Zach opened the refrigerator. Sure enough, the bakery box sat on the top shelf of the refrigerator, untouched cake inside.

'It's her favorite kind,' Nora offered, voice small.

'We'll figure this out,' Zach said softly. 'Don't worry.'

He turned, moved his gaze over the kitchen, stopping on a yellow and white toothbrush on the counter beside the sink. 'That yours?'

Camden looked at it, face turning chalky white. 'Gwen's.'

'You don't look so good, Nora.'

'It's the—' She paused, visibly pulling herself together. 'In the morning, Gwen brushes her teeth at the sink here. While the coffee brews. At night, she brushes in the hall bathroom.'

'She's pretty consistent about that routine?'

'It never varies.'

Which meant the last time Gwen Miller was here, it was morning. Question was, which morning?

Zach crossed to the sink, reached for the brush, stopping before making contact. It wasn't the source of the energy. In fact, the kitchen felt relatively neutral compared with the front room. His skin wasn't crawling the way it had been when he first stepped into the apartment.

The source of the energy didn't pass through this room.

To test the theory, he stepped back into the living room. Sure enough, the popping along his nerve endings returned along with the hum in his head.

'Let's check out her bedroom,' Mick said.

He nodded and followed her down the hallway. The closer he got to the bedroom, the louder and angrier the energy became.

They stopped outside the closed door. He drew in a deep breath and followed Mick inside. A big mess. Looked like a feminine tornado had struck – clothes and shoes scattered about, lotions, perfumes, cosmetics. Bed unmade.

But not the energy. Not like it had been in the hall.

He frowned.

'What?' Mick asked.

He shook his head and stepped back into the hall. Directly across from him was another closed door. He looked at Nora, hovering at the end of the hallway. 'What's in there?'

'Gwen's bathroom.'

'Have you been in there since you got home?'

Her eyes widened. 'I peeked inside. It looked the way it always does.' She moved her gaze between them. 'Why?'

Zach didn't answer. Queasy, growing light-headed, he crossed to the door. He suspected what would come at him when he walked into the room. He worked to prepare himself for it.

But nothing could have. The energy was raw. Angry. It hit him with the force of a wrecking ball. He braced himself with a hand to the vanity counter.

Mick seemed not to notice. She slipped past him; easing the door shut behind. She stopped, caught her breath. 'What the hell is that?'

Zach followed her gaze. On the back of the wooden door, someone had crudely carved the number seven.

The energy closed over him, smothering. Suffocating.

He lunged for the door, yanked it open and strode out of the apartment, down the stairs and outside. There, he puked into a trash barrel.

17

Micki found Zach bent over a trash barrel. She gave him his space until he straightened up. He was pale, sweating. 'You okay?'

'Yeah. It must have been something I ate.'

'Right.' She looked back at the young woman hovering in the doorway. 'Could you get Detective Harris a glass of water?'

She nodded mutely and hurried back up the stairs.

Micki turned back to him. 'We both know it's not something you ate. What's going on?'

He hesitated a moment. 'Energy. Big and bad.'

He was dead serious, Micki realized. She nodded, dealing with it. 'Like the energy you followed from the Ritchie scene?'

'Like that. Only stronger.'

What the hell did she do with that?

The roommate reappeared, a bottle of Kentwood water in her hands. She crossed to Zach and held it out.

He took it; Micki noticed their fingers brushed – and the tiny tremor that rippled over him. So small, that if she didn't know what he was, she wouldn't have noticed it.

'Thanks,' he said. He took a swig, swished water around his mouth, then spit it into the trash can. After doing that again, he took a swallow.

His color had returned. 'Ready to go back in?' she asked.

He nodded tersely. 'Let's do it.'

Leaving Nora in the living room, they headed down the hall, both donning Latex gloves.

'I shouldn't touch anything,' he said softly.

'Got it. You tell me what you need me to do.'

They entered the bathroom; Zach flinched but didn't bolt. A good sign, Micki decided.

The house was old, the single panel door solid. It had the look of wood that had been painted many times. The most recent color was a brick red.

The seven had been dug dead center into the door.

Micki leaned in. The jagged edges of the carving revealed the many layers of paint in a rainbow of colors.

Carving. The word conjured thoughts of an artist. Of deliberate, controlled actions resulting in a beautiful creation.

Whoever had done this had hacked at the wood as

if in a frenzy. Chips and splinters littered the floor around the door. With the carnage, drops of blood. Smears of it on the door, not as visible, blending with the red. A partial, bloody handprint.

Micki held her own hand up to the print. Comparing its size to hers, it most probably belonged to a man.

She turned to Zach, and found him staring intently at the door. 'Yo, dude.' She waved at him. 'Call HQ. We need to get an evidence crew out here.'

He shook his head. 'Not yet. I've got to get a better look at this monster.'

As if it wasn't evidence, but the perp himself.

He inched around her and squatted so he was eye level with the seven. He lifted his right hand, palm out.

Micki frowned. 'I thought you couldn't touch anything.'

'I want to try something.'

'Just so you know, I don't clean up barf.'

A smile touched his mouth. 'Neither do I. That's why I'm taking this slow.'

He moved in slowly, passing his gloved hand in front of the door panel, inching closer until his hand floated a fraction of an inch above.

His hand trembled. The trembling spread to his entire body. Something in the air changed. Became electric. The hair on Micki's arms stood straight up.

She rubbed them, feeling light-headed. She opened her mouth to suggest he back off when he tumbled backward, landing smack on his ass. He looked comically dumbfounded. She would have laughed if she wasn't certain she looked the same way.

'You okay, Hollywood?'

He got to his feet. 'Holy shit! Did you feel that?'

'That depends. What did you feel?'

'Like a shock of static electricity. But on steroids.' He flexed his fingers, as if trying to wake them up.

She wished she could tell him he was full of crap, but she'd felt the charge in the air, too. She rubbed her arms again. 'So, what're we dealing with here?'

'No frickin' clue.'

'And I believe in the Easter Bunny and Tooth Fairy too.'

'I'm being totally legit,' he said. 'This is twilight zone time for me too.'

'Great,' she muttered and yanked off her gloves. 'But you're still thinking Miller's disappearance is related to the Ritchie homicide?'

'I didn't say that.'

'You said it was the same energy—'

'I'm not so sure now.'

Better and better. 'Considering this,' she motioned the door, 'we can agree Ms Miller is in some sort of trouble?'

'Yeah. Definitely.'

'Is she alive?'

'I don't know.' He dragged a hand through his hair. 'What do you think?'

'Nothing here suggests otherwise.'

'Except that freaking bloody handprint.'

'Not Miller's,' Micki said. 'The perp's. How he got her out of here without a struggle, I don't know. But I'd bet my badge she left here alive.'

'What do we do now?'

'Talk to the neighbors. Maybe somebody saw or heard something. Get that evidence crew down here. And have another chat with Ms Camden.'

The young woman jumped to her feet as they entered the living room. She clasped her hands in front of her, looking anxious. 'What do you think happened to her?'

'I need you to take a look at something.'

She frowned. 'Okay.'

Micki showed her the door. The girl gasped. 'What *is* that?'

'You've never seen this before?'

'No.' She took a step back, looking frightened. 'I was right, wasn't I? Something's happened to Gwen.'

'Do you have any idea what it might mean?'

She shook her head, tears flooding her eyes. 'Oh my God, this can't be happening. I don't know what to do.'

'First, take a deep, calming breath,' Micki said soothingly. 'It may be nothing.'

'I need to sit down.'

A moment later, the girl sank onto the sofa and dropped her head into her hands.

'I need to ask you a few more questions. Okay?' Camden nodded and Micki went on, 'Any chance Gwen got really drunk or really pissed off and did that to the door?'

'God, no.'

'You're certain of that?'

'Yes.'

'What about Gwen's purse and cell phone? I didn't

see either when we searched the apartment. Did she keep it somewhere we might have missed it?'

'She usually dropped her purse wherever.' Her voice shook. 'Phone was mostly in it or a pocket.'

'Which most likely means she took both with her.'

'That's good news, isn't it?' The young woman moved her gaze between them.

Micki concurred. 'Now, think carefully, Nora. Is there anything else you can tell us? Something the number seven might mean to Gwen? Anything else at all?'

'No.' The girl teared up again.

'Does Gwen have family nearby?'

'Florida.' She wiped her nose with the back of her hand. 'The Panhandle.'

'Have you called them?'

'I didn't want to upset them.' She suddenly straightened. 'Maybe Gwen's with them?'

Micki didn't think there was a chance of that, but she agreed. 'Maybe so. I'll call them. I'll need their names and contact information, as well as the names and contact info for the friends she was with Saturday night. And also the ex-boyfriend.'

She jumped to her feet. 'I can get that. But you'll call her folks first, right?'

'Absolutely.' Micki smiled. 'With luck, Gwen's with them and we'll be done here.'

18

Tuesday, July 9
5:30 P.M.

'Miller's not with her family,' Micki said, re-holstering her phone. 'Now, they're on their way here. Shit.'

Zach, across the sidewalk cafe table from her, cocked an eyebrow. 'Did you really think there was a chance she would be?'

'There's always a chance.'

She pushed away the po'boy she'd been picking at. 'Crap. Families suck.'

He finished his sandwich and wadded the wrapper into a ball. 'Why? What's the problem?'

'Managing their emotions. I understand why they're freaking out, but I can't do my job and hold their hands at the same time.'

'You're saying they require time and a delicate touch?'

'Yes.'

'And you're a Mack truck?'

'Pretty much.'

'I'll take care of them.'

'Just like that?' She snapped her fingers. 'You really think so?'

'Sure.' He stood and lobbed his balled-up wrapper at the trash can. It dropped cleanly in. 'No problem.'

She looked at him, two very different emotions hitting her simultaneously: one, relief he would deal with Miller's family; two, gleeful expectation of his arrogance biting him squarely in the ass.

And she wasn't so nice not to say 'I told you so,' after it did.

The week's outlook just improved.

She smiled and stood. 'Appreciate it, partner. They're all yours.' She dropped her garbage in the can and fell into step with him. 'First stop, the friends Miller partied with, then the boyfriend. You've got the list?'

Miller's roommate had given them a list of names and numbers. Zach glanced down it. 'Nick, Angela, and Beth. The three rent a house together.'

'One-stop shopping,' she quipped as they climbed into the Taurus.

She should have known better, Micki realized a short time later – with police work, it was never as easy as that. Beth was at work and Angela had left for her night class. But Nick was home and eager to talk.

Micki had assumed that part of the roommate triangle would be a couple; it was clear after meeting Nick that the three were BFFs.

120

'This is devastating,' he said, drawing out the last word for dramatic effect. 'We were all together Saturday. We dropped her at her place. She was fine!'

'That's why we want to talk with you and your roommates. As far as we know, you were the last to see her—'

'Alive?' he whispered, then pressed his right hand to his chest. 'Lord, God, baby Jesus, tell me this isn't happening.'

'Mr Baldwin—'

'Nick.'

'—we have no reason to believe she's dead.'

He teared up. 'Excuse me. I need a tissue.' He returned a moment later with a big box of Puffs. 'I'm sorry.' He dabbed his eyes. 'I'll try to hold it together.'

Micki frowned slightly. 'You seem pretty upset about this.'

'I'm an emotional person.'

'We have no evidence to indicate she's been harmed.'

'Except that horrid door!'

'How do you know about the door, Nick?'

'Nora texted me a picture of it. My God . . .' He pressed the tissue to his eyes. 'Who does that?'

Even though Micki counted to ten, her response came out sounding as irritated as she felt. 'That's what we're trying to find out. Could I see that photo, Nick?'

He looked confused but pulled up his cell phone and showed her. Sure enough: the desecrated door, in all its glory. The text was time-stamped: 4:47 P.M.

Where the hell had the crime scene techs been when

121

Camden was snapping the photo like some ghoulish tourist?

'Do you know who else she sent this to?'

'Just the three of us.'

'"Just",' she muttered. 'Great.'

Zach stepped in, tone mellow. 'Nick, you might hold the key to finding Gwen. That's why we're here. So, I need you to hold it together and focus. Every detail you can recall, dude. One of them might be just the clue we need.'

The young man nodded, visibly pulling himself together. 'Where do you want me to start?'

'The very beginning. What time did you all meet up on Saturday?'

'We picked her up about two. We wanted to make a day of it. 'Cause of her birthday.'

'You drove?'

'Angela did. We parked near her place and walked into the Quarter. Ate lunch at Cafe Maspero, wandered around. Jackson Square. The French Market. Hit a few shops. The weather was awesome, so it was just nice to be outside.'

'Did you run into anyone you know?'

'At the clubs that night.'

'But not during the day?' He shook his head. 'Can you recall the name of the shops you went into?'

'A few. I bought a fabulous hat at Rewind, a consignment store not far from the French Market.'

Micki made a note. 'Any other shops?'

He rattled off a few names, none that Micki recognized. She was at home with places like JCP and Target.

'Tell us about the ex-boyfriend,' she said.

'Darren. The slimy weasel. She was destroyed when he broke up with her. And right before her birthday.'

'You ran into him that night?'

'It wasn't an accident. Going to Cayenne's was Gwen's idea, we all tried to talk her out of it.'

'Describe what happened.'

'She was pretty drunk. When he blew her off, she figured she'd show him and started making a scene with some guy.'

'Making a scene?'

'Crawling all over him, real exaggerated.'

'Who was the guy?'

'Just some guy.'

'You didn't get a name?' He shook his head. 'Was Darren angry?'

'I think so, yeah. He kicked us all out.'

Zach stepped in. 'How angry? Enough to retaliate? Get physically violent?'

The young man's face went momentarily slack with thought. Then he shook his head. 'The truth is, I don't think he cared all that much. He's just mean, dude.'

'How'd he break up with her?' Micki asked.

'Text message.'

Cold. Or gutless.

'Did Gwen draw the attention of anyone else in the bar?'

'Uh, like everyone. Like I said, she was over the top.'

'The guy she was "crawling all over", he get kicked out, too?'

'Nope.'

123

Interesting. 'You see him again that night?'

He shook his head.

'Did Gwen talk about seeing him again?'

'Not that I remember. She was all about Darren. Gross.'

'So, you got kicked out of Cayenne's. Did you call it a night, head back?'

'No way. We couldn't take her home like *that*, not on her twenty-first birthday. So we hit a couple more places, then went for coffee and beignets. By the time we took her home, she'd forgotten all about the jerk.'

Micki doubted that, but went on, 'How'd you get her home?'

'It wasn't easy.' He made a face. 'She threw up twice.'

What twenty-first birthday was complete without puking your guts up on somebody else's shoes? Those days seemed a lifetime ago. 'Think carefully, Nick, did Gwen interact with anyone else? Someone we should talk to?'

'Did you tell them about that creepy fortune teller?'

They turned. An apple-shaped young woman wearing scrubs and huge horn-rim glasses was dumping her book bag by the door. She headed their way, hand out. 'Angie Brennan. Class was cancelled.'

Micki stood, shook her hand and introduced herself. Zach did the same.

'Creepy fortune teller?' Zach said.

Angie frowned at Nick. 'Seriously, you didn't?'

'It didn't seem like a big deal.'

'It was a big deal to Gwen. It totally freaked her out.'

124

'Why don't you fill us in,' Micki said.

The girl dragged a battered ottoman over and plopped down. 'It was one of those tarot card readers who sits in Jackson Square, in front of the cathedral. We were walking by, and she called out to Gwen.'

'By name?'

She shook her head and her ponytail swung. 'Gwen must've looked her way. Then she said something like "Come, pretty girl, let me tell you the future." I remember it was super corny. We all laughed.'

Nick jumped in. 'At first Gwen wasn't going to do it, but since it was her birthday, we urged her to. Told her we'd even pay for it.'

'It was supposed to be fun.' Angie snorted. 'Fortune tellers always tell you good things. Always. Right, Nick?'

'Right.' He nodded. 'And since Darren just broke up with her, we figured hearing true love was waiting right around the corner was just what she needed to hear.'

'But that's not what this fortune teller did?'

Again, Angie's ponytail swung. 'If we'd known, we never would have encouraged her.'

'She looked like a witch.' Nick jumped in. 'And right away, she started pulling up these crazy, bad cards – death, the hangman, swords and stuff.'

'She put a good spin on them, but we could tell she was getting sort of weirded out.'

'And so was Gwen.'

'So the witch decides to read Gwen's palm instead. She takes her hand—'

'And that's when things really got messed up.'

'She makes this terrible face and jerks away from her. Ends the reading.'

Zach frowned. 'Terrible face?'

Nick rubbed his arms, his own expression turning queasy. 'Like it hurt to touch her.'

'Or was disgusting,' Angie added. 'I couldn't believe she could do that to Gwen. It was so mean!'

Nick leaned forward. 'Then she warns Gwen. "Be careful," she says. "Your enemy roams like a roaring lion, looking for someone to devour."'

'It was such a bullshit move,' Angie said. 'I was so mad. That was the last thing Gwen needed.'

Nick agreed. 'She was really upset.'

'The gypsy lady is packing up her crap, like literally, the folding table and chair—'

'We're totally pissed. Demand our money back—'

'Gwen is white as a sheet. She's begging the witch to tell her what she saw. What was wrong.'

'Then what,' Zach asked.

'She stuffs some money in my hand. Looks at Gwen and says "You'll meet your true love soon. He's waiting." She straps everything on her wheelie and goes.'

Zach turned to Nick. 'You didn't think this was important enough to tell us about?'

He flushed. 'She was just a head case, right? A phony psychic with a crazy, mean streak?'

'What if she wasn't?'

They all went silent, and Micki looked at Zach in disbelief. Maybe next time she should bring along a roll of duct tape, to keep *his* mouth shut.

'What Detective Harris means,' she said, 'is that in a missing person investigation, everyone who comes into contact with the victim is important.'

'This psychic, you got her name?'

'Not me.' Angela looked at Nick. 'Did you?'

'No. But Beth must have, 'cause she said she was going to report her. I could text her and ask.'

'That'd be great.'

Just then, the front door burst open and a tall girl with wild red hair barreled through. She all but skidded to a stop when she saw Micki and Zach.

'Hello,' Micki said, holding up her shield. 'Beth Adams?' She nodded. 'Detective Dare, NOPD. My partner, Detective Harris.'

Angela jumped in. 'They're here about Gwen.'

Nick followed. 'They're trying to find her.'

Beth's eyes lit up. 'Any leads yet? And what about that door? I've been thinking about the number seven, what it could mean. Hold on, I wrote a few ideas down.' She dug through her purse, and found what she was looking for – a crumpled sales receipt. She handed it to Zach. 'Sorry. I didn't have any paper.'

'Thanks,' he said, glancing at the list and handing it to Micki.

She quickly scanned it. *Seven deadly sins, seven wonders of the world, seven days of the week, lucky number seven.*

'That's all I came up with so far,' Beth said. 'I'm sure there're more. I could get online and—'

'No. But thank you, this is a great start.' Micki folded the list and slipped it into her pocket. 'Nick and Angie were telling us about your experience with the Jackson Square fortune teller.'

'What a poser! It was just awful what she did. I was going to report her when—'

Micki cut her off. 'Did you get her name?'

She seemed not to notice Micki's impatience and nodded. 'Oh yeah, I got it. Brite Knight. I remember because it seemed sort of cheesy, you know. Fortune-teller, illuminating the darkness. Puh-leese.'

Zach, Micki noticed, was having a hard time not smiling.

'You're certain?'

'Yes, ma'am.'

'Detective,' she corrected.

'Yes, ma'am, Detective.'

Zach made a choked sound to cover a laugh. Micki frowned. How the hell did he know her so well already? 'Could you describe her?' she asked.

'Don't have to.' Beth pulled out her cell phone. 'I took a picture of Gwen when the reading started. Before "Brite Knight",' – Beth made quotation marks with her fingers – 'went all psycho on us.'

Her two friends gathered around her, to get a look at the photo.

'The only thing is, you can't see her eyes. They were super-weird. Bright, like a cat's.'

'I thought they were colored contacts,' Nick offered.

'Had to be,' Angie agreed. 'Right, y'all?'

Micki recalled thinking exactly the same thing about Zach and his FBI buddy, Parker. During that first meeting.

Micki glanced at Zach, wondering if he had made that connection.

'Could you email that photo to me?' Zach asked. 'In fact, any you might have taken that day? It could be important.'

'Like maybe her abductor's pictured in one?'

'Exactly. You're good at this.' He smiled; Beth nearly swooned.

'I'm majoring in criminal justice.'

'Then you should realize,' Micki said, 'we don't even know for certain she's been abducted.'

Beth didn't acknowledge the comment. Instead, she batted her lashes at Zach. 'What's your email address? Or I could text them to your cell?'

No one missed the invitation in the question and Micki stepped in. 'Detective Harris doesn't have an email address yet. Here's mine.' She handed each of the three of them one of her cards, saving the flirty Beth for last. She looked her squarely in the eyes. 'Now,' she continued, 'we need to question each of you independently.'

Angela looked startled. 'Why?'

'So you don't influence each other's recollections of events. We've already talked to Nick, so—'

'Okay by me,' Beth announced. 'I get Detective Harris!'

19

Tuesday, July 9
7:15 P.M.

Micki had been in a hundred French Quarter bars exactly like Cayenne's. Cover bands every night, cheap beer on tap, young people looking for love and tourists looking for fun. They all smelled the same – of cigarettes, stale beer and sweat. The ones on Bourbon, Cayenne's included, kept the front doors thrown open so the music could pour out into the street.

Micki looked at Zach, standing beside her in the doorway. 'Ready?'

'Depends. What's your plan?'

'Question Lacoste. Arrest him if he confesses.' He should have smirked at that; he was still too green to know how ridiculous that comment was. Confess? Hardly even an option. Flee, fight, deny, dodge and lie their asses off – no, *those* were options.

'What do you want me to do?' Zach asked as they started for the bar.

'Try not to start a riot.'

One corner of his mouth lifted in amusement. 'Do I really deserve that?'

'"I get Detective Harris,"' she mocked. '"Pick me, pick me!" Stampede ensues.'

'Not my fault I'm devastatingly handsome.'

She rolled her eyes. 'Watch and learn, my young padawan.'

Micki sidled up to the bar. She motioned to the ruggedly good-looking bartender.

'Yo,' he said, smiling and setting a coaster in front of her. 'What can I offer you, beautiful?'

Implied in his tone was a promise that nothing she might desire was off the table. Micki pegged him as the sleazy scumbag Miller had been gaga over.

'*Anything* I want?' she asked, lowering her voice to a sexy purr.

'You bet, baby.' He rested his elbows on the bar and leaned toward her. 'Anything.'

She wanted to barf; instead, she held out her badge. 'Information, lover-boy. That's what I'm looking for.'

He straightened up so quickly, Micki figured he'd have a backache later.

'I didn't mean anything by that.'

'You so sure of that? I think you're making a little extra money on the side, selling a different kind of happy juice. Pills maybe. Yeah, that's it. Pills.'

'No way.'

The patrons on either side of her glanced in their

131

direction. The kid looked sick. Sometimes she freaking *loved* this job. 'So, I shake you down now, I don't find any contraband in your pockets?'

'That's right. I'm clean. One hundred percent.'

'Detective Dare,' she said. 'My partner, Detective Harris. We have a few questions.'

His relief was all but palpable. 'About?'

'Gwen Miller.'

He cocked an eyebrow.

'I understand she was in Saturday night.'

'So?'

'It was her birthday. You kicked her out.'

'She was out of control. Really making an ass of herself.'

'You were jealous, seeing her with another guy like that.'

He snorted. 'Hardly.'

'You were angry.'

'Annoyed.'

'After your shift you went to see her.'

He looked genuinely surprised. 'Excuse me?'

'You went to her apartment.'

'Did she tell you that?' He looked from her to Zach. 'Because whatever she told you is a lie.'

'I'm not convinced.' She looked at Zach. 'How about you?'

'You'll have to do a lot better than that, man.'

'I broke up with her.' He leaned closer, lowered his voice. 'Personally, I could care less if she fucked that guy on the dance floor, but my boss would've fired my ass over it.'

132

They didn't respond, and he shook his head. 'Stupid bitch. What did she say? That I raped her? Pathetic. Either order a drink or—'

Zach caught his hand, anchoring it to the bar. 'We're not finished.'

Lacoste froze. Micki looked at Zach in surprise. There'd been steel in his voice; gone was the easy-going charmer. He meant business.

Lacoste paled. 'What do you want to know?'

Zach answered. 'When's the last time you saw Gwen?'

'That Saturday night. When I kicked her out of the bar. That's the last time, I swear.'

'And after your shift ended?'

'I went home with somebody. Was with her all night.'

'Who?' Micki asked. 'We need a name.'

'All this because some bitch—'

'Gwen Miller,' she corrected and looked at Zach. 'He doesn't have a very good attitude about women.'

Zach agreed. 'He needs to learn some respect.'

Sweat broke out on Lacoste's upper lip. 'I went home with her.' He indicated his fellow bartender. 'Shelley. We do that sometimes. It doesn't mean anything.'

'She'll back you up?' Micki said.

'Yes, absolutely.'

Zach released his hand. 'I'll go test that.'

Lacoste watched him walk away and Micki snapped her fingers to get Lacoste's attention. 'Tell me about the guy Gwen was all over that night.'

'A regular. A real loser.'

Micki sensed that to Lacoste, everyone was a loser but him. 'Name?'

'Corey.'

'Last name?'

'LeFever.'

From the corners of her eyes, she saw Zach conversing with the other bartender. Heard her laugh. Obviously, completely charmed.

Pick me, pick me.

Freaking mumbo-jumbo.

'You have his contact info?'

'Don't know him that well. He comes in most nights.'

Zach strolled back. She saw him slip a folded cocktail napkin into his pocket. No doubt Shelley's phone number. That figured.

It shouldn't irritate her, but it did.

Several minutes later, they were back on the street. They climbed into the Taurus. 'Proud of you, Hollywood,' she said, as he cranked the engine. 'Nice move with Lacoste. You grew a pair in there.'

'I've always had 'em. Just picky about how I use 'em.'

She laughed. 'Whatever. What'd you learn?'

'Shelley confirmed they spent the night together. The whole "Friends don't let friends go home alone on Saturday night" thing. Kinda takes the romance out of it.'

'Speaking of romance, you didn't strike out.'

He looked momentarily confused. 'You mean Shelley?'

'Saw you slipping a napkin into your pocket.'

'I couldn't be rude, right?'

Irritated. Again. She shook it off. 'You get a bead on Lacoste.'

'Oh yeah. From the read I got, he didn't touch Miller Saturday night. But you'll like this. With him, what you see is what you get. Not much else going on there.'

'No way.' She laughed. 'He couldn't be *that* shallow?'

'Oh yeah, he could.'

'I wish I could've snapped the cuffs on him. The boys in holding would've loved messing with him.'

Zach yawned. 'What now?'

'Back to the Eighth. Run our mysterious fortune-teller through the system, see if we get a hit.'

'It can't wait until tomorrow?'

'Welcome to a life protecting and serving, Hollywood. Ain't it a gas?'

20

They did get a hit. Brite Knight had several arrests under her gypsy scarves. Small stuff. Disturbing the peace. Complaints about her business practices. Shoplifting. Pickpocketing.

It also gave them a last known address.

'Got her,' Zach said, grabbing his car keys.

'Oh no, you don't.' Mick hopped to her feet. 'I'll drive. I've had about all I can take of your P-O-S car for today.'

He grabbed his jacket off the back of his chair. 'Courtesy of the Bureau.'

'Bastards. They could do better.'

'My sentiments exactly.'

They exited the building, dodging fellow officers escorting several working girls inside. Mick led him

136

around the side of the building to a midnight blue Chevy Nova SS.

He whistled. 'Sweet wheels.'

'There's a story.' She slid inside, reached across to unlock his door. 'Maybe I'll tell you someday.'

'Waiting for that day, Mick.' She looked at him, eyebrow cocked. He smiled. 'No, seriously.'

'I suggest you buckle up. I'm not that good a driver.'

That wasn't true, he discovered. She handled the vehicle skillfully. But recklessly, weaving in and out of traffic, jackrabbit starts and sharp stops.

'How many miles to a gallon you get?'

'Depends.'

'On?'

'My driving.' She laughed and floored it. 'Right now, maybe six.'

She took a curve too fast and he braced himself. 'So, I'll drive next time.'

'Chip in for gas and we're good.' She glanced his way. 'What did you drive, back in your real life?'

His real life. As if this was a whim. A diversion. *Wasn't it?* he asked himself.

'BMW.'

'Convertible,' she guessed. 'Less than a year old. Maybe silver. A 300 series.'

'And they call me psychic,' he said lightly and grabbed the door handle as she executed a perfect U-turn, then slid to a stop in front of a rundown, shotgun-style double.

'Here we are.'

He let out a relieved breath. 'And who taught you to drive that way?'

'That, Hollywood, is another story.'

He snorted. 'Those stories are starting to stack up, partner.'

'Something for you to look forward to. Knight's is the unit on the left.'

Zach peered at the house. Light glowed from a single front window. 'Looks like nobody's home.'

'Let's find out.'

They climbed out of the vehicle, crossed to Knight's unit. Sagging front porch. Stairs he wasn't confident would take his weight. An X spray-painted on the front door.

He remembered seeing those Xs on a documentary about Hurricane Katrina. Search and Rescue teams left them as a record they'd been there.

'This neighborhood got slammed by Katrina,' Mick said, then rapped loudly on the door. 'Ms Knight,' she called. 'NOPD.'

Nothing. No light or movement from within. No sound.

'Brite Knight,' she called again, 'police!'

Still nothing.

'What now,' he asked.

'I say we wait.'

'I'm cool with that.'

She moved the Nova, parking across the street from the duplex. Clear view, but discreet. If anyone could be in this vehicle.

Zach indicated the store on the corner. 'I'm going to grab something to nosh on. Want anything?'

'A Mountain Dew.'

'Seriously?'

'I'm a country girl. Oh, and something salty.'

He shook his head and alighted the Nova.

A classic corner grocery. Like something out of a movie set in the old south, shelves stocked with a mish-mash of items: canned goods and snacks, diapers, batteries and boiled peanuts. A cooler with soft drinks, waters and a chocolate drink called Yoo-hoo. And one of those old-fashioned freezer boxes with ice cream bars.

The woman behind the counter eyed him suspiciously. Zach nodded in her direction, then crossed back to the storefront window. He peered out, could see the Nova, Mick inside.

He unclipped his phone, dialed Parker. 'It's me,' he said when the man answered. 'Where are you?'

'Washington. Until Saturday.'

'Got an update. That energy we labeled not-so-friendly, it's made another appearance.'

Zach sensed Parker's interest pique.

'Here's the thing,' he went on, 'seems Mr not-so-nice-on-steroids kicked my ass.'

'Where?'

'Missing coed's apartment. Left something interesting behind. The number seven, hacked into the bathroom door.'

For a long moment, Parker was silent. Long enough that Zach wondered if the call had dropped. 'You there, P?'

'I've got to go. Get me a full report, ASAP.'

And he hung up. Typical Parker. No time to waste

on pleasantries. Zach re-holstered his phone and peered out the storefront window. Mick at the wheel, nothing had changed.

He grabbed a basket and hit the snack aisle, tossing in chips, cookies – anything that caught his eye, including a PowerBar for him and the Dew for her.

He took the loaded basket to the counter. The woman behind it cocked an eyebrow. 'Eating disorder?'

He laughed. 'Just like having options.'

Tall and skinny, with the lined face of a sun worshipper and kind eyes, she fixed that gaze on him a moment, then began to scan each item. 'You new? I haven't seen you around before.'

'I haven't been around before.'

'Mysterious.'

'I'm a cop.'

'Well, that explains everything.'

He smiled and eyed her name badge. 'I like you, Millie. I'm Detective Harris. You can call me Zach.'

Her mouth twitched. 'All righty, Zach. That'll be twenty-six twelve.'

He extracted bills from his wallet, handed them to her. 'You know a fortune-teller named Brite Knight?'

She nodded and handed him his change. 'She's odd, that one is. Caught her shoplifting once.'

'You call the cops?'

'Nah.' Millie packed the items in two brown sacks. 'I felt bad for her. It was post-Katrina, tourists hadn't come back yet. She was hurting, so I fixed her up.'

He hadn't been wrong about those eyes.

Zach scooped up the sacks. 'Nice meeting you.'

She stopped him at the door. 'This neighborhood can be sketchy. You be careful, Zach.'

'Thanks, Millie. You, too.'

Moments later, he reached the Nova. 'That took awhile,' she said when he swung open the passenger door.

He handed her the stuffed paper sack. 'Your Dew's at the bottom. PowerBar's mine.'

She started unpacking the bag. 'How long you think we're going to be here? A week?'

'Can never have too many provisions.'

'Beef jerky?' she said, holding up the beef stick, eyebrows raised. 'Seriously?'

He settled into the bucket seat. 'You said you were a country girl.'

She rolled her eyes and dropped it back into the bag.

'Made a new friend. Millie. She knew Knight.'

'It's. A. Stakeout, Hollywood,' she said speaking super-slowly, as if to an idiot. 'You know, covert, element of surprise? She could be tipping Knight off right now.'

He ripped open a bag of pistachio nuts. 'She's not.'

Mick groaned and popped the Dew. 'Mumbo-frickin'-jumbo. It's gonna send me right over the edge.'

'Wasn't like that.' He cracked open a nut. 'Tell me about your family, Mick.'

'No.'

'You have any siblings?'

'What part of "no" don't you understand?'

'Your parents still alive?'

She reached across the seat and grabbed the bag of pistachios. 'You are so irritating.'

'Do you see them much?'

'Fuck off, Hollywood.'

'Where'd you get that chip, Mick?'

'Nut,' she said, holding one up. 'Not a chip.'

'The one on your shoulder, partner.'

'I know.' She shifted her gaze to the house. 'I was born this way. Came out of the womb with a bad attitude.'

'Why don't I believe you?'

'Trust issues?'

They both knew that described her, not him. He told her so.

For a long moment, she remained silent, gaze on Knight's home. When she finally spoke, her voice vibrated with emotion.

'Why would you have trust issues? It's so easy for you. Look 'em in the eye, grab their hand and – bam – you know just what they're made of. For some of us, it's a little more complicated than that.'

He saw a lifetime of hurt in her eyes. 'I suppose it is, Mick.'

She leaned her seat back, eyes once again fixed on Brite Knight's place. 'Got a question for you, Hollywood.'

'Shoot.'

'When did you discover your gift?'

'Before I could understand I was different from everyone else.'

'Your parents don't have it, no one else in the family?'

'I'm adopted. I don't know my bio parents.'

'Shit, sorry. I forgot.'

'Nothing to be sorry about. I've got great parents who had the means to give me the best of pretty much everything.'

'Where do you think it comes from? The gift, I mean. You must wonder.'

The question struck close to home. Close enough his answer came out more sharply than he intended. 'Of course I do. Most adopted kids wonder who they got their height or hair color from, I wonder who had the freak gene.'

'A freak. Is that the way you think of yourself?'

He didn't want to go there and used her dodge from earlier. 'There's a story. Maybe I'll tell you sometime.'

She fell right in line. 'Waiting for the day, Hollywood.'

He smiled, realizing he liked her. Chip and all.

For several moments, they silently snacked. Zach, the pistachios and her, a variety of items, going from one to another, sampling – chips, cookies, the jerky. He wanted to laugh, but decided that wouldn't be his best move.

He glanced toward the mini mart. 'I forgot water.'

She ripped open a pack of cheese crackers. 'Two sacks of crap, and you forgot something to drink?'

'Ironic, right?'

She held out her can. 'Dew?'

He grasped the door handle. 'Be back in two. You want anything?'

She indicated the carnage around her. 'Seriously?'

He grinned. 'Gotcha. Be right back.'

As Zach reached the store, a guy in a hoodie burst out, knocking into him.

Zach stumbled backward. An image formed. Terror. Pain. The quiet shattered.

Millie, Zach saw, cowering behind the counter. Holding her side. Blood seeped through her fingers. She met his gaze. He saw the terror in hers. Pain twisted her features. She pointed in the direction the kid had gone and mouthed '*Go.*'

Zach glanced toward Mick, saw her attention was fixed on Knight's place and made a decision. He nodded at Millie and started after the perp, unclipping his phone as he went.

He dialed Mick. 'Look my way,' he said when she answered. 'Dude just robbed the store.'

'Where the hell are you?'

'In pursuit.'

'Hell no, you stay and—'

'Get an ambulance, Millie's shot.'

'Shot? Wait! You stay with her, this is my—'

'Take care of Millie,' he said again. 'I've got this.'

21

Micki spotted Zach two blocks up, the perp a half block in front of him. Dark hoodie, moving fast. He had the look of a gangbanger. Which meant he wasn't alone. Those guys were never alone.

Son of a bitch, Zach so did *not* have this. Not by any stretch of the imagination.

Micki swept the snack smorgasbord aside, cringing at the thought of the mess on the Nova's floor, and started the car. The engine roared to life; she rolled away from the curb.

She radioed for back-up and an ambulance, then sorted through her options. She didn't want to startle the perp, didn't want her presence to aggravate the situation. And she had no idea what Zach might do next. The guy was a total frickin' loose cannon.

145

The perp suddenly stopped. He turned toward Harris, his hands jammed into the hoodie's pockets. Micki's pulse leapt, but before she could react, another vehicle, a souped-up Ford Mustang Cobra, came out of nowhere. It slowed, a door flew open. The perp dove into it.

Gangbangers. *She hated it when she was right.*

She saw Zach react, shout out.

This was going down now, and he hadn't even pulled his weapon.

The Cobra's tinted rear window lowered. She saw the silhouette of a gun. She had one option.

Not the Nova. Not her baby.

Shit. Damn. Son of a—

'Sorry about this, Hank,' she muttered and floored the accelerator. She hit the brights, barreling toward the Mustang.

A moment before impact, she yanked the wheel left; the Nova went into a spin, its rear end smashing into the other vehicle.

Her safety belt engaged, knocking the wind out of her. Her head snapped forward, then slammed back against the headrest. The Nova shuddered to a stop; she released the belt and stumbled out, weapon drawn.

And found Zach standing over the cuffed suspect, gun trained on him and a shit-eating grin on his face.

'I'm fine,' Micki snapped at the emergency room doctor. 'Just let me out of here.'

'You know the drill, Detective. You don't go anywhere until I give you my official okie-dokey.'

'Then give it to me,' she all but growled. 'I've got a job to do.'

The physician remained unmoved by her surly attitude. 'Seems to me, the job's what got you hauled in here.'

'Your point?'

'The more you complain, the longer it takes.'

Micki bit back what she wanted to say, instead following his directions to move this way and that as he poked and prodded.

'How is she, Doc?'

Harris. Her worst nightmare.

She glared at him. 'You.'

The physician answered, sounding chipper. 'Besides surly and completely unreasonable? I'm happy to say she's fine.'

'I'm right here,' she snapped.

'Yes, you are. You're going to be sore for a couple days. Bruised breastbone and—'

'Can I go now?'

'And,' he went on, 'you may have some neck trauma. Listen to your body and don't push it.'

Zach laughed at that; Micki sent him a look she wished could kill.

'I'll prescribe something for the pain—'

'Don't bother,' she said. 'I won't take it.'

'Ibuprofen then. Every four hours. Like clockwork. If that doesn't do the trick, I'll call in—'

'It will.'

He turned to Zach. 'Watch her. I'll be right back with her release papers.'

He left the room; she kept her gaze trained on the wall.

'Sorry about your car, Mick.'

'I don't want to talk about it.'

'I guess we should've taken mine, huh?'

'Shut up, Harris.'

'I'll make it up to you.'

'I told you, I don't want to talk about it.'

'I know you're pissed. And I think you should get it out. Just let me have it.'

He was right; she was pissed. If her entire body didn't feel like she'd been used as a punching bag, she'd use him as one. Tackle his ass and beat the crap out of him.

She glared at him. 'My car's dead, you realize that, right?'

'Not dead. Wounded in action.'

She went on as if he hadn't spoken. 'You always pull your weapon. If you're gonna confront a perp, you better be ready for war.'

'Yes, ma'am.'

She curved her hands into fists. 'And how the hell did you do that?'

'Do what?'

'Get the kid on the ground and cuffed like that? Without getting shot?'

He smiled in that way of his. *Charming. Ingratiating.* The jerk.

'When you slammed into them, the car door popped open and the kid tumbled out. Total face plant.'

Micki looked at him in disbelief. 'You are the luckiest son of a bitch I've ever had the displeasure of meeting.'

'I figured he was the lucky one. Kid could've been killed.'

'And so could you. You don't have nine lives. Keep that in mind for next time.'

'Yes, ma'am.'

'Stop that.'

'What?'

'The "yes, ma'am" shit. Like I'm your mother or something.' He simply cocked an eyebrow and she muttered an oath. 'What about the perp's homies?'

'Scattered like cockroaches. I pointed that out to Lamar.'

'Lamar?'

'The perp. He's only fifteen years old, can you believe that? Poor kid.'

She sputtered at that. The Nova was dead, she was battered and *he* felt sorry for the kid behind it all. 'He committed an armed robbery and shot the store employee!'

'It was only a flesh wound. Lamar didn't want to hurt her. He told me everything.'

Micki dropped her head into her hands, wincing at the movement.

'I rode over in the ambulance with him,' Zach went on. 'The Bloodhound Gangstazs recruited him. More like coerced him. He didn't have a choice, really. Tonight was his initiation. He was supposed to rob the store and kill any witnesses. He couldn't do it. Cried like a baby.'

She dropped her hands. 'And you believed that horse-shit?'

'He was telling the truth. I read him.'

'And your *read* never fails you?'

'Hasn't yet.' He paused. 'You saved my butt. Again. Thanks, partner.'

And again, he came out looking like a hero. Not a scratch on him. The guys down at the Eighth were going to have a field day with this.

'Why're you looking at me like that, Mick?'

'I hate you, Hollywood.'

He looked surprised, then laughed. 'Aw, c'mon, Mick. You can't hate me. I'm too damn cute.'

She couldn't, Micki realized. And he was. But she was working on it.

A girl had to have a goal.

22

Wednesday, July 10
9:50 A.M.

Zach sat on a wrought iron bench facing Jackson Square. Traffic on St Peter Street crawled by, the sound of the vehicles occasionally interrupted by the clip-clop of horses' hooves as they pulled tourist carriages.

He moved his gaze over the square, taking in the iconic statue of Andrew Jackson and the St Louis Cathedral's spire, the artists, psychics, and other entrepreneurs peddling their wares. Since the previous evening's stakeout of Brite Knight's place had proved a bust, he and Mick had decided to catch the fortune-teller here.

Mick was late. He glanced at his cell. No call, no text. And late wasn't her style.

She'd hardly spoken to him this morning. He didn't blame her for being pissed off, fed up with his antics. But it'd all turned out cool.

Except for her car. And bruises. And the squad room ribbing she'd taken from the likes of J.B. and Buster.

Yeah, he deserved to be dropped like a bad habit. She would if she could, but she had her orders.

And Micki 'Mad Dog' Dare took her orders – and her big-bad-cop role – seriously. Zach smiled to himself. He liked her. Thorns and all. Heck, the spiky little devils were almost endearing.

His cell went off. Not Mick, he saw. Parker. 'My man,' he said. 'S'up, dude?'

'I hear you were involved in a little excitement last night.'

'News travels fast.'

'Good work.'

'Thanks. But I had help.'

'I heard about that, too.' He sounded amused. 'Everyone's pleased with the program.'

He thought of the Nova. *Not everyone.* 'You find out anything on the psychic I told you about?'

'She isn't one of ours.'

'Ours?' Zach repeated. 'What do you mean?'

'The Bureau's.'

'Who else is there?'

'I'm being called back into a meeting, I've got to go.'

'Wait, Parker. Who else—'

He didn't finish because Parker had hung up. Zach frowned. Not one of the Bureau's. Not a Sixer. That was just weird.

'Why the frown?'

He looked up at Mick and smiled. 'Worried you'd decided I wasn't worth the trouble.'

'You aren't. Marching orders, Hollywood.'

'That's fair.' He stood. They started for the square. 'How're you feeling this morning?'

'Sore.'

'I've been thinking—'

'God help me.'

He went on as if she hadn't commented. 'If Brite Knight's the real deal—'

'Clairvoyant?'

'Yes. She might pick up on us and be gone before we even set eyes on her.'

'Seriously?'

'Yeah. Some clairvoyants can do that.'

'Can you?'

'No.'

'Too bad. So what do you suggest?'

'Let's split up,' he said. 'My guess is, these folks own their spot, either officially or unofficially. Miller's roommates said Knight's table was in front of the cathedral. You go from the right, I'll take the left. I think we'll have a better chance of staying off her radar.'

She was looking at him oddly. 'What?' he asked.

'Are you starting to think like a cop?'

'No worries of that, Mick.' He grinned. 'Still the same old Hollywood.'

They separated. Zach circled around to the left, Mick to the right. They would meet in front of the cathedral. Zach scanned the faces of the artists, psychics, and mimes as he passed.

The square was busy and most didn't notice him.

153

But a few looked his way, met his eyes and nodded. As if acknowledging a secret they shared. It made his skin crawl.

And then he found her. Just where Gwen's friends had said she had been that past Saturday.

And simultaneously, she found him. Just as those other few vendors had, she seemed to sense him and turned his way. She looked him dead in the eyes.

Or seemed to. He couldn't be sure because of the big dark glasses she wore.

When he started toward her, she stood and quickly gathered together her things. But before she could take a step away from her table, Mick had reached it.

He saw her hold up her shield and gave himself a pat on the back. Maybe he was starting to think like a cop after all.

'My partner, Detective Harris,' Mick said when he joined them at the small table. 'We have a few questions for you?'

'Answering questions, cher, it is what I do. Sit.' She motioned to the folding chair. 'Let's see what the cards have to say.'

She drew a deck of tarot cards from a small velvet bag and began to expertly shuffle them. Zach noticed she wore lace gloves.

Dark glasses. Gloves. Part of her schtick, Zach wondered. Or self-protection?

He was betting on the latter.

'We're looking for a young woman. Name's Gwen Miller.' Mick held out a photograph.

The woman fumbled the cards. 'Haven't seen her.'

'Could you take a better look?'

She glanced at it again. 'Sorry, cher. Maybe I give you a reading instead?'

'Maybe you should take off your sunglasses,' Zach said.

'It won't make a difference, I've never seen her before.'

'That's strange,' Mick said. 'We have three witnesses who say you did a reading for this girl on Saturday. It was her birthday.'

'Your witnesses have me confused with someone else.'

Mick held out her phone with the picture of the psychic with Miller. 'I don't think so.'

Brite Knight stared at the photo, then shrugged. 'Maybe I did do a reading for her. So what?'

'Why'd you lie, Ms Knight?'

'I see a lot of people. They run together in my head.'

'I find that hard to believe.'

'Believe what you like.'

'What did you tell her?'

'Same thing I tell everyone: what they want to hear.'

'Not this time.' Zach bent, forcing her to look at him. 'Whatever you told her shook her up.'

'I don't know what you're talking about.'

'Of course you do.'

Mick took over. 'Her friends described you as a psycho. Said you recoiled from her. You must remember that.'

The psychic paused. When she spoke again, her heavy Cajun accent was gone. 'She, this Gwen Miller, was just one of a hundred people I flag down every day. They run together.'

'She's missing,' he said.

'I don't know anything about that.'

'Of course not.' His voice dripped sarcasm. 'Take off your sunglasses, please?'

'Why?'

'Why not? You trying to hide something?'

She took off the glasses, expression defiant, and looked at them both. Miller's friends had called her eyes strange, freaky. Instead, they were a dark brown. Nothing special about them.

'You ever wear colored contacts, Ms Knight?' Mick asked.

'Sometimes. Why?'

'You wearing them now?'

'What if I am?'

Zach leaned in. 'You really do have the gift, don't you? You're special. Tell us about it.'

She snorted. 'You're more full of shit than I am. I'm nothing special, Detective. This is a job. The outfit, the accent, all of it. A job. I need to make money to keep a roof over my head.'

'I'd like a reading.' Zach took two twenties out of his wallet, tossed them on her table.

She stared at the money, then returned her gaze to his. 'Sorry, I'm done for the day.'

'Bullshit, Ms Knight.'

'Look, all I do is read people. What they're wearing, how they hold themselves. And I listen. Most tell me what they want to hear.'

'You're a fake. That's what you're saying?'

Zach sensed she hated saying it, that she had to force the words out. 'I'm good at what I do. It's a gift, just not supernatural. It doesn't hurt anyone. They walk away satisfied.'

'Not always,' Mick said. 'We checked your record. Not everyone's been satisfied.'

Her cheeks flamed red. 'Some people are just ugly. They don't want to be happy.'

'Sometimes you tell them things they don't want to hear. That's what happened with Gwen Miller, isn't it?'

'This is harassment. I told you, I don't even remember her.'

Zach held out his hand. 'Read my palm.'

She slipped her hands into the pockets of her brightly colored handkerchief skirt.

'Read my palm, and we'll go.'

She hesitated a moment, then cupped his outstretched hand in hers. He expected a jolt. Of energy, pure emotion.

It didn't come.

He readied himself for series of images, flashes of memory, something.

He got nothing.

'What's wrong?' she asked softly. A condescending smile touched her mouth, as if she had known what he expected and was amused by his surprise. Much the way a cat was amused by a mouse's attempts at escape.

It pissed him off. 'Just waiting for you to begin.'

She didn't move her gaze from his. 'You've been given everything. Everything but what you long for most.'

'And what is that?'

'You know in your heart of hearts.' She closed his hand into a fist. 'But what you seek is not here.'

Generic, Zach acknowledged. He could have rattled that off. Or Mick.

But her words rocked him to his core.

Everything but what you long for most.

What you seek is not here.

'Brilliant move,' Mick said as they walked away, 'getting her to take your hand. What did get from her?'

'Nothing.'

'Nothing?' she repeated, tone incredulous. 'For real?'

'Yeah. Not so brilliant after all.'

'I didn't know that could happen.'

'Neither did I.'

'Maybe it was the gloves?'

It wasn't. He'd felt the warmth of Knight's skin through them, had felt her steady pulse.

'Maybe,' he said anyway.

'She was lying. About not remembering Miller. I'm not surprised, though. People like Knight, living on the fringe, don't want any involvement with cops.'

Micki paused, studying him with narrowed eyes. 'Your reading, what she said. It's bothering you.'

What you seek is not here.

Answers. The truth.

He shook his head. 'No.'

'What aren't you telling me?'

That Brite Knight was different from anybody he had ever met. He had held her hand – and felt nothing. She had looked at him – and he had known she saw into the very darkest corners of his being.

That had never happened before.

Almost as if Brite Knight wasn't human.

23

Wednesday, July 10
8:50 P.M.

Zach glanced at Mick. She sat at her desk, bathed in the glow of her computer monitor, intent in her search for the meanings of the number seven. In the forty-eight hours since locating Knight, they had followed every possible lead in an effort to locate Gwen Miller. Questioned classmates and teachers. Family, friends, co-workers. Anyone whose path had crossed hers in recent weeks.

Nothing. Nada. It was as if she had fallen off the face of the earth.

Miller's family had proved to be as draining as Mick had warned. They were understandably frantic with worry, both needy and demanding. They'd had difficulty grasping the concept that he couldn't be looking for their daughter and holding their hands at the same time.

Holding their hands. The emotion that had transferred from their hands to his had been overwhelming.
Especially Miller's father. His baby. His little girl. Zach
had been assailed with images of the young woman
as a child – special, precious moments he'd had no
right to be a part of.

But he hadn't been able to shut them out.

And yet with Brite Knight, he'd clasped her hand
and felt the loudest nothing imaginable.

Almost as if she wasn't human.

'You're staring at me,' Mick said, not looking up.
'Why?'

He was, he realized and dragged a hand through his
hair. 'Let's call it a day. I'm beat.'

'You go ahead. I want to finish this search.'

'Anything so far?'

'More than I expected. Seven's a biggie. Lots of
symbolic meanings, both cultural and religious. Plenty
for some sick bastard to latch onto.'

'Call me if you find something.'

She looked up then, eyebrows drawing together. 'You
going anywhere besides home?'

'Not planning on it. Why?'

'Wondering if I need to be on high ass-saving alert.'

He laughed. 'I'll SOS you.'

'Be careful. This time I won't have the Nova to save
the day.'

'I'll keep that in mind.'

The French Quarter street outside the Eighth was
crowded. Mick had warned him that weekends could
get nuts, depending on what was going on in the city.

Festivals, a sporting event or convention. Mardi Gras, God help them. Basically, anytime tourists poured into the Quarter, their lives went bat-shit crazy.

Zach started toward his vehicle, then changed direction, heading deeper into the Quarter. He wove his way through and around the partiers – being bumped and jostled – wandering aimlessly. Oddly, there were more people in the Quarter than the other night, but less energy.

Or was he simply adapting to it?

He found himself standing in front of St Louis Cathedral, in the spot where Brite Knight parked her table. He smiled to himself. Not so aimless after all.

Brite Knight had the gift. She had seen something bad when she took Gwen Miller's hand. Bad enough that she had run away. Strong enough that she had been unable to protect herself against it. That she had been unable to hide her fear – no, horror – from Miller and her friends.

And Zach knew what it was. Because it had literally knocked him flat on his ass.

He started walking again. This time with purpose. The fortune-teller wouldn't evade him this time.

He remembered where she lived. Outside the Quarter, the fringes. Where people like Brite Knight always lived. It wasn't the sort of block one walked alone at night, though he reminded himself he carried both a badge and a gun. A gun he had drawn but was uncertain he would be able to use against another human being.

He reached Knight's home and climbed the couple

162

of sagging stairs to the front porch. The sound of a TV came from inside; a local news station.

He knocked; she came to the door, cracked it open and peered out. No gloves. No sunglasses. Eyes as bright as a cat's. Just the way Miller's friends had described them.

'I need to talk to you,' he said.

'Not interested.'

She moved to shut the door in his face; he stopped her, forcing the door open. 'I want answers.'

'"I want",' she mocked. 'Like a child. You'll have to find your precious answers somewhere else.'

'You're going to tell me the truth. I'm not leaving until you do.'

She narrowed those strangely bright eyes. 'Arrogant Half Light. Spoiled child. Given gifts you have no idea of. No appreciation for. You—'

'*Missing University of New Orleans student Gwen Miller—*'

He jerked his gaze past the fortune-teller to the TV in the living room beyond. Miller's face.

'*Anyone with information please call Crimestoppers at—*'

A reward. Her parents were offering a ten-thousand-dollar reward. They'd taken a second mortgage on their house to do it.

Zach looked back at Knight. She, too, was staring at the television, face as white as a ghost's.

'What do you know?' he asked softly.

'Leave me alone.'

'I can't do that.'

163

She shook her head. 'You're sticking your nose into things far bigger, far more dangerous than you have any idea of.'

'I know more than you think. It's got an energy . . . strong. Furious. You felt it, when you took Gwen Miller's hand.'

'Leave me alone! You'll get us both killed.'

'There's another girl. Her name's Angel. Angel Gomez.'

Her fear crackled in the air between them, racing along his nerve endings. The hair on his arms and legs stood straight up.

'There's no help for them.' Her voice shook and tears filled her eyes. 'The darkness is greedy and—'

'Are they dead? Are we too late?'

'—light is fleeting.'

'What do you mean? If they're not dead—'

'Goodbye, Detective.'

This time he allowed her to slam the door in his face. He heard the dead bolt turn into place. His thoughts were scrambled, whirling with what she had said.

She had called him a Half Light. Had said the darkness was greedy. That he would get them both killed.

Zach turned and walked away, sensing the fortune-teller watching him go. Feeling those bright eyes boring into his back.

Parker, he thought. They had to talk. But not by phone. Face-to-face. Saturday, when he returned from Washington.

24

Thursday, July 11
8:15 A.M.

Zach couldn't stop thinking about the things Brite Knight had said to him. What was a Half Light?

He'd been unable to sleep, so he'd done his own internet search: light and dark were symbols for life and death, good and evil. He got all that. Light – life – was fleeting. And darkness – death – was greedy.

Mumbo-jumbo, as Mick was fond of saying.

Or was it? Maybe something more. Something that could lead them to Miller and Gomez.

'Good morning, Mick,' he said and set a triple tall latte on her desk.

'Hey,' she said, reaching for the cup. 'Thanks.'

She took several sips. Made a 'Mmmm' sound and glanced up at him. 'What the hell did *you* do last night?'

'What?'

'You look like shit.'

'Don't act so happy about it. So do you.'

She took another sip of the coffee. 'Fell asleep at my desk.'

'At least you slept.' He propped himself against the desk. 'Couldn't switch off.'

She looked sympathetic. 'Why do you think pills and alcohol are so many cops' best friend?'

'Is that what you do, Mick? Anesthetize?'

'Nah. I figure I'll sleep when I'm dead.' She slid him several printed pages. 'Seven's a very popular number with mystics, numerologists, astrologists, and religious scholars. Lots of symbolism.'

He skimmed them. 'The seven wonders of the world, seven deadly sins, seven continents, seven levels of hell, seven days of the week . . .' he looked up, eyebrow cocked with amusement. 'Snow White and the seven dwarfs?'

'I was being thorough.'

'That's my Mick.' He flipped through the pages. 'This is pretty amazing, actually. Nothing about light and darkness?'

'Should there be?'

'Just a theory.'

She frowned. 'One you obviously haven't shared with me.'

'It occurred to me last night. The fortune-teller's name. Brite Knight. Light and dark.'

She took another sip and made another 'Mmm' sound and he bit back a chuckle.

'I may not be on the top of my game this morning, but I don't get it, dude.'

'I didn't say it was a good theory.'

'Pretty lame, actually.' She paused, met his eyes. 'Unless something prompted it?'

He didn't even blink. 'Just popped into my head.'

Her brow furrowed. She opened her mouth, then shut it. As if she doubted him. Which she had every reason to, since he was lying his ass off.

But only because he had to. For now.

'Have you talked to Parker?'

'Why?'

'Just thinking you might have.'

Because she was smart. And she didn't trust him. 'Briefly. He's in DC until Saturday.'

'Why?' she asked again.

'In DC? I didn't ask.'

'No.' She gave her head a slight shake. 'Why'd you talk to Parker?'

'Thought his take might be helpful.'

She curled her hands around the paper cup, expression thoughtful. 'Was it?'

'He had no take. Just wanted me to write it up.'

'Typical Bureau.'

'Exactly.'

Activity swirled around them, conversations, laughter, discussions. Warming up for the day, for the weekend ahead.

'I'd like to have a chat with him,' she said.

He played dumb. 'Who?'

'Parker. He's your contact. He's deep into this whole

Sixer thing. If this "big and bad" energy you picked up on is the real deal—'

'It is.'

'Then Parker knows something.'

Exactly. But you and Parker? No way. Not happening.

'Not necessarily.'

'You're not serious.'

'What do you expect to get from him?'

'Answers.'

'To what?'

'To what the hell's going on, that's what!'

'Don't go getting your knickers in a twist.'

'Knickers in a—'

'Look, I know Parker, he's not going to want to talk to you.' he lowered his voice. 'You're not Bureau.'

'That's bullshit. He damn well better talk to me. I'll hold him down and cuff him if I have to.'

Clearly, she had no idea of Parker's abilities. But still, the image of it made him smile.

25

Zach opened his eyes, instantly awake. *Parker. Approaching the front door.* He climbed out of bed and into a pair of shorts, then grabbed a T-shirt on his way to the front room.

He reached the door just as the bell sounded. He swung it open. 'What the hell, P? It's four in the freaking morning.'

'I need a drink.' Parker strode past him. 'I hate commercial flights. They completely blow.'

Zach watched him cross to the bar. 'What happened to Saturday?'

'Last time I checked, it was.' He held up a bottle of red. 'Do you mind?'

'Go for it.'

Parker peeled off the metal cap then cupped his hand

169

loosely over the top of the bottle. With a quick flick of his wrist, the cork released. He grinned and tossed it to Zach.

Zach caught the cork, but didn't comment. A parlor trick. All the Sixers had them.

'I thought you'd be happier to see me,' he said, pouring a glass of the wine.

'Four A.M.'s not my happy time.'

'Our chat couldn't wait until later. I'm heading out to the coast at noon.'

Zach nodded. 'Okay, then let's do this.'

They sat. Parker began. 'Tell me about the energy.'

'I want to start with the fortune-teller, Brite Knight. What is she?'

'I haven't met the woman, you have. You tell me.'

'I'm not interested in playing your FBI games, Parker. If I knew, I wouldn't ask. What is she?'

'If she's special—'

'She is.'

'Then she's one of us.'

'On the phone, you said she wasn't one of us.'

'Not a Sixer. But like us. The Gifted.'

The Gifted. As if they were a separate race, not just an anomaly.

As if reading his mind, Parker leaned forward. 'Did you really think there were only a handful of us?'

'How many?'

'Too many to count.'

'She was different from you and me.'

'In what way?'

'I got nothing from her but a heartbeat. No thoughts

or feelings, not one memory. That's never happened before.'

'Maybe that's her gift?'

Easy. Glib. Not one ruffled feather; not even a glimmer of curiosity.

None of this is news to him.

Zach narrowed his gaze. Perhaps this would be. 'Or maybe she's not human?'

Parker choked on the sip of wine. Zach smiled. 'I see I finally have your full attention.'

'That's ridiculous.'

'Is it?'

'I've seen it all when it comes to the gifted. And we're all human.'

Zach held his gaze. 'I went to see her. For answers.'

'But you didn't get any?'

He shook his head. 'She was scared. Not of me. Of what she saw when she held Gwen Miller's hand.'

'The energy that kicked your ass.'

'That's my guess.' Zach paused, recalling her words. 'She was scared and angry. At me. For interfering. She said I'd get us both killed.'

Parker said nothing, so Zach went on. 'She called me a Half Light. Said it as if it were a slur. A Half Light,' he repeated. 'What did she mean by that?'

Parker's brow furrowed. 'Something about your gifts, maybe?'

'You haven't heard that term before?'

He shook his head again. 'No.'

He sounded sincere. Absolutely convincing. Yet how could that be? Parker hadn't been surprised by Zach's

171

lack of response to Knight, or the description of the unusually strong energy, but he'd never heard the expression Half Light?

Convincing or not, Zach didn't buy it. 'She also said light is fleeting.'

'Life is fleeting?'

'No, light. And that the darkness is greedy.'

'She sounds like a new age whack-job. Which isn't surprising. The gifted often lose their way. Besides, you're focusing on the wrong thing. It's the energy source we're after, not a delusional fortune-teller.'

'What about the number seven?'

'It obviously has special significance for the UNSUB. What that is, we don't know yet. We need more information.'

Again, Zach wasn't quite buying Parker's response. But why would Parker lie to him about this? They were on the same team, after all.

Zach held his hand up, fingers splayed. 'You feeling strong this morning, P?'

Parker eyed him. 'You can control the transfer?'

'I don't know. It was big and badass.'

'Then I'll pass.'

'Scared, Parker?'

'Cautious.'

'Bullshit. Who're we after? You know.'

'I don't. If I did, I wouldn't need you, now would I?'

'Why don't I believe you're being straight with me?'

'Your problem, man. We're on the same team.'

'Are we?'

Parker indicated Zach's phone. 'Your partner's calling.'

A split second later, his cell went off. The sun wasn't even up yet. 'H'lo,' he answered, making his voice thick and sleepy-sounding.

'Wake up, Prince Charming. Another girl's missing.'

26

The missing girl had connections, Micki learned when she reached the scene. Patricia Putnam's dad was Senator Roland Putnam, head of the powerful Foreign Relations Committee.

She signed the scene log and glanced at Zach, standing quietly next to her, gaze fixed on the front door of the small duplex. 'Hollywood, it's about to rain Federal agents. We need to do our thing before they take over.'

He nodded, expression tight. Preparing himself, she thought. In a way no one else here had to. And unlike the Miller scene, they didn't have this one to themselves.

'Detective Dare?'

She turned. An officer, vaguely familiar. Perkins, his

badge said. He had a young man with him. Putnam's neighbor, she thought.

In the next moment, Perkins confirmed it. 'Jeff Spears. He called it in.'

'Hi, Jeff,' Micki said. I'm Detective Dare, this is my partner Detective Harris. I need to ask you a few questions.'

The young man was tall and skinny with a mop of dark curly hair. He stuffed his hands into the pockets of his khaki shorts, looking uneasy. 'Sure.'

'Could you tell me what happened?'

'I don't know what happened. I didn't have anything to do with it.'

Somebody doesn't like cops so much. 'I mean, what prompted you to call us?'

'Oh.' He let out a long breath. 'I heard noises coming from her place.'

'What kind of noises?'

'Like banging and stomping. It was really loud.'

'Where were you?'

'In bed. Trying to sleep. I'm a barista at PJs. I was supposed to open today.'

'What time?'

'Five.' He sighed. 'I hope I don't get fired.'

'I'll have Officer Perkins talk to your boss.'

'Thanks.'

She went on. 'Okay, so you heard banging and stomping, what did you do next?'

'Pounded on the wall. Figured she was having a party, it being her birthday and all.'

Micki looked up from her notebook. 'Did you say it was her birthday?'

'Yeah. Twenty-first.'

She glanced at Zach, saw that he had also connected the dots. This made three.

'What happened next?'

'It got worse. Like things really being slammed around, broken.'

'No music?'

His brow furrowed slightly, as if he hadn't considered that before – like how could it have been a party without tunes?

'No,' he said.

'Laughter?'

'No.'

'Screaming?'

'No, God. No.'

'Then what?'

'I was really pissed off, so I called her.'

'You're friends?'

'No. But we're friendly.'

'Gotcha.' Micki made a note. 'Go on.'

'She didn't answer. But the noise stopped.'

'Why didn't you just go to sleep then?'

'I tried, but then I started worrying, you know. I started thinking how weird . . .' He cleared his throat; shifted from one foot to the other. 'So I got up and came over, just to make sure she was okay.'

'What did you do first?'

'Knocked on the front door. Called out. She didn't answer, but – I knew she couldn't be asleep, not after all that racket. So I tried the door.'

He flushed, looked from one of them to the other.

176

'I'm not going to get in any trouble for that, right? I'm mean, I know her dad's some sort of big deal.'

'A senator. But no, you won't get in any trouble. The door was open?'

'No, locked. I almost went back to bed, but I just had this feeling. So, I went around back. To the kitchen door.'

He paused, as if struggling to speak. 'That's when I saw the mess.'

'The mess?'

'Like a tornado had gone through the kitchen, stuff everywhere. I ran back to my place and called you guys.'

'You see anyone coming or going?'

'No one.'

'You're certain?'

'Yeah.' He shrugged. 'But I wasn't watching.'

'Thank you, Jeff.' Micki closed her notebook. 'Detective Harris, do you have any—'

'Your partner left.'

She glanced sideways at the spot where Zach had stood moments before. 'Where'd he go?'

'Around back.'

Micki nodded and handed Spears a card. 'If you think of anything else, call me.'

Then she sighed and went in search of Zach.

27

Zach decided not to wait for Mick. From what the neighbor kid had said, the kitchen was ground zero. And he didn't want an audience for his reaction to this thing. His nerve endings were crawling and he hadn't even stepped inside.

He went around back. Like a lot of the homes in the area, this one sat on pilings. Three steps led to a small landing and the back door; through the open door, he glimpsed chaos.

He started up the steps, a pressure settling on his chest. With each step, the pressure grew stronger. It affected his ears, his equilibrium.

But he took the last step, crossed to the doorway. And stopped. Every cabinet door stood open, as did the refrigerator and freezer. Kitchen table and chairs on their sides. Bottles and jars smashed, food products spilled across the floor.

He stepped cautiously through. The physical chaos was nothing compared to the energy that swirled around him like a funnel cloud. Angry and aggressive. Like before. But bigger, More *insistent*. It clawed and tugged at him. Wanting in. Wanting *him*.

Not his physical being, he thought, head growing light. Something else. It felt as if his head was about to explode. As if—

Get out. Now!

He responded to the command without question, stumbling backward, outside. His ears popped; he dropped to the top step and brought his head between his knees. He breathed deeply – in his nose, out his mouth.

With each expelled breath, he promised himself he would not be sick. Not this time. This bastard was *not* going to get the best of him.

But how did he protect himself from it?

Use your light, Zach.

A woman's voice. As clear as if she was standing behind him. He looked over his shoulder, even though he knew he'd find no one there.

His cell went off. Parker, he saw. 'Yo,' he answered. 'Your sense of timing's sensational.'

'You're at the scene.'

'You know I am. Come on in, the water's warm.'

Parker didn't laugh. 'Feds are on their way.'

'So I heard. They know about me?'

'No. And they can't.'

'Great.' He paused, lowered his voice. 'Having my ass kicked here. I could use some help.'

'Figure it out. We need answers.'

The arrogance infuriated him. 'You know more about this thing than you're telling. Give me something, Parker. Throw me a bone.'

For a long moment, Parker was silent. 'Earlier, you asked who we're after.' He paused. 'Not a who, Zach. A what.'

Before Zach could respond, Parker was gone.

28

Micki found Zach sitting on the back steps. The steps led to the home's secondary entrance. It stood open; she saw it led directly into the kitchen.

She returned her gaze to his face. He didn't look good. 'Who was that on the phone?'

He confirmed what she'd suspected. 'Parker.'

'What'd he have to say?'

'Feds are on their way. They don't know about me. And they can't.'

She nodded. He sounded as off as he looked. She pointed toward the doorway. 'Find anything?'

'Haven't made it all the way in.' He paused. 'Don't know if I can.'

'The same energy?'

'Yeah. But worse.'

She cocked an eyebrow. 'What does that mean?'

'More pissed off.'

She frowned. 'After the way you reacted last time, I would've bet money it couldn't get worse.'

'You and me both.'

'I'll get started.'

'And I'll work on getting my shit together.'

Micki nodded and moved past him and into the kitchen. Big mess. As if someone had decided to go berserk. Groceries all over the floor. Cabinets opened and emptied. Furniture overturned.

Mick smiled grimly. At least they could rule out a cat burglar.

She picked her way to the center of the room, to a relatively clean patch of tile flooring. She moved her gaze over the destruction. Mayo, pickles, and grape jelly jars smashed. Smears of peanut butter and a carton of milk splashed all over the floor. A carton of eggs, dropped and stomped. Clear boot print. And ketchup at the center of the mess – like a heart. Also stomped. The red condiment had shot out like blood from an artery.

The items appeared to have been placed purposely, forming an uneven semi-circle.

Micki skimmed the circle again. 'Son of a bitch,' she muttered, then turned toward the door. Zach had come to stand on the landing. She indicated the semi-circle. 'Seven items. Not an accident.'

'His calling card?'

She cocked an eyebrow, torn between amusement and appreciation. 'You google that term on the way over, Hollywood?'

'Yeah.' He grinned, though it looked forced. 'Just in case, Mick.'

She returned her gaze to the items. 'Why? If the calling card's the number seven, why the crescent shape? Why not just use the ketchup to write it out? What's he trying to tell us?'

'Hell if I know.' He hesitated a moment. 'What if it's not a "he", Mick?'

'A woman?' She pursed her lips in thought. 'Can't exclude the possibility. But it doesn't feel that way to me.' She squatted to get a closer look. 'Let's see if he left anything else.'

Sure enough, what looked like drops of blood. She followed them to the refrigerator and found a smear on the door. 'Bingo. Sometime during this party, he cut himself.'

Zach didn't reply and she turned toward him once more. He stared blankly at her.

'You look so strange,' she said again. 'Are you all right?'

'Define all right.' He glanced over his shoulder, then back at her. 'Feds have arrived. In five . . . four . . . three—'

He stepped back from the door. Two agents, she saw. Both tall, dark, and crisply pressed.

'Detective Harris,' Zach said, greeting the two. Micki noticed he didn't offer them a hand. In fact, his hands were shoved deep into his pockets.

'My partner, Detective Dare.'

'Agents Culpepper and Roberts. You've been made aware of why we're here?' She agreed and they went

183

on. 'We understand you're investigating a similar incident from a week ago.'

'Yes. The girl's name is Gwen Miller. No political connections. She also went missing on her birthday.'

'We'll need you to bring us up to speed.'

'Of course.'

They stepped into the kitchen. The taller of the two muttered an oath. 'Was the previous scene like this one?'

'No. And yes.'

Roberts looked back at Zach. 'You coming, Detective Harris?'

'Can't. Severe peanut allergy.' He nodded toward the smear of peanut butter, then shifted his gaze to Micki. 'If you've got this, Mick, I'll start the door-to-door.'

29

Zach tightened his grip on the steering wheel. He glanced in the rearview mirror at the disappearing row of emergency vehicles. When Mick realized what he'd done, she'd tear him apart.

Abandoned the scene. No word to anyone. Not even her.

He'd had to get out. It'd taken all his concentration to keep up his cop-in-control facade for the two agents.

Now, his head felt on the verge of exploding. The blood thrummed so crazily at his temple his thoughts scrambled. Faster and faster. The pain grew brilliant, blinding. Bright white light.

Zach lowered the car windows. The mild morning air rushed over him, bringing him a sliver of relief. He sucked it in, shuddering. Not a who, they were tracking, Parker had said. A what.

Zach believed him now. Whatever that thing at the scene was, it'd tried to climb inside him.

The squeal of brakes and scream of a horn sent Zach careening back to the moment.

He'd run a red light. A mini-van barreled toward him. A woman at the wheel, kids in the back. Their eyes met. Her expression registered horror, realization.

Zach prepared himself for the impact, for the sound of crumpling metal and breaking glass, the force of the airbag slamming him against the seat.

They didn't come. The miss couldn't have been by more than a hair's breadth. He felt the vibration of her vehicle skimming past his.

The enormity of what could have happened hit him. He began to shake. Too close . . . too damn close. He could've killed that woman. Or one of her children.

He came to a side street and turned onto it. He stopped, cut the engine, and rested his forehead on the wheel.

What the hell was happening to him? He'd never experienced anything like this. An energy that could bring him to his knees? With the power to crawl into his head and scramble his brain?

He wasn't cut out for this superhero bullshit. He'd had a good thing going, pre-Sixers. Life had been easy. Fast car, fine threads, beautiful women.

It hadn't been enough.

He'd felt more alive the short time he'd been a Sixer than he had in all his years of living large.

186

Dammit! This wasn't what he'd signed up for. To give a shit? To take something so seriously, shrugging and walking away wasn't an option? No way. Zach Harris kept things loose. Kept his options open.

But who is Zach Harris?

He had to get a grip. Had to figure out either how to beat this thing or protect himself from it.

He leaned his head back on the seat and closed his eyes, told himself to focus. When his gifts first manifested, they'd turned him upside down. Physically and emotionally. He'd had to learn how to harness his abilities. How to control their effect on him.

He hadn't been helpless back then, hadn't been a victim. And he wouldn't be now.

Zach turned to what had worked in those early days and then again during his Sixers training. He drew a deep breath in through his nose and released it out his mouth, working to clear his head as he did. Visualizing gathering up the chaos, blowing it out. New breath. Clean. Sparkling and bright. Collect the mental garbage again. Dark and ugly. Pain and confusion. The stench of whatever that thing was. Dump it at the curb. Go back for more.

Minutes passed. His trembling eased; his heart rate slowed. Mind emptied.

Of everything.

Except light. Gleaming and bright.

The realization hit him like a thunderbolt. Zach opened his eyes and sat up straight. White light. When he emptied himself of everything else, that's what was left. It'd always been that way. He'd figured it was for everyone.

But what if it wasn't? Emptied, did some folks have a gray slate? Or colors? Like a painter's palette? Or even a deep endless black?

Zach thought about the voice in his head from earlier, urging him to use his light. A woman's voice. One he hadn't recognized. Even as a part of him denied the possibility it had been real, another accepted the notion.

Someone sent to help him? But who? And how?

Or simply a manifestation of his own psyche, another part of himself responding to the assault?

Arrogant Half Light.

Brite Knight. She would know. The darkness is greedy, she'd said. Light is fleeting.

Not a coincidence.

He jumped as his cell phone vibrated at his hip. He unclipped it. Mick, he saw.

She didn't give him a chance to speak. 'Where the hell are you?'

'Up the street.'

'What street?'

'I don't know. The one with the streetcar line.'

'Seriously?'

'Dead serious. Or almost dead, but that's another story.' He peered out the window. 'I had to pull over.'

'You're in your car?' Her tone was hushed, but vibrated with fury. 'You left the scene? Just climbed in your car and—'

'Drove off. Yeah. I had to get away from there, Mick.'

'You can't do that. You can't just decide you're

188

going to make a coffee run or something and leave the scene.'

She was sputtering – a fact he wasn't about to point out. 'We have to talk.'

'You bet your ass we do!'

'Not like this.' A woman pushing a baby carriage walked past, glancing in at him curiously. 'Face-to-face. Someplace private.'

'This is bullshit, Harris. I covered for you. Made up some crap about you checking out a hotline tip.'

'The energy attacked me. Stepping out of the kitchen wasn't enough.'

'Details. Now.'

'No, not like this. Meet me at the Eighth.'

'One hour,' she said and hung up.

The hour passed in what seemed to Zach like a blink of an eye. He sat across an interview room table from her; she was looking at him like he'd sprouted a second – and third – head.

He went on anyway. 'It felt like it was hammering at me. Trying to find a way inside me.'

'The energy?'

'Yes.'

She drew her eyebrows together. 'To do what?'

'Ruin my day, steal my soul. How the hell do I know? I've never had anything like that happen before. And believe me, nobody, including Parker, warned me something like this was even possible.'

She stood. Began to pace. 'But I felt nothing. Culpepper and Roberts felt nothing.'

'Just my lucky day, I guess.'

'Talk to me about the energy. You say it's the same as before.'

'Yes,' he agreed. 'But more aggressive. Angrier.'

'And that's it?'

He shoved his hands into his pockets. 'For now.'

'For now,' she repeated acidly. 'Wonderful. It's like being partners with frickin' Houdini. What're you trying to hide from me now?'

'Nothing.'

'Bullshit.'

'I think I can beat this thing.'

'How?'

'I don't know yet. A feeling.'

She didn't believe him. He saw it in her expression, the slight tightening of her jaw, the thinning of her mouth.

'What about the rest of the scene,' he asked. 'What did you find?'

'Other than the kitchen, nothing out of order. No numbers carved into doors.'

'Both girls were celebrating their birthday.'

'All three girls,' he corrected. 'I think Gomez is the one who got away.'

'Based on what?'

'The energy on her ID. And she disappeared.'

Mick shook her head. 'She didn't disappear. She checked out.'

'Think about this,' he said. 'She leaves her home and abandons her job. Pretty drastic, wouldn't you say?'

'Isn't that the MO Teddy described? She decided it was time to move on.'

190

'Or she ran for her life.'

Mick snorted. 'Again, based on what?'

'Look.' He stood and crossed to her. 'If this thing is as big and bad as we think—'

'Back way up, Hollywood. We're looking for a perp. Flesh and blood, two arms, two legs, the whole bit.'

'That's what you're looking for, Mick. That's not what I'm tracking.' He held her gaze a moment, then turned away. 'And I believe she came into contact with it.'

'We find her, maybe we find our perp.'

He agreed. 'So, where'd she go?'

'Family member. Friend. Maybe she left the area.'

He hoped not. 'Where're Culpepper and Roberts?'

'Presently, going over the Miller report. If they spot something we missed, it's really gonna chap my ass.'

'They won't.'

'You didn't shake hands with 'em. Why?'

She didn't miss a thing. He'd have to remember that. 'I couldn't. My system was getting ready to completely short circuit. And without me and the energy, we've got pretty much zilch.'

'You've got confidence, Hollywood. I'll give you that. But I promise you—'

His cell went off; he held up a hand stopping her. 'Detective Harris.'

'What are you going to do now, Half Light?'

'Ms Knight?' He motioned Mick, mouthed her name. She grabbed a notebook.

'I heard about the new girl.'

'New girl?'

'Putnam. We need to meet.'

'You know something about the girls?'

'Maybe.'

'You know who snatched them?'

'I know they're in danger.'

'What kind of danger?'

'Tonight, Half Light. Midnight. Café du Monde.'

'I'll be there.'

'Just you. No cops. No feds.'

'I am a cop.'

'This is between you and me. No one else. Or I don't show.'

'Why would I do that?'

'Angel Gomez. I know where she is.'

Gomez. He'd been right, she was the one who got away.

She could lead him to the energy.

'Okay, I'll be there.'

He re-holstered his phone and looked at Mick. 'Knight wants to meet. Midnight. Café du Monde.'

'Why?'

'Something about the missing girls. She wasn't specific, but said they're in danger.'

'Tell me something I don't know.'

'She said she knows where Gomez is. Which answers our question of a moment ago.'

'She ran to Knight.' Mick hesitated a moment on that, then nodded. 'Okay, good. We'll be there.'

'Just me. She was insistent on it.'

'Oh hell no, Hollywood. That's so not happening.'

30

Zach sat at one of Café du Monde's outdoor tables. He'd chosen a seat at the outer edge of the patio, in full sight of Mick. She'd refused to wait behind but had agreed to keep her distance, finding a spot on the Moon Walk above and behind him.

He wondered why Brite Knight had picked here to meet. The safety of a public place? The fact that here, no one would give them a second glance? Zach smiled to himself. Or like him, an unhealthy obsession with the sugary dough bombs?

The waiter deposited his order, collected payment, and hurried to the next table. Zach checked his phone. Still not quite midnight. He dialed Mick, saw the connection had been made and laid his phone on the table. Low tech spy gear, he thought. Mick would be able to listen to their conversation, no warrant or wires required. Unless, of course, the fortune-teller caught on.

Zach had dealt with the fact that Mick might hear something he'd rather she didn't – things that he'd deliberately kept from her – but he figured the inevitable end to that was coming anyway.

He took a giant bite of a beignet and powdered sugar went everywhere. He heard Mick's snort of amusement, and he grinned. So much for absolute silence on the line.

He wiped his mouth, then dropped the used napkin over the phone just as the cathedral bells began ringing out the hour.

She's coming.

Zach scanned the thinning crowd of Saturday night revelers and caught sight of her. Knight stood at the corner of Jackson Square and Chartres Street, waiting for the crosswalk light to change.

Their eyes met, hers so bright tonight he could make out the color of her irises from here. She nodded slightly in acknowledgement. Traffic cleared and she started across. Suddenly she stopped, causing the drunk behind her to nearly topple over. She lifted her face slightly to the breeze, as if to catch a scent. The way an animal in the wild did at the presence of a hunter.

In the blink of an eye, she turned and headed in the opposite direction. He swore and leapt to his feet. 'She's bolting,' he said, snatching up his phone and starting after her. 'I'm in pursuit.'

Knight was faster than he would have imagined she

could be in her long gypsy skirt. Zach darted across the street, dodging vehicles and earning the blare of horns, all the while trying to keep her brightly colored scarves in sight.

Into the park she went. Zach followed, pressing. When he cleared its iron gates, he caught a glimpse of red rounding the corner of the cathedral.

He was closing the distance between them.

Zach pushed harder. Feet pounding on the pavement, heart and breath coming fast and hard. She ducked onto St Peter Street, going behind the church, onto Royal. Only moments behind, he too made the turn. And stopped cold.

The fortune-teller had disappeared. Zach drew his eyebrows together. How could that be? Had she ducked into a shop or . . .

No. Everything on this little strip of Royal Street was closed, locked up for the night. Like another world from where he had just been: quiet, eerily peaceful. Empty.

But not.

Zach made his way forward. Something electric rippled over his nerve endings. The hair on his arms and at the back of his neck stood up.

Knight was here. He felt her presence.

Zach made the corner, heading back toward the Square. Moving slowly now, scanning dark doorways and shadowed alcoves, tuning out everything but the place inside him that had ahold of her.

He stopped at the entrance to a short alleyway. Cobbled. Old-fashioned streetlights, casting a feeble glow.

Gotcha.

He stepped into the alleyway. 'Brite,' he called, 'I don't want anything from you but the truth.'

Nothing but silence, deep and somehow unnatural. He took several more steps forward, his senses jumping like crazy.

'Was that you I heard in my head?' he asked. 'Telling me to use my light?'

Go. Run. The voice in his head. Urgent, rising to a screech. *Now!*

Zach responded automatically. A rustling stopped him. Followed by a soft gasp. The sound of a struggle.

'Brite!' he shouted and swung back.

And spotted her. Pressed deeply into a shadowed alcove.

No, not in a shadow. Covered by one, he saw. Blacker than the blackest night, pulsing with energy. Pressing her back, seeming to swallow her. Her face stood out pale white against the darkness of her attacker; she looked to be in agony.

'You! Back off! Now.' He drew his weapon and charged forward. 'Police! Step away and—'

Zach flew backward, lifted off his feet by an invisible force. He smashed into a café table and chairs, toppling them and sending him sprawling. Pain shot through his shoulder and he saw stars.

But he hadn't lost his grip on the gun. He dragged himself to his feet, stumbled forward, gun out.

'Police! Step away from the woman now or I'll shoot!'

The shadow evaporated.

Brite Knight sank to the cobblestones.

Zach ran to Knight's side. She lay in a strange, twisted position and he eased her onto her back. Her head lopped to the side and he saw the strangest wound right below her collarbone. Circular, like a cross between a bite and a hickey. She didn't seem to be breathing. Panicked, he searched for a pulse and found none.

'Mick, ambulance! Now!'

He started CPR. Counting. Thirty pumps, blow air in. Nothing. Thirty more. Still nothing. Then again.

'Zach!'

Mick. The sound of sirens. He kept pumping, mind racing.

You'll get us both killed, Half Light.

Not a who, Zach. A what.

The paramedics arrived, pulled him away from her. Zach knew they weren't going to be able to help her. Whatever that thing had been, it'd made sure of that. She'd been dead before she hit the ground.

Mick caught his arm. He looked at her, drowning in regret. 'She said I'd get her killed. And I did. It's my fault, Mick. My fault.'

'Slow down, partner. What happened?'

'It killed her. This thing, it—'

'Whoa, dude. A *thing*?'

Mick was waiting. Gaze steady on his.

He had to tell her. No more lies and evasions. 'This is going to sound nuts.'

'Try me.'

He told her, starting from his pursuit of Knight.

Relaying how he had sensed her presence, called out to her. 'I heard what sounded like a scuffle. And that's when I saw her. And it.'

'This . . . thing?'

'Yes.' He struggled to recall exactly what he'd witnessed, worked to exorcise his own emotions from the description. Certainly, his own disbelief.

'Like a dark cloud,' he said flatly. 'But blacker. At first I thought it was her, a silhouette, but then I saw her face. Clearly.'

A ripple passed over him at the memory. 'She was in excruciating pain. The thing, it covered her, pressed her into the corner . . . pulsing with energy.'

Mick's gaze wasn't so steady now. Concerned. Disbelieving. 'You've had a shock. You're upset, and . . .'

'Detectives?' They turned to the paramedics. 'There's nothing we can do for her.'

'Any idea what killed her?' Mick asked.

'Cardiac arrest is my guess.'

'No,' Zach shook his head. 'She was attacked.'

The young medic frowned. 'We didn't see anything to indicate a physical assault.' He shifted his gaze to Mick. 'No body trauma, blood or other wounds—'

'What about the wound on her right shoulder?'

'We didn't see a wound, Detective.'

'Just under the right collarbone, circular. Real nasty-looking.'

His stomach sank at the strange way the young man was looking at him, as though he had a big-time screw loose.

'It was there.'

'Show me, maybe we missed it.'

They hadn't, Zach saw. Where the angry bruise had been – nothing but smooth, unmarred skin.

He stared at the spot, for once at a loss for words. The paramedic slapped him on the shoulder. 'The light and dark play tricks on us, Detective.'

Zach watched him walk away. *The light and dark play tricks?* How weird, him saying that.

'Coroner's on his way,' Mick said, coming to stand beside him.

'It was there, Mick. The wound. I saw it with my own eyes.'

'Look, Zach—'

'I'm not crazy. This was no heart attack. She was murdered.'

'Nobody said you were crazy.'

'Yeah, you did. Without words.'

She shifted her gaze slightly. 'It's been a crazy couple days. Let's just wait and see what the autopsy tells us.'

31

Patricia Putnam's disappearance had made the national news. The details had been kept from the press, but Micki figured it was only a matter of time before they started leaking out.

It wasn't every day a Senator's kid went missing, and it was proving to be a press event. Full circus, big top and sideshows included. Major Nichols was so far up their asses, Micki wondered if she or Zach would ever walk upright again. She didn't blame him, he had both the chief and the mayor up his.

No one cared about the death of a French Quarter fortune-teller.

No one but Zach.

The autopsy report had just arrived. It was official, her partner was a full-on whack job. Coroner had

200

determined Knight died of natural causes. Cardiac arrest. Knight had been neither young nor in good shape; the coroner suggested the attack might have been precipitated by her flat-out run as Zach pursued her.

Not even close to his version of what happened.

Micki glanced his way. He sat at his desk, buried in paperwork. They hadn't spoken much; she'd been grateful for the space. To think things through. What he'd said. What he hadn't said.

She'd decided there was a lot he hadn't said. And she meant to find out just how much he'd been hiding from her.

Micki stood and crossed to his desk. She dropped the coroner's findings in front of him. 'Read it and weep, Hollywood.'

He studied the report. She watched as an angry flush climbed his cheeks. He lifted his gaze to hers. 'I know what I saw. And it wasn't a woman having a heart attack.'

'Medical examiner called it, dude. He found nothing to indicate anything other than death by natural causes.'

'She may have died because her heart stopped, but the reason it did was anything but natural.'

She lowered her voice. 'And the perp was a pulsating shadow that appeared to be swallowing Knight. He picked you up and tossed you across the alley.'

'Nuts as it sounds, yeah. And I've got the bruises to prove it.' He lifted his shirt, revealing the bruises on his side.

The man sported a swoon-worthy six pack, which she would've taken a few more moments to appreciate if she wasn't on a mission. 'Are those supposed to prove something?'

'Seriously?'

'Yeah, seriously. You could have gotten those anywhere.'

'But I didn't.' He made a sound of frustration. 'Brite Knight was murdered. And we're just sitting here.'

'What do you suggest we do? Feds plucked the case out of our hands, you have orders to keep all your super-special powers super-secret, and I don't have a huge urge to believe a partner who's been playing games with me.'

'I don't know what you're talking about.'

Micki folded her arms across her chest. 'Which part?'

'The game-playing part.'

'Now, that just pisses me off.'

She held his gaze. Silently daring him to man up and admit he hadn't been honest with her. Certainly not transparent.

When he hesitated, she snorted with disgust. 'Last night you told me Knight said you'd get her killed. Exactly when did she tell you that?'

'I was kind of hoping in all the excitement you missed that.'

She wasn't amused at his attempt at levity. 'First off, I miss nothing. Second, the ice you're treading on is damn thin. You want to answer my question now, Hollywood? And no bullshit.'

'Not here,' he said softly. 'Interview room.'

She followed him; he closed the door behind them. She waited to see if he meant to stand or sit. When he sat, she took the chair directly across from his and met his gaze evenly. 'Whenever you're ready, dude.'

He nodded slightly and began. 'The night you were researching the number seven, I went to see Knight.'

'Why?'

'I felt drawn there.' He paused a moment, then went on. 'I didn't set out to go see her. I just started walking, thinking things through.'

'And ended up at her place? On Esplanade? That's a stretch.'

'No. Her spot on Jackson Square. That's when I knew I had to talk to her, right then.'

'Why?'

'I knew she was lying, about Miller's reading. She saw something that scared her. I wanted to know what that was. I thought *we* needed to know.'

'We,' she repeated. 'Ironic. Considering.'

He winced slightly at the sarcasm. 'That's not the only reason I needed to talk to her. The other was— It's difficult to explain.'

'Take a whack at it, Hollywood. If anyone can explain something away, it's you.'

He let out a slow breath. She saw something in his expression she never had before – insecurity and doubt. 'You know I said that when I took her hand, I got nothing.'

Micki waited, torn between being pissed and fascinated. Doubtful and spellbound.

'I should have picked up something,' he went on. 'It was like a dead channel. It threw me . . . I wondered—'

'What?'

He shifted his gaze. 'If she wasn't human.'

'You didn't just say—'

He met her eyes then. 'Yeah, I did.'

For a moment, she simply stared at him. He was dead serious. She saw it in his unflinching gaze, the set of his mouth. 'And we've now crossed over the rainbow.'

'Exactly my thought.' He rubbed his jaw. 'I remembered where she lived, and headed there. She answered my knock, was obviously unhappy to see me there, but I refused to go.'

'That's when she made the comment about dark and light?'

'Yes.' A rueful smile touched his mouth. 'You really don't miss anything, do you?'

If he thought he could distract her with compliments, he was in for a big surprise. 'What came next? The Scarecrow or Cowardly Lion?'

'She told me the darkness was greedy and light was fleeting.'

'What does it mean?'

'I didn't know. And I still don't.'

'More bullshit, Hollywood?'

He shook his head. 'Parker claims he doesn't know either.'

'And you believe that?'

He hesitated. 'No. But I have no way of proving it.'

'Go on.'

'Knight was obviously distraught and didn't want

204

to talk to me. When I refused to take no for an answer, she called me arrogant.'

'Finally, somebody speaks the truth.'

'I thought you'd like that. To be exact, she called me an arrogant Half Light.'

'Half Light,' she repeated, frowning. 'Did she explain?'

'What do you think?'

'That's when she said you were going to get her killed.'

'Actually, she said I'd get us *both* killed. And now she's dead.'

Micki heard the angst in his voice. She shook her head. 'She had a heart attack. Not your fault, partner.'

He ignored that and went on. 'She denied knowing anything about Miller. Then slammed the door in my face.'

'But she was lying.'

'I thought so then. She confirmed it when she called Saturday night. She said they were in danger.'

'And that she knew where Gomez was.'

'Yes.'

Mick frowned. It linked the three women and indicated that Zach had been correct about Gomez being the one who got away.

Three young women. Not two.

Of course Zach had been right. He'd had inside information.

Inside information. It got her back up. It ran counter to what she'd built here, what she held on to day in and day out. Us against them. Right against wrong.

Family.

'Why'd you keep it from me?'

'Which?'

'All of it.'

He spread his hands. 'It's complicated.'

'No, it's not. It shouldn't be. We're partners.'

'At the time, it seemed like . . .' He hesitated. 'Sixer business.'

The words landed with a thud. Angry heat stung her cheeks. 'We're not on the same team.'

He looked uncomfortable. 'I didn't say that.'

'No, you're always careful about what you say. The picture you present. It's what you do that tells the real story, isn't it? You *act* like my partner, then turn around and operate behind my back.'

'You don't get it.'

'You're right, I don't.' She stood, furious. And hurt. The former, she grasped. The latter, she buried. 'We're partners. Or we're not. We play for the same team. Or we don't. You're a stand-up guy. Or you're not.'

He faced her. 'In my world, nothing's black and white. And it's gotten a whole lot grayer in the last couple of days.'

'Hocus-pocus, self-indulgent bullshit. There're rules for living, Hollywood. Boundaries to be honored.'

'*Your* rules, Mick. Your boundaries.'

'So what do you live by?' she shot back. 'What do you live for? Oh wait, I think I know. For yourself.'

'Walk a mile, baby.' He ground the words out. She'd broken through his easy-going, charmer facade. She wondered at the darkness of what lay beneath.

'Poor little superhero. Always got everything he wanted. My heart bleeds.'

He seemed to freeze a moment, then crossed to stand directly in front of her. 'You want it all? The whole truth?'

'This isn't a game.'

'And I'm not playing.'

He was angry. But so was she. She met his gaze defiantly. In challenge. And immediately recognized her mistake.

She couldn't look away. Something about those eyes, that blue. As endless as a summer sky and as deep as the ocean.

Magnetic. A connection. Between the only two people in the world. They were bound by something greater than their physical bodies or corporeal time. Limitless. Perfect.

A shudder rippled over her, rousing her from her stupor. His magic, she realized. This was what he used to get others to do his bidding. To turn them to mush.

What he had promised he would never use on her. Look away, Micki, she told herself. Break free. *Do it.*

She mustered the will. It rose up in her, painfully. The connection snapped.

She felt hot, then cold. Starkly alone.

'You son of a bitch,' she said, voice raspy. 'You gave me your word you wouldn't do that. Not to me.'

'I had to get your attention.'

'Always with an excuse, Hollywood. What's your word worth to me?'

'Parker called me at the Putnam scene,' he said softly.

'About the missing girls. Who had them.' He paused. 'But that's the thing, Mick. It's not a who, it's a what.'

That penetrated. She blinked once, then again.

'Doesn't fit into your neat black-and-white world, does it? Where's the boundary with that one? I'd sure as hell like to know.'

Black.

And white.

She shook her head, fighting for equilibrium. To clear her thoughts. Focus. She took a step back. 'I can't be here right now.'

'After last night, I believe him. That thing I saw on Knight, it killed her. At the Putnam scene, it wanted to kill me.'

Not a who.

A what.

She turned to go. He caught her arm. 'Running away, Mick? I thought you wanted on my team?'

She trembled. 'Take your hand off me.'

'No boundaries. All shades of gray. That's my world, Mick. You still want in?'

His hand on her arm burned, heat that went clear to her core. Her thoughts spun, like a merry-go-round on crack.

She searched for a sarcastic comeback. Something both caustic and glib. Trademark Mad-Dog Dare.

She had nothing. Nada, except for this kaleidoscope of confusion. 'I'm out of here,' she said, yanking her arm free and walking away.

32

Zach watched Micki go, thoughts racing. A throbbing in his blood, like an awakening. New life. Pulsing. Their connection.

He had felt the power of her anger, the depth of his betrayal of her. The strength of her immense will. And something more. Something he couldn't put his finger on. Not yet.

Always with an excuse, Hollywood. What's your word worth to me?

He got it. He did. But did she get the unique position he was in? Yes, he'd excluded her, acted without her knowledge, but he straddled two agencies, two allegiances. And, apparently, two worlds. This one and the one populated by a pulsing, murderous shadow.

Which sounded like a bucketful of excuses. Even to him.

Annoyed with his own thoughts, he grabbed his jacket and exited the interview room. And ran smack into J.B.

'Whoa, Hollywood, where's the fire?'

'Sorry, man.' He moved around him.

J.B. caught his arm. 'Saw your partner head out of here like a bat out of hell. Lovers' quarrel?'

'Screw off, J.B.'

'Sounds like I struck a nerve.'

Zach shook off J.B.'s hand. 'You're such an asshole.'

'Thanks for noticing, pal,' the man called to his back.

Zach ignored him. He paused at Sue's desk. Looked her in the eyes. 'Following up a lead. Meeting Mick there.'

Moments later, he was on the French Quarter street. And was assailed by energy. Not the dark energy they were tracking, but the chatter he'd experienced his first night in the city. The roar of it in his head.

It took him by surprise and he stopped cold. People streamed by him on the sidewalk. Most paid him no mind, a few sent him irritated glances.

He shook his head, worked to focus. Force it back. Quell the momentary panic. Dull the roar.

He succeeded and turned toward Jackson Square. Why now? he wondered. What did it mean?

He caught his reflection in a shop window and stopped again, stared at it. Not quite clear, a shadow reflection.

What's your word worth to me, Hollywood?

What was it worth? To her? Or anybody else? The reflection seemed to beckon him closer. He responded. Straining to see. To know. What did he stand for? At his very core, *who* was he?

At a sharp rap on the window, he jerked back. The saleswoman. Motioning him to take off. Looking at him like he was either crazy or high. He turned quickly away, embarrassed. Maybe he wasn't superhero material. Maybe he should stick with what worked for him, what had always worked for him.

Use his freak factor to live the good life. Take the path of least resistance. Quit the Sixers. Leave this beautiful old city with its psychic chatter, murdering energy, and prickly partners that demanded boundaries and loyalty far behind.

His cell went off. *Parker*. Zach considered ignoring the call, but knew the man would find him no matter where he tried to hide.

'Yo,' he answered, 'Park-man.'

'What the hell are you doing?'

'California dreamin', dude.'

'Stop it. You don't have that luxury.'

'Screw you. Brite Knight's dead. Did you hear?'

'Yes.'

'My fault. She said I'd get her killed. And I did.'

'So, that's what this pity party's all about.'

He'd picked up his psychic vibrations. 'Think you have a bead on me, P? Don't get over-confident.'

'Where are you?'

'Outside the Eighth.' He resumed walking. 'You?'

'The airport. Landed ten minutes ago.'

'Coming or going?'

'Coming.'

'Pathologist called Brite's death natural causes. A heart attack.'

'I heard that, too.'

'We both know that's bullshit.'

'Do we?'

'I was there.' Zach paused for effect. 'I saw it, Parker. The thing that murdered her.'

For a long moment, the man was silent. 'Then we need to talk.'

'We do. Mick needs to be included.'

'Not her area.'

'She's my partner.'

'Only at the Eighth. Everything else, I'm your partner. Your allegiance is to me, the Sixers.'

'That's not going to fly. Sorry.'

'Excuse me?'

'You heard me. Day in and out, she's the one on the street with me. And where are you, Parker? Flying all over the freaking globe.'

'She can't know any of this, Harris. Not yet.'

'When?'

'When the time is right.'

'And when will that be? Never's my guess.' His voice had risen; he saw a few folks look his way and lowered it. 'More of your bullshit, Parker.'

'This is bigger than her being pissed off.' He paused. 'It's bigger than the Sixers program.'

Zach stopped on that. *Bigger than Sixers? Parker's pet project.* 'How's that?'

'You'll know soon.'

'That thing tried to kill me. I want to meet. Now.'

'I have another meeting this afternoon. Tonight. Seven-thirty.'

'Where?'

'Your place. In case I'm running late.'

'And you'll tell me everything?'

'I'll tell you what I can.'

'That's such a load of—'

Parker hung up.

'Crap,' Zach finished, holstering his phone.

Parker had been stringing him along this whole time – from their first meeting in the bar until just now. Portioning out information as if he was a Dickens waif asking for more please. Jacking him around, leaving him hanging.

Partners his ass. Partners shared. They had each other's back, a bond of loyalty.

He sounded like Mick. Allegiance. Loyalty. Commitment. To something. Someone besides yourself.

Son of a bitch. He got it.

33

Tuesday, July 16
3:05 P.M.

Micki sat outside her friend Jacqui's apartment building, engine running. The back seat of the piece-of-shit sedan was loaded with groceries from the nearby Winn-Dixie. She'd picked up all the staples her friend might need, as well as all Alexander's favorites: Goldfish crackers, Stouffer's mac 'n' cheese, chicken nuggets, and Oreos.

Jacqui would not be happy about the last, in particular.

But every kid needed at least one adult in his life who understood the importance of sandwich cookies being eaten guts first.

Micki fixed her gaze on a spot in the distance. Her confrontation with Zach – if that was even what she could call their bizarre exchange – had sent her reeling.

All of it, from his otherworldly claims – murdering alien energy – to her anger at his two-faced deception, and her shocking physical reactions to his gaze and grip on her arm.

She'd felt herself a hair's breadth away from totally losing it. Like a pressure cooker about to explode.

So she'd left the department. Without a word to anyone. Let Hollywood Houdini pick up the pieces for a change, she'd thought. She had needed time to think, sort out facts from feelings. Steady herself. Her black-and-white world had been shattered. She wanted it back. The security and comfort it had provided.

Fake security. A giant lie.

Something was out there, with the ability to take a life without marking the body. *If* she chose to believe her partner, a man who had proved himself to be both a poor cop and a skilled liar.

Not a whack-job, she thought. Not a fraud. In one week, she had seen too much to totally write him off.

Believe the lie? Cling to the security of it? Or face the truth, as outrageous as it might be?

'What do you think, Hank?' she asked. 'What would you do?'

A tap on the driver's side window startled her out of her thoughts. Jacqui looking in, smiling. Teeth startlingly white against her ebony skin. The concerned expression in her eyes belied her smile.

Dammit, her friend knew her too well.

'What's up?' she asked as Micki opened the door. 'You were talking to yourself.'

'Was I?' Micki stepped out, gave her friend a quick hug, then motioned toward the car's back seat. 'I come bearing gifts.'

Jacqui peered through the window, then frowned. 'Groceries, Mick? I told you before, you don't need to do this anymore. As much as I appreciate it, Alexander and I are making it just fine.'

Micki opened the rear door and started handing the other woman bags. 'I want to, okay? It makes me happy. Besides, it might be the one thing that keeps me from going straight to hell.'

'Give yourself some credit, Mick.'

'I suppose you're right.' She grinned. 'There isn't anything big enough to get me through those pearly gates.'

Jacqui shook her head. 'I know we'll be up there sipping Starbucks together and there's nothing you can say to change my mind.'

They started for the building, both loaded down with bags. 'Where's Alexander?'

'Napping. He had a playdate today. Swimming, picnic, then more swimming.'

'All tuckered out.'

'You've got that right.' Jacqui had left the door cracked and nudged it the rest of the way open with her hip. She held a finger to her lips and listened intently. Satisfied her little man was still asleep, they headed for the small, serviceable kitchen.

She started unpacking the bags. 'Saw this strange car parked in front of my place, couldn't believe it was you. What's with the crappy wheels?'

'Department loaner. The Nova's in the shop. Wounded in the line of duty.'

'Want to talk about it?' She opened the bag of cookies, snagged one, then slid it across the counter to Micki.

'Not so much.' Micki helped herself to one of the Oreos, knowing she sounded as glum as she felt.

'Did it have anything to do with your pretty boy with powers?'

Micki almost choked on her bite of cookie. 'What did you say?'

'Pretty boy. With powers.'

'Where did you hear that?'

'From you.' She crossed to the refrigerator, then began placing the cold foods inside. 'The other day, when I called.'

Then Micki remembered. She had muttered those words at Major Nichols' comment about Zach being easy on the eyes. How could she have been so foolish?

'Forget I said that, Jax. I was just being stupid.'

Jacqui cocked an eyebrow and started stowing the non-perishables. 'He's not pretty?'

'No.'

'What about his powers?'

'The only power he has is his ability to drive me crazy.' She paused. Looked at her friend. 'Forget what you heard, okay? It's important.'

'If that's what you need me to do.'

'It is.'

Groceries stored, Jacqui carried the cookies to the small round table. 'Have a seat. Water?'

217

'Yes, thanks.'

A moment later, Jacqui sat across from her. 'The guy, who is he?'

'My new partner.'

'What!' This time it was Jacqui who nearly choked. 'But Carmine—'

'Has been promoted.'

Jacqui reached for a cookie. 'When did all this happen?'

'You called in the middle of it.'

'Shoot, Mick. Did you have any warning it was going to—'

'Happen?' she finished for her. 'Nope. We were both blindsided.'

'That sucks.'

'You don't know the half of it,' Micki muttered and picked up her glass. The ice clinked as she tipped it to drink.

'Well?' Jacqui prodded.

'What?'

'How is he? Besides pretty.'

She wished she could tell her the whole truth. It trembled there on her tongue; it would feel so good to let it fall off. But, dammit, orders were orders. 'He's from outside the NOPD.'

'Practically the devil himself,' Jacqui said lightly.

She frowned. 'Make jokes, but he's a major pain in the ass.' She paused. 'One of those cowboy types.'

'What's wrong, don't like someone venturing into your territory?'

'I'm a team player, Jax. All the way.'

218

'As long as it's your way.'

That hurt. 'Thanks, Jax. Appreciate the love.'

Her friend didn't allow herself to get pulled into her 'poor me' party. 'You're saying he's not a team player?'

'That's what I'm saying. You know how important trust is between partners. I've got to *know* he'll back me up. I can't trust that he will.'

'Trust's a two-way street.'

'I've given him plenty of reasons to trust me. It's his fault the Nova's near death. I had to sacrifice the car to save him after he made a bone-headed, cowboy move.'

'And you've never screwed up?'

Frustrated, Micki snatched up her glass and carried it to the counter. 'I thought you'd at least try to understand.'

'I am. But I also seem to remember you complaining about Carmine at first.'

'I did not.'

Jacqui laughed softly. '"He's like a bull in a china shop,"' she mimicked. '"The man moves at a turtle's pace. I have to keep circling back. It's so annoying!"'

Micki grimaced, remembering those complaints – and more. 'Thanks for taking my side.'

'I didn't know we were taking sides.' Jacqui searched her gaze. 'What aren't you telling me, Micki?'

'Nothing, I . . .' She looked away, then back at her friend. 'Do you think I'm too rigid?'

'In what way?'

'My thinking. About the world. How it's supposed to work.'

'You're strong in your beliefs. What you expect from others. And yourself. In what's right and what's—'

'Wrong,' Micki finished for her again, thinking of Zach's shades of gray. 'I'm a black-and-white girl.'

'There's nothing wrong with that.' Jacqui frowned. 'Why? Does this have something to do with the new partner?'

'Nah, just hormones.'

They turned at the sound of small footsteps. Little Alexander, face creased from sleep, hair a mass of wild light brown curls.

He caught sight of her and squealed in delight. 'Auntie Mouse!'

He came running and she scooped him up in her arms. Before Alexander, she hadn't gotten the whole kid thing. How seemingly grounded adults could be so gaga over them.

She got it now.

Micki stayed another hour, until he'd been fed. She and Jacqui didn't talk about Micki's partner issues again, instead focusing their attention on Alexander.

Her friend walked her to the door. 'If you need me, you know where to find me.'

'I'll figure it out. No worries.'

'Trust's a two-way street, Micki. Don't forget that.'

She nodded, stepped out of the apartment, then turned back. 'Jax?'

'What?'

She opened her mouth to tell her she loved her, that she and Alexander were the most important people in her life. That she didn't know what she would do without them. Instead she said, 'Thanks, I needed this.'

'I know.' Jacqui smiled. 'Love you, too.'

Micki walked away. Reached the sedan, climbed in. And sat. Lost in thought. Ending this visit the way she had begun it.

Black and white. Black plus white.

Shades of gray.

They existed. It was all possible. She started the engine, thinking suddenly of Alexander. Black and white. And the beautiful shade that had been created by mixing them.

She shook her head, shifted into drive. Face the truth, she thought. As scary-crazy as it seemed to be.

Starting now.

34

Tuesday, July 16
5:55 P.M.

Micki turned onto her Riverbend neighborhood block. Despite the heat, several of her neighbors lounged on their front porches or steps. They smiled and waved, grateful to have a cop living on their street. More than one, actually. Her friend and fellow detective Stacy Killian lived a block over. She'd known Micki was house shopping and had called her the moment the sign had gone up.

The Riverbend area nestled in the Uptown bend of the Mississippi River, on one of the city's ridges. Natural high ground, it hadn't flooded in Katrina, which had begun a neighborhood transformation. Pockets of ramshackle rentals had been snapped up by young professionals, then renovated. She had been damn lucky to snag it.

Hers was a century-old, shotgun-style, in-the-process-of-being-restored money pit. But like the Nova, Micki loved it.

Zach, she knew, was waiting for her there. No special powers needed; he had texted her.

At your place. We need to talk.

Yes, she supposed they did.

His P-O-S was parked in front; she pulled her nearly identical crappy car into her narrow gravel drive. He sat on her small front porch, on the top step, shaded by the crepe myrtle tree. The neighborhood stray tiger cat sat beside him, like an orange and white sphinx.

She climbed out the car and crossed to the steps. 'How'd you get my address?'

'Sue.'

'Figures. She has the hots for you.'

'I know.'

'Of course you do. Duh.' She dug out her house key. 'Why don't we go inside?'

'I'd rather stay out here, if you're good with that? It's sort of pretty tonight. Almost cool.'

'You're out of your mind, Hollywood. It's muggy and buggy. But whatever. Make room.'

He did and she sat. Their shoulders brushed. She felt the heat emanating from him. And something else. Magnetic. Magical.

She frowned at her thoughts and scooted a fraction farther away from him.

Zach indicated the cat. 'She have a name?'

'She's not mine. Just a stray that comes around.'

'Still, you must call her something.'

'Kitty.'

'Original.'

The feline looked at her archly. As if she agreed mightily with Zach's assessment.

Micki shifted her own gaze back to Zach. 'Do your gifts include communicating with animals?'

He laughed. 'Not that I know of. Why?'

'Kitty here seems to have developed a special rapport with you.'

'Really?' He scratched the feline behind the ears and it rubbed its head against his hand and began to purr.

'I'll be damned. I've never seen her do that.' Then she realized what was going on and busted out laughing.

'What's so funny?'

'You and females, Harris. Any age, any species. They can't resist you.'

'Except you, Mick.'

Her smiled faded and she glanced away. That had been true. At first. But not anymore, not completely.

She turned back to him, looked him dead in the eyes. 'I'm in.'

'In?'

'One hundred percent. This whole whacky thing. Pulsing clouds of death, you just knowin' things for no reason at all. The fact that somehow you always come out smelling like a rose and I, well – I end up on YouTube.'

He opened his mouth to speak; she held up a hand stopping him. 'But there are boundaries. There have to be. Honesty. Transparency. Respect. And trust.'

224

'Mick, I—'

She stopped him again. 'Before you make some lame-ass excuse that pisses me off again, let me finish. I've got to be able to trust you that same one hundred percent. You give me your word you won't use your super mojo-vision on me, you keep it. And I'll give that trust right back to you. Then I'm in.'

'Can I speak now?'

'The floor's yours, Harris.'

'I need you, Mick. You can do what I can't. Without you, I'd probably be dead already.' He didn't wait for her to agree and went on. 'Excluding you the way I did was messed up. Lying, also messed up. And the mojo thing, it was a mistake. It just happened. It's something, a trick, I've pulled out of my bag for so long . . . it's become an automatic response.'

'When you don't get your own way.'

'When I want to get my own way.'

'So, what are you saying?'

'That I can't promise I won't slip up. But I can promise I won't consciously set out to use it. And if I do slip up, I'll stop immediately. How's that for honesty and transparency?'

'On the right track.'

'But?'

'It was damn creepy, Harris. Preparing myself for another slip-up.'

'Creepy, huh?' He rubbed his jaw, expression bemused. 'I've never actually affected a woman . . . quite that way.'

'That you know of.'

He laughed, then shook his head. 'You've got me there.'

But she didn't. And never would. 'I think we've already established I don't react to you like most women do.'

'Almost as if Parker and company knew that when they chose you.'

'But how could they have?'

'I don't know. Maybe we should ask him?'

'We?'

'Yeah, you and me. Partners. I'm meeting with Parker at seven-thirty.'

'Tonight?' She looked at her watch. 'It's six-thirty now.'

'Yup. You want in?'

'Hell yes, I want in.'

'I thought you would.' He rubbed his palms together. 'This is going to be tough. He already told me he wouldn't talk to you.'

'So, I sneak up on him.'

'You can't sneak up on a guy like Parker.'

'He's FBI, so what? I've got skills too.'

'He's special, Mick.'

'What do you—' Then she understood. 'He's like you. A Sixer.'

'The original. And he's psychically very sensitive. He'll pick up your presence before you get anywhere near him.'

'Where's the meeting?'

'In the Marigny. My apartment.'

'I'm there in the apartment, maybe in back. Or down the—'

'He'll sense you.'

'What about the thing we tried with Knight. Our phones—'

'Parker's picked you up through the phone before.'

'Seriously? Son of a bitch.' She shook her head. 'So what's your plan?'

'The sneaky-direct approach.'

'The sneaky-direct approach? Dude, in case English isn't your first language, those two things don't go together.'

'They do here. It'll also require the element of surprise and some old-fashioned arm twisting.'

'My part, I'm guessing.'

She'd meant it as a joke; he didn't laugh. 'First step is getting the two of you in the same room.'

'How do we get him to talk?'

He smiled grimly. 'That's my part. The tricky part.'

'And?'

'It'll either work or we'll both be out of a job.'

35

Tuesday, July 16
7:30 P.M.

Zach sat on his couch, eyes on the clock, waiting. Parker, he knew, would be right on time. At precisely seven-thirty, Mick would exit the Jax Brewery Parking lot and start for the Marigny. That would give him and Parker about ten minutes alone before the man sensed her approach. During that time, he would gauge how open Parker was ready to be.

When she arrived, the real fun would begin.

The clock struck seven-thirty; his front bell pealed. Zach stood and went to the door.

'Right on time.' Zach stopped, shocked by how rough the man looked – cheeks sunken, bloodshot eyes rimmed by dark circles. Like he hadn't slept since they'd last spoken, or had gone on a major bender. 'What happened to you?'

'I'm fine.'

Zach stepped aside so the other man could enter. 'The hell you are.'

Parker shrugged out of his suit jacket and loosened his tie. 'Let's get to it. Tell me what you saw.'

'I'd rather we start with you telling me what you know.'

'That's not how this is going down, Agent Harris.'

No it wasn't. His buddy was in for a big surprise. 'Okay, I get it. I tell you what I saw, then you reveal just enough information to explain it.'

'Astute, Harris. Information on a need-to-know basis. That's absolutely the way the game is played.'

Zach held Parker's gaze, defiantly, all the while counting down in his head. Not wanting to appear to give up too easily. When the clock in his head struck zero, he began. 'I told you most everything on the phone. Knight was murdered. The perp was a dark cloud of energy. When I tried to intervene, it picked me up and threw me across the alley.'

Parker had no reaction to that, and Zach went on. 'Knight had a wound on her right side, just below her collarbone. Like a hickey. Only more defined. By the time the paramedics arrived, it was gone.'

'Detective Dare didn't see the wound?'

'No. But as I said on the phone, she—'

'Speak of the devil and up she pops.'

'Where?'

'The sidewalk across the street. Now crossing.'

'She's a strong asset,' Zach said. 'I can't do the job without her.'

'We went over this.'

'If I don't bring her on board, she may bail on the program.'

'Let her. I'll find someone else.'

'She was your first choice, you must have had a reason for that.'

'Entering the building now.' Parker looked at him. 'She can't know what we know. Not yet.'

'You said this was bigger than the Sixers program. What did you mean?'

'Get rid of her and I'll tell you.' He held Zach's gaze. 'She's here. Trust me.'

'Why should I?'

'We're the same, you and I. She's not one of us.'

'That's true. She's not.'

'Did she see the wound before it disappeared?'

'No. She saw nothing. But I told her everything.'

'Unfortunate, but we can deal with it.'

'How?'

Before Parker could answer, Micki rapped on the door. Zach reached to answer it; Parker laid a hand on his shoulder. Zach looked at him.

She can't know. Not yet.

He held his gaze, then nodded. Opened the door. She stormed past him, into the apartment, then stopped, the picture of fury. 'You son of a bitch! I told you I wanted in. I guess it's business as usual, Hollywood?'

He hesitated. How this went down depended on how he answered. He and Parker were alike. They shared something few did. It united them. But Parker demanded trust he refused to return. Besides, something stronger united him and Micki: shared humanity.

'What did you expect, partner? I'm a Sixer first.'

'I told you before, I'm either all in or I'm out. I can't be partners with someone who only tells me half the story.'

Zach went to stand beside Parker. 'I can't change what is.'

She looked at Parker. Zach saw the determination in her gaze. 'Are you certain you want to do this? You're forcing my hand. And you need me.'

'I don't think I do,' Parker said. 'Actually, it's you who's making a mistake. Giving up your chance at glory. To be on the cutting edge of a new era in law enforcement. And, I suspect, you'll lose your job as well.'

'You don't give a crap about anything but your precious program and what its success means for your career.'

'I'm sorry you feel that way.'

'I was there that night, when Knight died. I saw—'

'What, Detective? A woman who died of natural causes?'

'What about the missing girls? You know something that could help us find them. I saw— '

'Nothing,' he said, cutting her off. 'You saw nothing.'

Suddenly Zach realized Parker's advantage. Understood his confidence. Mick *couldn't* have seen the murder – the wound before it disappeared, yes – but not the murder itself, even if she had been standing right there.

Because only the gifted could see.

'Let me tell you what the truth is, Detective Dare.

Brite Knight was alive, and then she was dead. No wounds or signs of body trauma. The poor woman suffered a heart attack. It's only your partner here claiming otherwise. And who would believe him when even I don't?'

'The thing that got Knight—'

'Thing?' Parker laughed. 'I don't know what you're talking about, Detective Dare. You and Harris are looking for a flesh and blood human being.'

She looked at Zach. 'And you have nothing to say?'

'Nothing except do whatever you're going to do.'

That was the signal. Zach grabbed Parker's left hand and brought his right one to it. Mick was ready with the handcuffs.

Before Parker realized what was happening, she had them cuffed to one another.

'Sorry, P,' Zach said, forcing their cuffed hands together, palm to palm, 'you left us no choice.'

'You crazy son of a bitch, you have no idea what you're—'

But whatever else Parker was about to say was drowned out by the roar of blood in Zach's head as the transmission began. At the base of his skull small shocks, like fireworks, exploded against his skin. Running down his arm, melding his and Parker's palms. His blood burned, raced; the sensation was at once searing hot and blisteringly cold. He began to shake.

He was aware of Mick's stunned expression. And of the fact that he had done something incredibly stupid. He was not in control of this transmission. *It* was.

The thing that had killed Brite Knight. That had tried to kill him.

His head filled with dark images, of anguish and destruction. The darkest place he had ever been, the deepest black. A place devoid of hope.

Desolation surrounded him. Heavy. Suffocating.

He became aware of Mick screaming at him to stop.

Zach opened his eyes. His vision cleared. Convulsions rocked Parker, one after another.

It was killing Parker.

Through him.

Something rose up in him, from the center of his being. It rushed forward, bright and hot. Zach felt as if he were flying backward.

Light flashed before his eyes. His head filled with the image of a woman. Beautiful. With the bluest eyes he'd ever seen. She smiled.

And then he saw nothing at all.

36

When Zach came to, he and Parker were on the floor, about ten feet apart. The other man was as pale as a ghost. There was the faintest scent of something acrid in the air.

Mick stood to the side, looking from one to the other, eyes huge. 'What the hell was that?'

Zach tried to laugh; it came out a croak. 'Water,' he managed instead. 'Please.'

'Make that two.'

She nodded and left the room. Zach looked at Parker. 'I suppose saying I'm sorry won't cover it?'

'You stupid son-of-a . . . You could have killed us both! You nearly did, you irresponsible asshole!'

'Point made.' A shudder racked him. 'How about I promise to never be that stupid again?'

'Don't make promises you can't keep.' Parker lifted at his hands. The snapped handcuff dangled from his left wrist. 'Look at me, I'm shaking like a leaf.'

'And your hair's standing on end.'

It was. Literally. The always immaculately groomed Parker looked as if he'd stuck his finger in a live socket.

Zach supposed that in a way he had.

Parker reached up. 'Damned if it isn't.' He shook his head. 'I'd heard about their power, but I'd never felt it.'

'Heard about whose power?' Mick asked from the kitchen doorway.

She crossed to them, handed Parker a glass, then Zach. When Parker still hadn't responded, she snorted. 'After what I just saw? Really? You're still going to try and keep me out of your secret FBI superpowers club?' She arched her eyebrows in disbelief. 'My partner was *glowing*.'

'I was glowing?'

'Like a light bulb. And I don't mind telling you, I'm a little bit freaked out right now.'

'*You're* freaked out?' Zach turned to Parker. 'It's time for some real answers.'

Parker shook his head. 'There are people I answer to. Directives I've sworn to follow. I'll make some calls, see if I can get the okay to bring in Detective Dare.'

'Bring her in? If *Detective Dare* hadn't snapped me out of whatever state I was just in, you'd likely be dead right now.'

'And if she hadn't been here, you wouldn't have pulled this bullshit stunt!'

235

'Don't be so sure about that,' he shot back, getting to his feet. His legs were rubbery and he grabbed the back of the couch for support. 'It's not like you've been exactly transparent with me.'

Parker followed his lead and stood. He, too, braced himself against the couch. 'Show a little more respect and maybe I would be.'

Mick stepped between them. 'Stop! We're way beyond petty finger-pointing.' She looked at Parker. 'Here's the deal, dude. I'm all in, whatever that means. Whatever it takes. You can trust me.'

For a long moment the two stared at one another. Zach figured if Parker didn't capitulate, Mick might go the handcuffs route again.

But he did capitulate, though not without a heavy sigh. 'I need a drink. And frankly, you will too.'

They assembled around the kitchen table. Parker set a bottle of Scotch and three glasses in the center. He poured himself two fingers and indicated they should help themselves. Mick declined and Zach decided on more water instead.

Parker sipped. After a moment, he set down his glass and looked at them. 'What I'm about to tell you, very few people know. Even among the gifted.'

'And here I am, an ordinary schmuck,' Mick muttered. 'Don't I feel special.'

'Actually,' Parker said, expression deadpan, 'Zach's the one who's special.'

'Why?'

Zach realized what he meant. 'Because I can see whatever that thing is.'

'Yes. And connect with its energy.' Parker lifted his glass. The amber-colored liquid rippled, catching the light. 'As human beings, we believe in what our five senses tell us is real. We need to prove things based on scientific fact. When we can't, it doesn't exist. Or we fabricate beings to explain what we can't understand.'

'Such as?'

'Vampires are currently popular.'

'The wound I saw on Knight,' Zach said. 'Near her throat. Like a bite.'

'But not.'

'Can ordinary people see it?' Micki asked.

He nodded. 'But it disappears so quickly, it's as if it never was.'

Zach looked at Mick. 'Not so crazy now, am I?'

She didn't laugh. 'Thinking maybe *I'm* crazy. Or having some trippy PTSD flashback.'

'I can assure you, Detective Dare, you're not tripping. These things are real. The history of art is well stocked with attempts to give them physical form. Henry Fuseli's masterpiece *The Nightmare* is one of my favorites. Delacroix comes to mind, as does de Goya. Gargoyles and Griffins. The grim reaper. Every period to the present day.'

Parker paused. Zach realized he was holding his breath, and slowly released it. 'So what the hell are they, P?'

'We call them Dark Bearers. And they want us dead.'

37

Micki stared at the two men. She realized her hands were shaking and dropped them to her lap. Was this really happening? She'd seen a whole lot of screwed-up stuff in her time on the force. But it'd all been real-world shit – here and now, touch it, feel it, wrap her frickin' mind around it.

But this? Murdering, non-physical entities that few could see? A partner who could transmit energy through his hands and – oh-by-the-way – glow in the dark as well?

A part of her figured she should pack up her toys and go home. Who needed badges, guns, and the investigative process when there were superhuman freaks like these around?

The other part acknowledged this was the coolest thing she'd ever been involved with.

Zach reached for the Scotch. She asked him to pour her one as well. He did and set it in front of her. Without speaking, they simultaneously sipped. The alcohol burned; her thoughts raced.

'Why,' she asked. 'Why kill Brite Knight? Why want Zach dead?'

'Simple. We pose a threat to their existence. Only we can stop them.'

'We,' Mick repeated, 'as in the gifted. Hence, the Sixers.'

'Yes.'

'And that thing you two were doing before, all you special folk can share like that?'

'No. Zach and I are the only two I know of. But there may be others.'

She digested that. 'What're you called?'

'Who? Zach and I?'

'People like you. Like Brite Knight. The gifted.'

'Human beings.'

'That's not what I mean. Dark Bearers have a name – or, at least you've *given* them a name.'

'So?'

'So, what do they call you?'

'I don't know that they call us anything.'

He was still withholding information. She sensed Zach thought the same thing. 'How'd they kill Knight?'

'Caused her to go into cardiac arrest.'

'How?'

'It's what they do.'

'Not good enough, Agent Parker.'

'It'll have to be, Detective Dare. How they do it isn't germane to this investigation.'

She let it pass, though she would've loved to argue. 'What does this thing, this Dark Bearer, want with Gomez, Miller, and Putnam?'

He frowned and stood. 'You'll have to excuse me, Quantico's calling.'

A split second later his phone went off. Freaking amazing, she thought, watching as he stepped out of the room.

She turned to find Zach studying her. She cocked an eyebrow. 'What?'

'Just impressed.'

'Really? With what? My non-existent superpowers?'

His eyes crinkled at the corners with his smile. 'Yeah, I guess so.'

'Get real.' She shook her head. 'What he's *not* telling us is the real story.'

'I agree.'

'What did Knight call you?'

'A Half Light.'

'And this thing's a Dark Bearer.' She thrummed her fingers on the tabletop. 'Light and dark, yin and yang, life and death.'

'Opposite sides of the same coin.'

'Exactly. Neither can exist without the other, nor be in the presence of the other.'

'Bad news for me, partner, 'cause that thing's a hell of a lot stronger than I am. No wonder Knight said

I'd get us both killed.' He paused. 'Look at me, batting five hundred.'

'It's not your fault.' Micki insisted. 'She called you.'

'About Gomez. Not Miller. Knight said she knew where she was.'

'Why the coeds?'

'Why indeed, Detective Dare?'

They both turned toward Parker, standing in the kitchen doorway.

'That was the director,' he said. 'I've been authorized to tell you whatever necessary to ensure the senator's daughter's safety.'

'That's big of him,' Micki muttered. 'Good thing Miller's in such good company. Otherwise she'd be screwed.'

He ignored her sarcasm. 'Zach, the "thing" you saw murder Knight is not what abducted the young women. You're looking for a flesh and blood being. A male, we're certain. In his twenties. Good-looking.'

'Yes,' Micki said. This, she understood. This, she could wrap her arms around. 'The male – he's how that thing attracts the young women. He picks them up while they're out partying. The clubs and bars in the Quarter.'

'Whoa,' Zach said. 'Back up. The energy links the scenes. I felt the same energy around that Dark Bearer, when it killed Knight.'

'The perpetrator is being manipulated by the Dark Bearer. They're both feeding on the girls' pain, suffering, and fear. There's more. Gomez isn't a part of this. Neither was Brite Knight.'

'That can't be right.' Zach drew his eyebrows together. 'Gomez disappeared on her birthday. The same energy from the Miller and Putnam scene clung to her ID.'

'Her path did cross the Dark Bearer's. We're not sure when or how. Knight was murdered, perhaps because of Gomez. Or simply because that's what Dark Bearers do.'

'Kill people like us.'

'Yes.'

Micki sifted through the things Parker had shared, piecing them together. She stopped on something he'd said moments ago. 'You said the perpetrator, our twenty-something male, is feeding on Miller and Putnam's fear. Present tense. You believe the girls are alive?'

'For now.'

'How much longer?'

'We're not sure, but we think until the last Saturday of the month.'

'Why then?'

'Neither the Dark Bearer nor his puppet will need them anymore.'

Micki's thoughts raced. She voiced them. 'July, the seventh month of the year. Saturday, the seventh day of the week. Four Saturdays in July. Four girls.' Her heart sank. She met Parker's gaze. 'Two more girls are going to be abducted.'

It wasn't a question, but he answered anyway. 'We believe so. Unless you can locate and stop him.'

Zach had been quiet. He suddenly spoke up. 'You say

"he won't need the coeds anymore". How do you know?'

'The seven left at each scene. The divine number of completion.'

'What will be complete?'

'The transformation of the puppet, Detective. A new, full-blown Dark Bearer will be born.'

'Another one?' Zach dragged a hand through his hair. It trembled slightly. 'Not good.'

'Not good, indeed,' Parker said.

Micki leaned in. 'Can we stop the transformation from becoming complete?'

'Yes. Up to the stroke of midnight that final Saturday.'

'And the girls? We can save them?'

'Sunday, July twenty-seventh, they'll all be dead. Until then, they have a chance.'

'Give us something,' Micki said, feeling the urgency thrumming in her blood. 'Something that will help us locate him.'

'You work as a team. Dare, you use your investigative skills. Harris, you're tracking the Dark Bearer's energy.' Parker took a sip of his Scotch. 'It's going to be more difficult for our UNSUB to attract girls. The transformation is painful, excruciating at the end.'

'He's losing it,' Zach said.

'Yes. Mind and body. Desperation clings to him. The charm is now surface only. Look into his eyes: they will be flat, dead.'

'Like a shark.' Zach looked at Micki. 'A hunter.'

'The process,' she said, 'is painful. Excruciating. I don't understand. Is he dying?'

'Physically? No.'

'Then, what—'

'His soul, Detective Dare, for the lack of a more concrete explanation, is being stolen from him.'

38

Parker had refused to say more, other than that they were on their own. And that everything he'd revealed to them was classified.

No pressure. Only four young women's lives at stake.

Micki sat at her desk, gazing at the image on her computer screen. The painting Parker had mentioned. Artist Henry Fuseli's *The Nightmare*. A sleeping woman. Or was she swooning? Whatever state, she was completely vulnerable. A gargoyle-like creature crouched over her. Dark and atmospheric. No hard lines, the quality of a dream. Creepy.

Mind. Blown.

Major Nichols had called Zach and her into his office first thing. They were officially back on the missing coeds, at the FBI's request. But was the request

245

from the FBI that believed in monsters? Or the one that didn't?

Zach returned from a lunch run and set the bag of take-out and two bottles of water on her desk. 'You okay?'

'Hell, no. Freaking the fuck out.'

'It doesn't show.'

'Thank God.' She tilted the computer monitor his way. 'Is that what it looked like? The Dark Bearer?'

'No. And yes.'

She frowned and reached for the bag of food. 'Explain.'

'As a literal representation, no.'

'No gargoyle then. That's a relief. So, what's the yes part?'

He popped open the styrofoam box, dug a fork into his salad. 'The foggy, indistinct quality of it. And the way the image makes me feel.'

Vulnerable. Threatened. She suddenly wasn't hungry and pushed away her sandwich. They hadn't talked much since they parted the evening before. Mostly superficial. As if by keeping it light, they didn't have to deal with what Parker had shared. Not in any kind of real, to-the-core way.

They would have to deal with it soon; they had no choice. The two of them were on monster detail. Which meant, sooner or later, that bad boy was going to pop up and force the issue.

'Got the Bureau's file while you were gone. Made us both a copy.' Mouth full of salad, he just nodded. She handed him one of them.

'They've done with Putnam what we did with Miller. Traced her steps, interviewed friends, family, and neighbors. Connected with everyone she came into contact with.'

'What about video surveillance footage from that night?'

'Done.' Micki shuffled through the pages. 'They searched for a place the two women's paths intersected—'

'Besides partying in the French Quarter on their twenty-first birthday.'

'Yes.' Appetite returning, she reached for her sandwich. She looked from it to him. 'Is this a *wheat* wrap?'

'You won't even notice the difference. Whole grains, partner. The only way to go.'

'Dude, really? Remind me to make the lunch runs from now on.' She sighed and took a bite.

He watched her chew, swallow, then take another bite. 'Well?'

'Not completely awful.'

He grinned. 'Pretty soon you won't want anything else.'

'Doubt that.' She gave her bag of baked chips a skeptical look then ripped it open. 'As I expected it would be, their investigation was thorough, down to a search of the national databases for like crimes.'

'Any?'

'None that hit all the search criteria.'

He ticked them off. 'Coeds. Twenty-first birthday, the number seven.'

'Exactly.'

He took another forkful of salad, chewed in silence. Obviously thinking it through. 'They've no doubt narrowed it down. What does their UNSUB look like?'

'A lot like ours. Male, early twenties to thirty. Dark hair—'

'Whoa, dark hair? How'd they come to that conclusion?'

'Friends and family of the victims indicated that's what they gravitate toward in boyfriends.'

'Typical. Notice nobody ever says tall, blond, and handsome?'

'Seriously, you're going to go there? The way I see it, you've got 'em lined up.'

'Just fighting against stereotype.'

She rolled her eyes, then checked her notes. 'Strong, strongly built. He overpowers the girls and gets them out of the apartment without leaving behind evidence.'

'He's charming,' she read on. 'Charismatic. A regular to the club scene or in the service industry. Bartender, bouncer – someone like that. He picks his victims at random; his ritual is evolving and he's unorganized.'

Zach scraped the last of his salad out of the styrofoam container, then reached for her chips. 'It's evolving all right. And about to get a whole helluva lot more unorganized.'

He slid the chip bag back her way. 'So, how do we . . . nudge our task force friends in the right direction?'

'Take a look at this.' She cleared the top of her desk to make room for a map of the French Quarter. 'I marked all the bars Putnam and Miller visited. Red for Miller, blue for Putnam, and purple for the ones they both spent time in the night they disappeared.'

He studied the map. 'Bourbon. Conti. St Peter. They're all right here. They can crisscross the blocks, going back and forth between places, even taking their drinks with them. Party central.'

'Exactly. FBI called it. Our guy's either a regular to the scene or in the service industry. I'm betting on the latter. These,' she tapped the map, 'the clubs that are in close proximity, are the places we infiltrate. You and I start immediately. You'll . . .' – she glanced up, scanned the activity around them, then returned her gaze to his – 'do what you do best, and I'll do what I do. Task force meets tomorrow in anticipation of the weekend. My guess is they're planning to have a small army of undercover agents placed throughout the Quarter, some of them undercover celebrating their birthday. I intend to be one of them.'

Zach's cell went off. He stood to take it. A moment later he returned to her desk.

'Who was that?' Micki asked absently, not lifting her gaze from the map.

'Desk officer downstairs. There's a Fran from Teddy's Po'boys here to see me. Won't talk to anyone else, she said.'

That got her attention. 'Angel Gomez's friend?'

'The very one.'

It was a break. Maybe. 'I'll get an interview room. You bring her up.'

Ten minutes later, the young woman was sitting

249

across the interview room table from her. She was scared. And weepy.

'I didn't know what to do. So I came here.'

Micki offered her the box of tissues. She took one, then another.

'We're glad you did. How about a Coke? Or something to eat?'

She shook her head. 'I'm good. I just left work.'

'Tell us what happened.'

'Angel showed back up.'

'When?' Micki asked, working to mask her excitement.

'Three days ago. Showed up at my apartment in the middle of the night.'

'Is she there now?'

Fran nodded. 'Hiding.'

'From who?'

Fran hesitated. 'She said I couldn't tell anyone.'

Zach stepped in, voice silky. 'But you know that's not the right thing to do,' he said softly. 'That's why you're here.'

Her eyes welled with tears. 'Yes. And she's freaking me out.'

'Why's that, Fran?'

'She said something tried to kill her.' She lifted her teary gaze to Zach's. 'Did you hear what I said – not someone. *Something*!' She curved her arms around her middle. 'A creature, she said. A monster.'

Micki met Zach's eyes. She saw the excitement in his. Unless Gomez bolted, they had a break in the case.

'I don't know what happened to her. She was always

. . . different, you know. But now she's so out there.' Fran grabbed another tissue and started to shred it. 'It's my fault. I never should have taken her to that party. I bet someone slipped her something, and she's had a bad reaction . . . some sort of psychotic break.

'Half the time she's doubled over in pain. I don't know if she needs a real doctor, or if it's all in her head. She won't leave my apartment, says the thing's going to get her.'

Micki leaned forward. 'Did she say where she's been?'

'It didn't make a lot of sense. I thought for sure she was tripping, and . . .' Her voice rose. 'I'm done. Somebody else has to take care or her 'cause I don't know what to do!'

'Look at me, Fran,' Zach said. She did, and he went on. 'Everything's fine. I've got this. Detective Dare does, too. We'll take care of her, Fran. No more worries.'

One look into Zach's magical blue eyes and the girl became as calm as a sleeping kitten. Micki shook her head. Hocus-freaking-pocus. Still amazed the crap out of her.

39

Located in Mid-City at the edge of Tulane Avenue and above a Korean Restaurant, Fran's apartment was shabby but surprisingly spacious. Angel, Fran told them, had been sleeping on the floor of the back bedroom.

'It's sort of creepy,' she whispered, sticking her key into the lock. 'She put garbage bags over the windows, so nothing could peer in. Nothing,' she repeated. 'Creepy.'

'She's going to be just fine, Fran. Trust us.'

She nodded, opened the door. 'Angel,' she called out, stepping inside, 'it's me. I brought you Mickey D's.'

Although the girl didn't respond, Zach knew she was here. He picked up her energy. Her fear. It rippled along his nerve endings.

He looked at Mick. 'She knows we're here. And she's afraid.'

'Angel,' he said softly, 'my name's Zach. I'm a police officer and I'm here to help you. My partner's with me. Her name's Micki.'

Still no response. He moved farther into the apartment. 'I know you're scared, but we're here to help you.'

He looked at Fran. She pointed toward the kitchen. He nodded and started that way. 'Fran told us what happened. So we could help you.'

'I'll cover the exit,' Micki said. 'This seems like your area.'

He agreed. 'Talk to her, Fran. Reassure her.'

'Don't be mad at me,' Fran said. 'I had to. I didn't know what else to do.'

Two bedrooms off the kitchen, a bathroom between them. The first bedroom belonged to Fran. He paused at the bathroom door, eased it open. Shower. Toilet. Sink. No place to hide.

'Zach's really nice,' Fran said. 'And he's super-cute, too. He's going to help. He promised.'

The second bedroom door was only partly closed. As he neared it, he could hear the girl breathing. The sound was ragged with fear.

'I'm coming in, Angel.' He carefully eased the door open. Their eyes met, hers as wild as a trapped animal's. 'Angel,' he said again, softly, 'I'm here to help—'

In the next instant she was on him, scratching and kicking. He stumbled backward, head thumping against the doorframe. He saw stars and before he could right himself, she flew past him, heading for the front exit.

He righted himself and followed, envisioning Micki wrestling the poor kid to the floor, cuffing her hands behind her back.

But instead, he found them both on the floor, Micki's arms around Angel, holding her while she sobbed, her gun still tucked snug in its holster.

Zach shook his head, bemused. He thought he had a bead on Mad Dog Dare; turned out he might still have a little to learn.

Just over an hour later, he and Mick sat in her living room, watching Angel suck down a frozen coffee drink called a Mochasippi. They'd decided they couldn't take Angel to the Eighth – no way to explain why she was there – and his place wouldn't be appropriate. So they'd settled on Mick's.

He looked around. The house was a work in progress. Floors, windows, walls – all either being replaced or restored. And all very comfortable and homey in a way she would never be.

'Feel better?' Micki asked.

'Yes, ma'am.'

Definitely from the south, Zach thought. Deep south, old time manners.

'You gave us a scare, you know that?'

'No, ma'am.' She looked up at her. 'How so?'

'We were worried something bad had happened to you. A bad man had your ID card. When we went looking for you to return it, Fran told us you'd disappeared.'

A bad man? Zach wanted to chuckle. Where had this softer, gentler Mad Dog come from? He felt as if he'd landed in an alternate universe.

Angel captured the frozen drink in the straw, then tipped her head to suck it out. 'Who had it?'

'A man named Martin Ritchie.'

Zach stepped in. 'He was a drug dealer, Angel.'

'I don't do drugs.'

'Of course not.' He said it deadpan, realizing with surprise that he was playing the bad cop in this scenario.

'I don't!'

'And a pimp, Angel.'

Her eyes widened. 'I don't . . . I never did *that*!'

'He's dead now.'

'Oh.'

'Any idea how he got your ID?'

'No.' She frowned. 'I just knew it was gone.'

'Tell us about your birthday,' Mick said softly, coaxing. 'What happened that night?'

'I went to a party with Fran. She ditched me to go off with some guy and I didn't know anybody. They thought I was weird. Everybody does.'

She said it simply. A lifetime of truth in her words. Zach understood. He had been there.

'So I left.'

'Just like that. You didn't try to find Fran or tell anyone?'

She shook her head. 'I wasn't feeling well, either. My side hurt. Real bad.'

Micki stepped in again. 'Fran's worried about you. She thinks you may need a doctor.'

'It's just my ink.'

'Your ink?'

'My tattoos. They do that sometimes. Hurt. Burn.'

Mick looked concerned. 'Where are they?'

She twisted slightly and lifted her shirt, revealing her left side and back. Several tattoos. Black and white. A smattering of color. 'The new one's been bothering me the most.'

Micki looked at him. The tattoos looked fine. But there were a lot of major organs in that area of the body and persistent pain there could be a symptom of something serious.

Zach refocused on the sequence of events the night of her birthday. 'You left the party. What happened next?'

'I cut across the Tulane campus. I thought I'd catch the streetcar downtown. Then I started hearing things.'

'What kind of things?'

She hesitated. 'Like someone was stalking me.'

He searched her gaze. 'You mean, sounds like someone was following you?'

Angel stopped sucking on her straw, face pinched in thought. 'At first, maybe. I even thought a couple of those stupid frat guys might have followed me. You know, to mess with my head. But after the shadow started to grow—'

'Shadow?'

'Never mind. It sounds crazy.'

'Tell us, Angel,' Micki said. 'We're going to believe you.'

She seemed to consider that a moment, then shrugged.

'A shadow from the statue at the center of the Quad. Like it was reaching for me. A voice in my head told me to run. So I did.'

She said the words almost defiantly. Zach thought of his own experience, when a woman's voice had urged him to do the same thing.

'You say a voice in your head told you to run. You mean like your own voice?'

She looked at Mick, exasperated. 'No, not my voice. Somebody else's. I told you people think I'm weird. This stuff happens to me.'

'Was it a man's voice?' he asked. 'Or a woman's?'

She looked surprised by the question. 'Man's.'

'You're sure?' She nodded and he went on, 'So, you listened and started to run.'

'Yeah. But it was like, wherever I ran, whatever direction, it stayed with me.'

'With you. You mean a steady distance behind you.'

'No. Above me.'

'Above you? Flying?'

'Yes. Huge and dark like a— It sounds so stupid, the whole thing was probably my imagination.'

Zach looked her dead in the eyes. 'You don't believe that, Angel. And neither do we.'

She tipped her chin up slightly. The expression in her eyes was defiant. As if daring him to laugh. 'Okay. Like one of those dinosaur birds.'

'A pterodactyl,' Micki offered.

She nodded. 'Or a dragon. But I didn't look up. I was too scared.'

'Then how did you know what it looked like?'

'I felt it. It made this horrible sound—' She shuddered and rubbed her arms, as if to ward off the gooseflesh. 'Eli saved me.'

'Eli?'

'Elijah. He was there, in the parking lot.'

'Back up. What parking lot?'

'The one the voice lead me to. There was a light. But when I ran toward it, it went out.'

She moved her gaze between them, defiance gone, replaced by desperation. To be believed, Zach thought. As if this was the part of the story *she* wanted to believe in as well.

'Then there he was. He opened his car door.'

'And you hopped in.'

'Pretty much.'

'Tell us more about him,' Micki said.

'He was super hot. Even if he was sort of old.'

'Sort of old?'

'About your age. Too old for me.'

'How old did you turn on your birthday?'

'Eighteen.'

Zach exchanged a glance with Mick. Angel's age didn't fit either of the other two girls'.

'What happened then?'

'Eli talked to me. Convinced me it was dangerous for me to go home. He called somebody and they decided I should go to Brite's house.'

Micki cocked her head. 'He was a complete stranger and you seem like a smart girl; how did he convince you to do that?'

Angel frowned. 'I knew I could trust him.'

'How?'

'I just did.'

'No,' Zach said. 'You've been around. You don't trust easily.' He leaned forward, in challenge. 'How did you *know* you could trust him?'

Her lips trembled. She suddenly looked scared. 'Because he's my brother.'

40

For a moment, the only sound in the room was the last of Angel's drink being sucked noisily up the straw.

Zach looked at Mick, then back at Angel. 'Eli's your brother?'

'Uh-huh. Just not my blood brother.'

'Now I'm really confused.'

'I was too, at first. He explained it. We're both special, different from most folks.'

The gifted. Of course.

'So's Brite. There are others, too.'

'I know, Angel.' He paused. 'I am, too.'

'I wondered.'

'Did you?'

'Uh-huh.' She looked at Micki. 'But you're not.'

'Sadly, no.'

Angel looked back at Zach. 'What can you do?'

He understood what she meant. 'I know stuff about people. Things that have happened to them. I can touch someone and sometimes, see what they've seen. Just quick snapshots. Especially if there was a strong energy attached to that experience.'

'But only sometimes?'

'A lot. But not always.'

He thought of Brite Knight. How he'd picked up nothing. Perhaps Angel would be the same?

'Cool. That's why you want to hold my hand.'

'How did you know I wanted to do that?'

'I saw it.' She looked at Micki. 'I was afraid he was a pervert.'

Micki laughed. 'He sort of is.'

'Hey! That wasn't nice.'

'I couldn't help myself, partner.' She grinned at Angel. 'He's not a perv, just overreaching and annoying.'

Angel giggled. 'I know.'

'So, can I hold your hand?'

'You want to see if you can get a look at that thing that tried to get me.'

'That's right.'

'I would but . . .' She shook her head. 'I don't know if that's such a good idea.'

'Why not?'

'I might hurt you.'

'Why do you say that?'

'Brite told me. She told me I had to keep my distance. Eli, too. All of them.'

All of them. The words took his breath.

'What do you mean? How many?'

'I don't know; I had to stay in a back bedroom. But I listened as best I could. They said I was dangerous because of that thing that tried to get me.'

'You can't hurt me. And I really need to do this.'

Micki looked at him sharply. He understood why – she was worried what happened with Parker might happen here.

'Okay,' Angel said and jumped to her feet, 'but I've got to pee first.'

Micki told her where the bathroom was, then turned to Zach. 'Are you crazy? Don't do this.'

'I have to.' He took a deep breath, rubbed his hands together. 'They were talking about the Dark Bearer's energy. It must have been all over her.'

'Which is why they didn't touch her. And why you shouldn't either.'

'I can do this.'

'What if you kill her?'

'It's more likely she'll kill me.'

'Great. I'm so reassured.' She stood, crossed to the window, then marched back. 'I was there. I saw what happened. This isn't a good idea.'

'That thing with Parker, it's something only he and I can do. I can transmit what I've picked up to him. This isn't a transmission.'

'What about Miller's apartment? Getting too close to that thing's handiwork knocked you on your ass. And at Putnam's—'

'It's been what, ten days since her encounter with

262

it? Time diffuses the energy. Besides, I'm right here and not feeling even a ripple.'

'What are you hoping to learn?' she asked.

'I'm hoping to get a look at the thing that was after her that night. See if it was the same thing that killed Knight.'

'What do you mean?' They turned. Angel stood in the doorway; eyes wide, face pasty. 'It . . . that thing killed Brite?'

She didn't know Knight was dead.

As they gazed at her, her eyes filled with tears and her chin began to wobble. Mick went to her. Put an arm around her and led her back to the couch. 'I'm sorry, sweetie, we thought you knew.'

She shook her head, turned her face into Mick's shoulder. But she didn't cry.

'I'm so sorry,' she said softly.

'I didn't like her very much. I feel bad about that.'

'Don't,' Zach said. 'I met her. She wasn't an easy person to like.'

'But she took me in. She didn't want to, but she did.' Angel blinked back tears. 'You don't think that it was my fault that she—'

'No,' Micki said. 'Absolutely not.'

Zach crossed to where they sat, squatted down in front of the girl. 'If you didn't know Brite had died, why did you leave her house and go to Fran's?'

'She told me to leave. That it was coming for me.' She paused. 'In my head.'

'Telepathy,' he said. 'When was that, Angel?'

'I don't remember. The days . . . I get confused.'

'Deep breath,' Micki said. 'Clear your mind. Count back.'

She stilled, Zach heard her deeply drawn and expelled breaths. One. Two. Then three.

'A few nights ago. Saturday. I was watching *Saturday Night Live*. It was almost over.'

Saturday. The evening Brite Knight died. Zach fitted the timeline pieces together: *SNL* ended at midnight, the time he and Brite were scheduled to meet, when she had turned and run.

Run not from him or because she had sensed Mick's presence. But from the Dark Bearer.

She had been running for her life. And maybe for Angel's, too.

Zach looked at Micki. She had put all the pieces together, as well.

'Why'd you go to Fran's?'

'She's my only friend.'

'Why not Eli?'

'I didn't know where to find him. He said he was a graduate student at Tulane. But that's all I knew.'

'And he didn't try to contact you. In any way?'

'If by that you mean . . . telepathy, no. I tried to reach him that way, but it didn't work.' Her voice quivered. 'I thought maybe if Brite could do it, I could, too.'

'It takes practice. I'm not very good at it and I've practiced a lot.' He held out his hand. 'You ready?'

She looked nervous. 'I don't want to hurt you.'

'You won't.'

She started to take his hand, then jerked hers away. 'Wait! What should I do with my mind?'

He smiled and tapped her forehead with his index finger. 'Keep it right in there.'

She rolled her eyes. 'I mean, what should I think about? That thing?'

During Sixer training they'd experimented with their gifts, trying every variable and variation to learn what worked – and what worked best. The only thing that had seemed to help – or hinder – his memory retrieval was time: closer to the actual event, the stronger the psychic vibration.

But that had been before Mr Big-and-Badass had come on the scene. The rules of the game had changed. He just wasn't certain what they had changed to.

'No. Don't try to conjure it or the memory. Relax. Pretend you don't know who I am or what I'm trying to do.'

'Okay.' She let out a long breath, then grasped his hand. A series of images cascaded across the back of his eyes. A baby, abandoned on the steps of a church. A little girl with big brown eyes and dark hair. Crying. Hiding. A man with a belt looking for her . . . the streets. Alone . . .

He tried to skip past the images, move forward. Her story. Not his to take. The images shifted. Another night. Recent. The frat party, he thought. Then pain, blistering. Her side.

A heavy darkness. Ominous. Watching.

Stalking.

A silhouette. Black as pitch against the night sky. A sound. The flap of huge wings. A groaning, like an ancient door opening.

Fear. Hers. Panic. No, terror. Heart thundering. Breath coming hard.

Hers. And now his heart thundering, in his head and chest. Breath rushing, heaving past parted lips.

Then a brilliant light, piercing the darkness. Like a shock, so beautiful it stung.

Zach released Angel's hand. He sat back, working to compose himself. She stared at him, impossibly young and vulnerable. And lucky, he realized. So very lucky to be alive.

41

Angel had fallen asleep in front of the television. Micki had gotten her set up in the back bedroom with clean sheets, toiletries, towels – the whole bit. The same as she'd done for Jacqui four years ago.

But those circumstances had been so very different.

'You have a way with lost teenage girls,' Zach murmured when she returned to the living room.

'Yeah, I guess I do.'

'Where'd that tender streak come from, Mick? Could've knocked me over with a feather.'

She plopped down onto the battered recliner. She ran her fingers over the worn fabric, remembering Hank's big, calloused fingers doing the same thing. 'Paying my debts, I guess.'

'I bet there's a story in that.'

'There is.'

'And you'll tell me someday?'

'Maybe.' She smiled slightly. 'Do you think we're doing the right thing, having her stay here with me?'

'She has nowhere else to go. Not any place I'd call safe, anyway.'

'Have you thought . . . it might not be safe for her here? Maybe we should call Parker?'

'No, not yet. I don't know why, but I think she's better off with us. For now anyway.'

Silence fell between them, broken by the rumble of a car passing in front of the house. 'Well,' she asked.

'Well what?'

'What did you see? When you took her hand?'

'Our Angel hasn't had an easy life.' He stopped a moment, as if lost in thought. 'The energy, it wasn't the same as what killed Brite. Or the energy from the Miller and Putnam scenes.'

'How so?'

'Not as angry. Not chaotic, not at all.'

'What does that mean?'

'Hell if I know.' He stood and stretched, then sat back down. 'You know that painting you showed me earlier?'

'The Fuseli. What about it?'

'The thing, flying over her, it was more like that.'

She pursed her lips, studying on that a moment. 'Zach?'

He looked at her.

'Something different happened when you held

268

Angel's hand. Different from when you held anyone else's we talked to.'

He frowned. Waited. She went on. 'Together, you made a light where your hands met.'

'C'mon, Mick, seriously?'

'Dead serious here, partner. Ever have that happen in training?'

'No.'

'Did it feel any different?'

He shook his head, opened his mouth as if to say something, then shut it again. 'I should go, get some shuteye. You'll be okay?'

'Sure.' She met his eyes. 'Think I can take that thing down if I empty a magazine into it?'

'Truth?'

She nodded, though she already suspected what his answer would be.

'No. Sorry.'

'I'll try anyway.'

A smile touched his mouth. 'I know.' He stood, crossed to the door and stopped. 'Call me if anything weird happens.'

'Will do. And Hollywood, tomorrow we try to locate Eli.'

'The University should be able to give us what we need. How many grad students named Elijah could they have?'

'More than one. We don't even know his area of study.' She leaned her head against the recliner's high back. 'Institutions like schools and hospitals are really touchy about giving out information without a judge's order.'

269

'They'll give me what I want.'

Cocky. Overconfident from a lifetime of getting whatever he wanted. She wondered what that must be like, knowing with a glance or a touch your will would be done. Almost like being a god.

'Don't be too sure, even with your superpowers.' She tilted her head to look at him. 'I bet Parker could get us one in a snap.'

'I don't want him involved, Mick. Not yet.'

'Why, Harris? Really, what's your hesitation here?'

'I just have this feeling that once he has Gomez, we'll lose access. And we need her.'

'In what way?'

'Don't know that, either. Just this feeling. And . . .' He stopped, as if uncertain if he should voice the thought, then did. 'This feeling she needs us, too.'

They fell silent. She thought of their original plan to hit the French Quarter clubs in advance of tomorrow's team meeting and sighed.

'What?'

'Plan A shot to hell.'

'Not necessarily. I could head out, hit the clubs. See if I get a bead on the Dark Bearer's energy.'

She met his eyes. 'I could go instead.'

'We both know that in this situation, my abilities trump yours.'

'I know. And it pisses me off. Big time.'

He laughed. 'Not used to being the kid left behind, twiddling your thumbs.'

'You got that right.'

'I don't think we should leave her alone tonight. And you don't either.'

Her eyes narrowed. 'Reading my mind, partner?'

'Nah. Just starting to understand you. I'll report in.'

42

Wednesday, July 17
11:15 P.M.

Zach made a list of the bars on Mick's map. He began on the Canal Street end of Bourbon, working his way toward the Esplanade Avenue end, planning to hook around to the Jax Brewery complex, ending his club crawl there.

Wednesday nights in the middle of July, he discovered, weren't happening. Even the decibel of energy-chatter was low, like the hum of a fluorescent light.

He went into one club after another, in and out, crisscrossing the street as he imagined Miller and Putnam had. At each, he ordered a cocktail he had no intention of drinking, chatted with the bartenders, danced when the right opportunity presented itself, and generally worked his way around the room in search of the Dark Bearer's energy.

Mr Big-and-Badass was nowhere to be found.

Kudzu's was the last on Zach's list. Located on the second floor of the Jax Brewery complex, it had the biggest crowd he'd seen so far.

He entered the club and the hum in his head ceased. Just stopped dead, like a faucet had been turned off. Nada. Nothing.

Weird. *Very.*

Zach curled his way through the partiers, heading toward the bar and the open stool at the far end. He reached it and sat. Three bartenders, he noted. Two males, one female.

He caught the eye of one of the guys, signaled him. He noticed a slight tingling in the tips of his fingers and flexed them.

The bartender came over, set a coaster in front of him. 'Hey, man. What can I get you?'

Twenty-something. Handsome. Dark hair and eyes. Easy smile, bright white. Fit the profile to a T.

'Club soda with lime.'

The smile widened. 'You a cop, brother?'

'Why would you think that?'

'Club soda.'

He laughed. 'Gotcha. You probably don't serve much of that in here.'

'Especially from dudes out alone on a weeknight.'

Who, Zach wondered, was profiling who? 'It's my fifth stop, man. I've got to work tomorrow.'

The bartender fixed the drink, set it in front of him. Leaned against the bar. 'What kind of work you in?'

'Sales.' Zach took the glass, curved his fingers around

it. Cold, damp, and energy free. He took a sip. 'Software.'

'Haven't seen you in here before.'

'First time. I'm new to town.'

'Where you from?'

'California.' He took another sip. 'This place has it going on. Everywhere else I stopped was dead.'

'We're the place to be, no doubt about it.'

He started off; Zach stopped him. 'How's Friday night? Worth my while?'

'Depends on what you're looking for. Trends young.'

'Like the just turning twenty-one crowd?'

Something in the bartender's eyes changed, as if they were liquid pools of black. They seemed to dilate, become darker. Zach blinked. Gave his head a shake. 'You okay?'

An ordinary brown gaze. Nothing reflecting in them but curiosity. 'Went a little fuzzy-headed for a moment.'

'Good thing you switched to soda water.' He smiled. 'In this heat, you've got to watch out for dehydration. It'll level you, partner.'

Partner. Mick. Why had he called him that?

He left to wait on another customer. Zach studied him discreetly. He noticed something about the man he hadn't before. Every couple of minutes, he'd twitch. A very subtle jerk of his head or shoulder. Almost as if uncomfortable in his own skin.

Something about the guy's vibes wasn't quite right.

Zach reached for his drink. His hand shook slightly; he frowned and drew it back. What was up with that?

Maybe he was dehydrated, he thought. When was the last time he'd had a glass of water?

A fine sheen of sweat formed on his upper lip. He wiped it away, catching the female bartender studying him. He reached for his glass again. It was full.

He didn't remember ordering a refill. Or had he? Why couldn't he remember?

'Last call. Refill?'

The female. Mid-twenties, steady gaze. Pretty.

'Already?'

'I've been here since nine, darlin'. That's not an already for me, it's a finally.'

She had a southern twang. He thought of Micki. He should check in with her. He glanced at his watch. Three-forty-five A.M.

He blinked. That couldn't be right. He'd been here about twenty minutes; he'd walked into the club at midnight.

'What time is it?' he asked.

'Quarter to four.'

'I guess time flies when you're having fun.'

His words slurred slightly. She didn't seem to notice. 'What's your name?'

'Mike. What about you?'

'Amanda.' She dropped her gaze to his hand, then met his eyes again. 'No ring. You single or just acting that way?'

'Single. Very.'

'Glad to hear that.' She smiled. 'Considering the way you've been flirting with me tonight.'

'I just met you, Amanda.'

She laughed. 'I guess you did. Like I said, it's last call. Can I get you anything?'

An invitation behind the question. He ignored it. 'I'm good. Thanks.'

'What are you doing out alone tonight?'

'New in town. Checking out the mid-week party scene.'

She bent and propped her chin on her fist. Her blouse gaped, offering him a glimpse of her breasts. 'Picks up a bit tomorrow, and the weekend's insane. During Mardi Gras or one of the festivals, forget about it. Absolutely nuts.'

A perfect opportunity. 'That bartender,' – he indicated Mr Twitchy – 'what's his story?'

'Kenny? Why?'

'Not very friendly, that's all. Asked me if I was a cop. I mean, do I look like a cop?'

'Only a Hollywood cop.'

Hollywood. He gave his head another shake. 'What did you say?'

She laughed. 'You know: Bradley Cooper, Brad Pitt, Matthew McConaughey. Hollywood cops.'

'I'll take that as a compliment.'

'I meant it as one.'

'So, what about Kenny?'

'You asked me this before.' She laughed. 'How long ago did you switch to soda?'

No recollection. None.

He lowered his gaze to his drink, realization landing with a thud. Somebody, at one of his stops, had slipped something into his drink. He shifted his gaze to Kenny.

In an animated discussion with the other bartender. His heart began to race.

'Humor me.'

The words reverberated strangely in his head, as if he shouted them through a tunnel.

Amanda seemed not to notice anything amiss. 'He's okay. His girlfriend dumped him recently. He's been a little off ever since.'

A little off? Zach wondered if that description encompassed coed-abducting, numeral seven-gouging, and dark bearer-morphing? It obviously included twitching.

'Poor guy,' he said.

'You know it.'

From the corner of his eye, he saw Kenny duck out from behind the bar and make a beeline for the front of the club.

Amanda motioned his empty glass. 'Sure I can't offer you another? On the house?'

'Thanks, but I've got to go.' Zach laid two twenties on the bar, he caught her gaze, held it. 'I'll be in tomorrow night. But you won't remember me.'

'Okay.' She scooped up the cash. 'I look forward to that.'

43

Thursday, July 18
3:50 A.M.

Zach slid off the barstool. His legs felt rubbery and he paused to steady himself.

Pull it together, Zach. If Kenny's the guy, he may lead you to where he stashed Miller and Putnam.

He hurried out of the club, opting for the stairs instead of the elevator. From the second-story vantage point, he'd have a clear view up St Peter Street, of Jackson Square and Café du Monde.

He stepped out onto the landing, swayed slightly and grabbed the railing for support. Two girls moving past him giggled. The sound echoed in his head; he realized they were laughing at him. That they thought he was drunk.

Ignore them. Power through, Zach.

He clutched the rail. Traffic, both vehicular and

pedestrian, had thinned considerably. As the night breeze hit him, he caught the stench of something foul.

He looked in the direction of the smell. The bartender. Heading toward the wharfs. But not quickly. Stumbling, bent over. As if he was drunk. Or sick.

Having just seen the man, Zach could eliminate the former. Which meant he was sick. Parker had said the transformation to Dark Bearer was excruciating. That holding together his facade would become more and more difficult. Damn near impossible at the end.

Zach started after him. Cautiously, not wanting the man to pick up his presence – and for fear he might collapse himself. He couldn't lose him now.

Kenny ducked down a side street. Zach followed, but several minutes behind. The man, it seemed, knew the most deserted streets, the ones with few lights. A residential area. Rows of shotgun-style homes, all raised, most with small front porches.

Did the man live in one of these nondescript homes? The kind of place no one would suspect? Like that house of horrors in Cleveland? Did he have Putnam and Miller chained up in one? In a closed-off room or attic?

He tried to notice the street names as he cut from one to another. To remember, bring Mick and the others back.

The bartender mostly out of sight, Zach followed the sound of his labored breathing, the slap of his shoes against the pavement.

The occasional whiff of death.

The street narrowed, the homes on either side grew, elongated.

Closed in on him.

He stopped. So did Kenny's footsteps. His gasping breaths.

Zach struggled to catch his own breath, slow his heartbeat. Struggled to remember the last time he had caught a glimpse of the bartender. How long had it been? Two minutes? Ten? More?

He realized his mistake. He should have called Micki when he'd had the chance. Or Parker. He needed back up.

He couldn't stop now.

Suddenly, the world went deathly silent. A heavy energy rippled along his nerve endings, cold as ice against his overheated skin.

The end of the block went black as pitch. The Dark Bearer, he realized. Waiting for him. He felt its presence. Its pull.

He had gone from being the hunter to the hunted.

He turned and stumbled in the opposite direction. His heart raced in a way it hadn't when he was at a flat-out run. Fear. Real fear, like he had never experienced before. It coursed through his blood, pushing him on.

Was this what Brite Knight had felt that night? This smothering energy? Its relentless pull?

The feeling that no amount of resistance would be enough? That she was going to die?

Parker . . . I'm in trouble . . . I need . . .

This was it, the end. He had nothing left, nothing more to—

Help . . . Parker—

A safe house. St Mary's at the old Ursuline convent. Where?

Ursulines and Chartres. Can you make it?

Zach nearly collapsed in relief. He'd seen that cross street. He knew he had. *I don't know,* he answered. *Maybe.*

A side door. With a gold bell. I'll tell them you're—

Static drowned out Parker's response. Zach ran. His heart felt as if it might burst from his chest, his lungs burned, muscles fatigued.

He wasn't going to make it, Zach realized. He was going to die here on the street, murdered by a monster that shouldn't even exist.

His steps faltered, slowed. Would his death be classified a heart attack, same as Brite Knight's? Or did the Dark Bearer have other plans for him?

He could all but hear the monster's triumphal laugh. Fear choked him. Stole his will to fight. And what of Mick? She would know the truth but be unable to prove it. Would she be punished for his stupidity? Demoted?

Would she miss him?

Let go of your fear, son. He feels it, then controls you with it.

The woman. From before. Not Brite. Who—

She called him son.

His mother.

The one who had given him up. Who he had spent his life longing to know.

Breathe, my love. You're not dying tonight. Follow me.

The street opened up before him. Like a light to chase, showing him the way. Zach blindly followed, oxygen returning to his lungs, feeding his heart and muscles.

Dumaine, crossing St Phillip, turning onto Ursulines. Hard right onto Chartres Street. A church ahead. Rising up out of the night, monolithic. Rose window, gold letters on the stucco facade: ST MARY'S CATHOLIC CHURCH.

Almost there, he thought. A few more steps. A sound from the darkness. A howl or roar. Or was that the screaming rush of blood to his head?

Zach went around the side. An entrance. A bell. He rang it, then pounded on the heavy wooden door.

It opened. Zach slipped through. Collapsed on the cold stone floor.

A priest. Old and stooped. Bending over him. Eyes the color of a spring sky.

Mother. Don't go.

A sound from beyond the church walls. The scream of the wind. A siren.

An ancient evil.

Don't leave me, Mother.

The heavy door thudding shut. The priest's kind eyes. Others he sensed but couldn't see. An echoing quiet.

Then nothing at all.

44

Zach awakened to the obnoxious squeal of his cell phone. His head hurt. Sledgehammer-meets-blade kind of pain.

He blindly reached for the phone, knocking it off the nightstand and onto the floor. It stopped squealing.

Nightstand. He cracked open his eyes, moved his gaze over the room. His apartment. Light streaming through the blinds.

It stung and he moaned and rolled onto his side. Every muscle ached. Chest and lats, neck and shoulders, arms.

What the hell? Why—

Kudzu's. Mr Twitchy. Numb fingers, wobbly legs.
But what after?

Zach pulled himself into a sitting position, wincing.

He climbed out of the bed. Feet on floor, full weight on them. Agony.

He sat back down, checked them. Blisters on his feet. Raw. Weeping.

Zach stared at them.

Running. Feet pounding on pavement. Heart thundering.

Fear. Mind blowing.

His pulse quickened in response to the memory. He dragged a hand through his hair and stood again, fighting past the pain. He pulled on gym shorts, a T-shirt over his head.

He stank. The smell caused his eyes to water. He remembered. The dark night. Sweating. Near collapse.

He moved carefully to the bathroom. Started the shower, relieved himself, stepped under the spray. Zach stood, letting the hot water pound against his sore neck, shoulders, and back. The pain in his head eased some, stiff muscles began to soften.

His mind raced. He struggled for details. The handsome bartender. Kenny, he remembered. His bright smile and weird, liquid eyes. The way he had twitched.

As if uncomfortable in his own skin.

The other bartender – Amanda – flirting with him. His drinks, refilled without his remembering. Time passing.

Kenny exiting the bar. Following him.

Then nothing.

Nothing but my feet pounding the pavement. And fear.

There must have been something else. He sensed it

there, lurking on the edges of his consciousness, but just out of reach.

Zach soaped his body, washed his hair. Let the water sluice over him until it went cold. He stepped out of the shower. From the bedroom came the insistent call of his cell phone. Micki or Parker, he thought, letting it ring.

Sitting on the edge of the tub, he tended his blisters, using antibiotic cream, then bandages. He shook his head at his handiwork.

Zach Harris, superhero.

As he reentered the bedroom, his cell went off again. He scooped it up from the floor. Micki, he saw.

'Yo, morning.' His first words of the day. More frog croaking than human language.

'Where the hell are you?'

Typical Mick. 'Home.'

A moment of stunned silence. 'You have any idea what time it is?'

He cleared his throat. 'Absolutely none.'

'It's nine in the freaking morning. After, actually.'

He limped into the hall, to the kitchen.

'I've called you five times—'

'Hold a sec.'

He set down the phone, started coffee, downed two full glasses of water and three Advils, then picked the device back up. 'I'm back.'

'You better start talking, Harris. Last we spoke, you were heading to the French Quarter for some recon with a promise to check in. What happened to *that*? I imagined you dead in a ditch, for God's sake—'

'Aw, Mick,' he managed without the croak, 'you were worried about me?'

'In case you've forgotten, protecting your butt is my job.'

He stood, poured himself a coffee and sat back down. 'Someone slipped me a Mickey, messed me up good. At least that's what I think happened.'

'Explain.'

He shared about his bar crawl, noticing his numb fingers as he arrived at Kudzu's, losing time, and his rubbery legs. 'I woke up here, no memory of how I got home, every muscle feeling like I went twelve rounds with the devil himself and my feet tore up with blisters.'

He went on before she could comment. 'The good news is I made him, Mick. Our guy. I know where he works.'

'Hot damn. Where?'

'Kudzu in Jax Brewery. Fits the profile to a T.'

'FBI's? Or ours?'

'Both. Right age, handsome with dark hair. Charming. But with a twitch.'

'A twitch?'

'Yeah, like a random shudder. He gave off these strange vibes, like he was sick. Having a hard time holding it together.'

'And the Dark Bearer's energy. Did he—'

'No.'

'No?' she repeated.

He heard surprise in her voice. Disbelief. It had been their ace in the hole. 'Didn't pick it up. Not anywhere.'

'That can't be right. Not on anything?'

'I think it's him anyway. Something about his eyes . . . I said something about the Friday night crowds, kids celebrating their twenty-first birthdays . . . his eyes did this weird thing. Like the pupils expanded and contracted. Totally creeped me out.'

'You got his name?'

'First only. Kenny.'

For a long moment, she was quiet. 'How certain are you he's our perp?'

'As certain as a guy who's been drugged with who-knows-what can be.'

'Did he make you?'

'I don't think so. I think he was sick.'

'Why?'

'He left the bar suddenly. Just bolted. I followed him—'

'Wait. Followed him? Without back up? What the hell, Harris! Anything could have—' She bit the last back and swore. 'You're certain he didn't know you were tailing him? If he made you, we're blown. He could be anywhere now.'

Coffee downed, Zach made his way back to the bedroom. 'No way, we're cool. I kept my distance. He never glanced back or changed pace, other than to stumble or double over.' He began to dress. 'I lost him somewhere in the Quarter. By that time, I was pretty messed up.'

'And that's it?'

'By the look of my feet, it's not. But it's all I remember.'

287

She muttered something he couldn't make out, but knew better than to ask her to repeat. 'We stick to our plan,' she said. 'First step is heading uptown to Tulane, see if we can locate Angel's mysterious Eli. I'm at the Eighth; get your ass here as soon as possible.'

'My ass,' he said, 'is on its way.'

45

Tulane University's Office of the Registrar was located in Gibson Hall. The eyes of the pretty young woman manning the desk lit up when she saw Zach.

A piece of cake, Micki thought when she saw her. Let the spell casting begin.

'Good morning,' the brunette said as they approached the desk, attention fully on Zach. 'How can I help you this morning?'

'Detectives Dare and Harris,' Micki said, holding up her shield. 'We—'

'—hope you *can* help us,' Zach jumped in, tone silken. 'We're looking for one of your graduate students.'

Her eyes opened a little wider. 'Oh.'

'He's not in any trouble. We just need to talk to him.'

289

Zach smiled. Obviously drawing her into his web. It was all Micki could do not to roll her eyes.

'What's his name?' she asked.

'That's the problem. We only have a first name. Elijah.' He leaned a bit closer, charm oozing from every pore. 'But I was certain, if you just searched your database—'

'What's his discipline?'

'We don't know that either.'

They'd caught the attention of another woman behind the desk. She had the look of someone who had eaten a very large, very sour pickle for breakfast.

She marched over to the counter. 'Jeanette, I'll take care of this. I'm Mary Maripaus, the Registrar. How can I be of assistance?'

Zach had his work cut out for him. To his credit, he didn't even blink. 'Detective Harris, my partner Detective Dare. How are you today?'

'Identification, please.'

They obliged and she studied them as if she was an expert in forgeries. Satisfied, she nodded. 'You're here why?'

'We're trying to locate one of your graduate students. Name's Elijah, goes by Eli. Unfortunately that's all the information we have on him.'

'Well, I'm sorry to hear that. I can't help you.'

'Ms Maripaus, Mary,' he said, looking directly into her eyes, 'I understand our request is out of the ordinary, but I'm sure you *can* help us. I'm certain you want to.'

She gazed at him. He had her, Micki thought. In the

290

next moment, that pickle mouth pursed. 'I'm certain I do not. Those eyes and smile might work on a young lass like Jeanette, but they're not going to work on me. You're asking me to access our student database, essentially giving free rein to harass any student named Elijah. As the registrar, I can assure you we have a number of them.'

Zach's surprise was almost comical. Micki quickly stepped in. 'Ms Maripaus, Detective Harris meant no disrespect.' She lowered her voice. 'We need to question this Eli in regard to the two coeds who have gone missing, one of them, as I'm certain you know, a Tulane student. It's our belief this Elijah's path crossed one of theirs. Any information he could share might lead us to them.'

Her mouth softened slightly, but she shook her head in refusal. 'If you really are detectives, I'm sure you know the university is legally bound to protect the privacy of our students. That said, we will, of course, follow the letter of the law. If the court requests the information, we will provide it.'

'Time's of the essence. Anything you could do . . .'

'There's nothing I can do. But it's been my experience the legal system moves quickly when there's more than just speculation involved.'

'Ouch,' Micki muttered as they cleared the office, casting a glance at Zach.

He didn't reply and she forced back a grin. 'Welcome to the world of ordinary humans, partner. Sucks, doesn't it?'

'I don't want to talk about it.'

'Sure, I miss the magic making my life easier, but just witnessing someone resisting your charms—'

'Detective Harris!'

Pretty Jeanette from the Registrar's office hurried after them. When she reached them, she was slightly out of breath. She handed Zach a folded piece of paper. 'I know one Eli on campus. He's one of Professor Truebell's graduate assistants, the Philosophy Department. I thought of him right off because you remind me of him a little. Your eyes.'

She smiled, an adorable dimple appearing in her right cheek. Micki decided she hated her – and all girls with adorable dimples and to-die-for-smiles. Life just wasn't fair.

'I better go before Mrs Grumpy-pants realizes I didn't run to the restroom.'

She started off, then looked back. 'Oh, and that's my phone number. Call me!'

Zach smiled. 'You were saying, partner?'

'I don't want to talk about it.'

'If it makes you feel any better, I'm pretty sure Mrs Grumpy-pants liked *you* more.'

'Shut up, Harris. We have a lead, let's follow it.'

Fifteen minutes later, they were standing outside Professor Lester Truebell's office. Luckily, they'd caught him during his regular office hours; unfortunately, a student was with him.

They didn't have long to wait. The student exited and the man greeted them. He was a cross between Santa and one of his elves – spritely, with a full white beard, but small, slim and wiry.

His face defied age, but considering his thinning hair and its color, Micki guessed he had to be at least fifty.

'Hello,' he said, smiling. 'I'm Professor Truebell.' He cocked his head. 'Neither of you are in any of my classes. Are you lost?'

'No. I'm Detective Harris, this is my partner Detective Dare. NOPD.'

His eyebrows shot up. 'Can I help you in some way?'

'Professor, we're looking for one of your graduate assistants. Elijah Wetekamm.'

'Eli? What on earth for?'

'Just to question him. His path may have crossed one of the missing coed's. Any information he could offer would be appreciated.'

'I'm certain he would be happy to speak with you, but he's left.'

'Left?' Micki repeated. 'For the day? The week?'

'The entire summer session, I'm afraid. A family member needed his help, so he went. He withdrew from his classes.'

'When was this?'

'Monday morning, first thing.'

She frowned. 'I find that odd, Professor.'

'Life, Detective, is not about what we can do for ourselves, but what we can do for others.' He smiled, gaze moving between them. 'Spoken like the philosophy geek I am.'

Something about the elfin man made her think she'd enjoy passing a couple hours with him at Shannon's Tavern, swapping stories and life philosophies over beer and peanuts.

Clearly, that wasn't happening. Ever.

'Could we get his contact information from you?' she asked. 'A cell phone number, email . . .'

'An email address, of course. He'll be checking in. But he doesn't have a cell phone. I'm sorry.'

Micki looked at Zach. He looked as doubtful as she felt. 'That surprises me, Professor Truebell. To most young people, their cell phones are as important to them as their limbs.'

'Exactly why he doesn't have one. And why I don't, either. To live actively in the moment, one needs to experience it. Can't do that if you're attached to an electronic device.'

'More philosophy?'

He smiled. 'Always. Let me get that address.' He went to his desk, jotted it on a sheet of paper, and handed it to Micki. 'I wish I could help more.'

'If he checks in, could you please have him call one of us? It could be a matter of life or death.'

Truebell took the card. Zach stuck out his hand. 'Thank you, Professor.'

Truebell eyed it a moment, then took it. 'You're very welcome. Good luck with your investigation.'

Micki watched Zach's face: whatever he was picking up from the lively professor, it was causing the corners of his mouth to twitch, as if he was holding back laughter.

They were nearly to their car before she asked. 'What was so funny?'

'The good professor thinks you're hot. Apparently, he likes his chicks badass.'

'Chicks?'

'His word, not mine. The whole gun thing, very turned on.'

'Fabulous.' She rolled her eyes. 'Nothing else? About Eli or Angel, anything?'

'Nothing. He was telling the truth. Eli left to help a family member in distress.'

'This Eli might not even be the one we're looking for.'

'My guess is, he is.'

'Because of what Jeanette said? About your eyes?'

'That and the coincidence of him having a family emergency around the same time Knight was killed.'

'Where's that piece of paper Jeanette gave you?'

'Close to my heart,' he teased. 'Why?'

'I'm going to google him.' He unlocked the Taurus, they slid inside and buckled up. 'What was his last name?'

'Wetekamm, Elijah.'

'You're going to have to spell that one.' He did and she punched it into her smartphone. 'Yup, there he is. He's got the trademark baby blues.'

He started up the vehicle, then leaned over. 'Let me see.'

She held out her phone for him, then scrolled. 'He's a do-gooder. Associated with a charity devoted to helping displaced and disenfranchised youth.'

'That fits with what Truebell was saying.'

'Here's a picture of them together, some event. Truebell's receiving an award.'

'There's one way to be a hundred percent certain he's our guy.'

'Show Angel his picture. Just what I was thinking.'

'Holy crap.' He backed out of the parking spot. 'Does that mean . . . could it be we're on the same page?'

She snorted. 'In your dreams, Hollywood Houdini. The way I see it, you're on *my* page now.'

He slid her an amused glance. 'The right page?'

She smiled. 'Damn straight. Task force meets in an hour. I'm thinking we should divide and conquer.'

He nodded. 'You speak their language, Mick, I don't. All I'd bring to the party is super-freak and let's face it, they wouldn't get it.'

She laughed. 'Thinking you're right, Hollywood. You check on Angel, show her the photo. I'll take the meeting. We meet up after.'

'On your page, Mick.'

46

After he and Mick parted company at the Eighth, Zach headed uptown toward her place. He made a couple stops on the way. The first, Teddy's to reassure Fran that Angel was safe, and to instruct her to tell anyone who might ask that she hadn't seen her. Snagging lunch for Angel and himself had been an added benefit. Next, he'd swung into a CC's Coffeehouse for one of the frozen coffee drinks she loved.

He found her sitting cross-legged on her bed, a sketch pad in her hands. 'Hey,' he said from the doorway. 'Can I come in?'

She looked up and her silky dark hair fell away from her face, like a curtain being opened. 'Sure.'

He pulled the small, rickety chair up beside the bed. 'What're you doing?'

'Sketching.'

That time, she didn't look up. He'd assumed he'd find her watching TV or on the internet, not bent intently over the four by six inch spiral. 'Can I see?'

'You really want to?'

'Yeah, I do.'

She handed it to him, then quickly looked away, as if nervous of what she might see in his face while he looked at them.

The book was almost full. He flipped through. Some had been sketched in pencil, others ballpoint pen, still others in marker. As if she had used whatever implement handy that day or moment. The images were dark, poetic. Rife with symbolism and angst: the ugly and the beautiful, life and death, joy and pain.

They were amazing.

Zach told her so and she looked at him almost shyly. 'You really think so?'

'I wouldn't say it if I didn't mean it. You've had lessons?'

'That's funny.'

'Why?'

'Where would I take drawing lessons?'

'I don't know. But then I don't know much about you.'

'If I could be anything, I'd be an artist.'

'From the looks of this, you are. These are good, Angel.'

Her cheeks turned pink and she shrugged. 'I just dream them. That's not being a real artist.'

'Wait, you dreamed these images?'

She nodded. 'At night, they grow. When I'm awake, they come to me.'

'Every night?'

'Not every night.'

He handed the tablet back. 'What do you mean they grow?'

'I'll show you.' She flipped back. An image of a heart. With what looked like roots growing around it. She flipped forward. The same image, but with flames in the heart. Then forward again, to see wings. Then next, constellations orbiting the heart in a semi-circle.

He tilted his head. There was something familiar about the image, though he was certain he had never seen it before. 'Is it finished?'

'I don't know.' She rubbed her side. 'But I don't think so.'

'Is your side bothering you again?'

'A little, not bad. Maybe it's because we were talking about it.'

'It?'

'My tattoo.'

'You had this drawing tattooed on your side?'

'I thought it was important. In case I lost my sketch-book.' She shifted her gaze slightly. 'I know that's sort of weird.'

'I'm not judging you, Angel.'

She sneaked a quick glance up at him. 'It doesn't feel good when people do. I don't like it.'

'I don't either.'

She fell silent a moment. 'Yesterday, you said we

were alike because we're different from everyone else, same as Brite and Eli are.'

'Yes.'

She frowned slightly, as if she was studying intently on the fact. 'I wonder about something?'

'What's that?'

'In my whole life, I never met anyone else like me.'

'Me either. So what?'

'Why now?'

Her question surprised him. 'You really are a little Yoda, aren't you?'

She laughed and wrinkled her nose. 'I don't know about that, but seriously, what do you think? Why now?'

Sixers, he thought, then rejected the answer. 'I don't know. What did Eli and Brite tell you?'

'Just that I was special.' She rubbed her side again. 'I already knew that.'

'How bad's your side hurting?'

'Not as bad as that night.'

'When that thing tried to kill you. The night you met Eli.'

She nodded. 'Did you find him?'

'Maybe.' Zach took out his phone, called up the picture. He handed the device to her. 'Is that your Eli?'

'Yup. Is he okay?'

'He's fine. How come you didn't tell me he had eyes like mine?'

She handed him the phone back. 'I didn't think it mattered.'

'I suppose it doesn't.' He stood. 'I brought us some lunch. From Teddy's. And a Mochasippi for you.'

She burst into a smile and scrambled off the bed. 'Great! I'm starving!'

He laughed and trailed her to the kitchen. She dug into the roast beef and gravy po'boy, dunking her chips in the debris left on the paper wrapper. He joined her, amazed at how much she could eat. And how fast. She was slurping her coffee drink before he'd even started the second half of his sandwich. He decided to wrap it back up and leave it for her for later.

He told her so and she smiled. 'Thanks. Micki doesn't have much around here to eat.'

That didn't surprise him. 'I have to go now. Is there anything you need before I do?'

'What if I need to reach you?'

'I'll give you my number.' She grabbed her pencil and sketch tablet; carefully wrote the number and his name beside it. 'You can call me anytime, Angel. No matter what.'

She looked up at him, expression quizzical. 'But you're coming back?'

'Yeah, sure. Mick too.'

'Good.' She cocked her head. 'I like you, Zach. At first I wasn't sure, but now I do.'

He smiled. 'I like you, too.'

'You promise you'll come back?'

'I promise.' He crossed to the kitchen doorway, stopped and looked back. 'Angel? How do you know what you do isn't being a real artist?'

She pursed her lips in thought. 'Real artists can draw what they see and make it look right. I can't do that.'

'Not always. Have you ever been to an art museum?'

301

She shook her head. 'No, but I used to look into the windows of art galleries in the Quarter.'

'Would you like to go sometime, when all this settles down?'

'And I'm safe?'

'Yes.'

She nodded. 'There's one here, in New Orleans?'

'Yup, at City Park.'

'I'd like that. Thank you, Zach.'

'You're welcome. Remember, don't leave the house or open the door for anyone.'

She promised she wouldn't.

He let himself out, and found Parker waiting for him at the curb, car engine running. He reached across the seat and opened the passenger side door. 'Get in,' he said.

47

'Where are we going?' Zach asked, buckling his seat belt.

'There are some people you need to meet.'

'Who?'

'That you'll learn when we get there.' He pulled away from the curb. 'I know you have the girl.'

'What girl?'

'Playing dumb doesn't suit you, Harris. You're better than that.'

'Who told you?'

'Friends.' Parker glanced at him. 'There's nothing you can do that I won't eventually find out about.'

'But eventually can be a very long time.'

'Or no time at all.' Parker made the jog from St Charles

303

Avenue onto Carrollton. The streetcar, bright red, rumbled past them. 'Gomez is at Dare's. Correct?'

'Yes.'

'Good. She should be safe there. At least for a while.'

'From the Dark Bearer that tried to kill her.'

He nodded. 'How did you locate her?'

'Her friend Fran called me. She ran there after Brite warned her the Dark Bearer—'

'Was coming for her.'

'How did you know that?'

Parker ignored his question. 'You should have contacted me immediately. Why didn't you?'

'A feeling,' he said, deciding on a partial truth. 'That she was better off with me and Mick.'

'You were right.'

'She's safer at Mick's because she's not one of us.'

'Yes.'

'Is it dangerous for me to be in contact with her?'

'For the moment, no. But you'll need to move her. Someone Dare knows and trusts. Someone you've never met.'

'Why? What's going to change?'

He didn't take his gaze from the road. 'You'll know soon enough.'

'More evasions?' Zach snorted. 'Getting damn tired of them, P.'

'You sound like Dare.'

'She's not so bad. At least I know where I stand.'

'That's what this is all about.'

Zach didn't bother to ask Parker what he meant; he knew the man wouldn't give him a straight answer.

They fell silent. Zach gazed out the window, counting the streets they passed, noting their names: Oak, Willow, Spruce.

An interesting area, he thought. As they neared the I-10 connection, the sprawling live oaks and gracious old homes lining the avenue gave way to a sorry-looking commercial development.

To Zach's surprise, Parker didn't take the interstate, but continued on Carrollton, going under the overpass and emerging on the other side, the character of the landscape changing again. Residential. Old shotguns and southern-style cottages. A look of disrepair.

'Mid-City,' Parker said. 'It got slammed by Katrina, but is coming back in a big way.'

After seven blocks, Parker made the turn onto Canal Street. Zach saw the change then. New life in the form of old homes repurposed into businesses. An advertising agency, a bed and breakfast, law offices, restaurants. Funeral home. Most with sparkling windows and shiny signs, neatly tended gardens and freshly painted shutters.

'We're almost there.'

'The people I need to meet—' He shook his head. 'Over-the-top cloak and dagger, P.'

'You have no idea.'

He studied the man a moment. 'This isn't a hit, is it?'

Parker grinned. 'We're the Bureau, not the mob.'

'That's reassuring. For a minute there, I wasn't sure.'

'Mandina's,' Parker pointed to one of the restaurants. 'Best fried oyster po'boys around. But go early, while the oil's really fresh. That's when they're best.'

He pulled to a stop in front of one of the repurposed homes. On the boulevard's neutral ground, two streetcars passed each other going in opposite directions, a red blur from the corners of his eyes.

His focused on the building. Two story. Victorian. At least a century old. Stained-glass side window, though he couldn't make out the imagery. A lovely shade tree in the small patch of green in front, a concrete patio table with sea-glass-blue umbrella. A single wooden placard swayed in the breeze.

LOST ANGEL MINISTRIES.

He couldn't help thinking of Angel Gomez. She had been lost. He and Mick had found her.

Now, here he was.

They climbed out and slammed their doors in unison. Parker looked at him. 'C'mon. They're waiting.'

Parker, Zach realized, wasn't in charge of this meeting. He was simply a courier, here at the behest of someone higher up the food chain.

The realization piqued his curiosity. They stepped through the iron gate. Zach noticed it was wired to alert those inside that visitors had arrived; at the front door, a surveillance camera transmitted their image.

Parker rang the bell, looked up at the camera. Whoever was watching buzzed them in.

They entered. A charming parlor. Colored light from the stained-glass window falling on the cypress plank flooring. A double-landing staircase, the railing old and solid-looking.

Something skittered along Zach's nerve endings. Like shards of glass. But it didn't pierce or sting. It sang.

306

There was energy here. A lot of it.

As Zach processed that fact, Professor Lester Truebell appeared at the top of the stairs.

'Hello, Detective Harris. Welcome to LAM.'

48

Thursday, July 18
3:05 P.M.

Truebell: the friend who had told Parker about Gomez, Zach realized. He looked at Parker. 'He's one of us?'

'That depends on what you mean by "us",' Truebell answered, bounding down the stairs. He held out a hand. 'It's good to see you again, Zachary.'

Zach took his hand. *Nothing. No feedback whatsoever.* He yanked it back in surprise. 'What the hell? This morning—'

'You read me.' He smiled. 'I recognized you immediately. I'm familiar with what your gifts are, so I manipulated them.'

More like, manipulated him. It rankled and Zach narrowed his eyes. 'I'm at a disadvantage.'

'One we are ready to correct. Come. We're meeting in the conference room. Eli's bringing some refreshments.'

'Eli? So you lied to us.'

Truebell motioned him into the small conference room. The oval table would seat eight comfortably, ten in a pinch. A flatscreen monitor hung on one wall; an old fireplace occupied another.

'Everything I told you this morning was true. Eli did withdraw from school to tend to a family situation. It was you who assumed home was someplace else.'

'And the family emergency?'

'Our sister Brite's murder and our concern for Angel's whereabouts.'

'But now I know she's safe.'

Zach turned. Eli in the doorway, holding a tray. No wonder Angel had called him hot. Strikingly handsome. Built like a Greek statue. Blond hair. Vivid blue eyes. Easy smile, brilliant white.

That smile grated. Hard. 'I don't know what game you're playing here, but you have about two minutes to explain it in a way that doesn't piss me off more than I already am, or I'm out of here.'

'Sit down, Zachary,' Truebell said. 'Let us smooth those ruffled feathers.'

Zach sat. Eli put the tray of water and glasses on the table, along with a plate of assorted summer fruits.

Truebell began. 'We decided it was time to bring you into the fold.'

'The fold,' Zach repeated. 'Which means I haven't been.'

'You weren't ready.'

'But I am now?'

'Maybe. Maybe not. But you've forced our hand.'

He frowned slightly. 'Because of Gomez.'

'Yes. She's important to us. Our cause. But also because of last night. What happened.'

'What do you know about last—'

'Remember, Zachary.' He held Zach's gaze, said it again. 'Remember.'

And he did. It came roaring back, filling his head. The Dark Bearer. Hunting him. Being certain he was going to die. Telepathically contacting Parker for help. A safe house. The old priest looking down at him. Voices.

'My God.' He looked at Parker. 'It tried to kill me.'

'It almost succeeded.'

'You saved my life. The safe house—'

'We'll get to that.'

Truebell again. Zach looked at him.

'Like I said, it's time to bring you into the fold.'

'Not Sixers?'

'No, not Sixers.'

Zach folded his arms across his chest. 'What is this place?'

'Lost Angel Ministry. LAM for short. Officially, we're a not-for-profit I founded twenty years ago. We cater to young people who have lost their way. Addiction issues. Family or abuse issues. The abandoned, disenfranchised, homeless.'

'And unofficially?'

'The youth we seek out and minister to are like Angel. And you, Zach.'

'The gifted?'

'Half Lights.'

The name Knight had called him. The one that had sounded like a slur on her lips.

Eli spoke up. 'Discrimination runs deep, Zach. Even within our own kind. Brite was one of the old guard, but she was working with us anyway. Trying to help.'

'Are you kidding me?' Zach said, looking at Eli. 'You're reading my mind?'

'Sorry.' He lifted a shoulder. 'I'm trying not to, but sometimes things break through my filter.'

He looked at Parker. 'You son of a bitch. You knew all along. When I asked you about Knight, about what she called me, you—'

He stopped, head filling with what Eli had just said: *Discrimination runs deep. Even within our kind.*

Our kind.

Brite Knight's hand. Truebell's from a moment ago. He'd picked up nothing. He remembered thinking that it was almost as if Knight wasn't human.

Zach told himself to get a grip. Truebell and Knight possessed unique gifts, perhaps exceptional ones. As in all cultures, forms of discrimination existed. The haves and the have-nots, the coolest kids from the rest of the herd.

'Okay,' he said, 'you have a special little club, just for the gifted. I'm happy for you, but not interested.'

He started to stand. Truebell stopped him. 'We're not a club, nor an organization.'

'Then what the hell are you?'

'We're Light Keepers, Zachary. And so are you.'

49

'Okay,' Zach said, moving his gaze between the three men, settling finally on Professor Truebell, 'I'll bite. What's a Light Keeper? Some sort of creature from outer space?'

'Sort of,' Truebell said lightly. 'We're mortal angels, Zach. Guardians of the light.'

Zach laughed. One of those spontaneous *You've-got-to-be-fucking-kidding-me* laughs. 'I wish I'd known I was going to take a ride on the crazy train today, I'd have dressed for the occasion.'

'This isn't a joke,' Parker said. 'Far from it.'

Zach shook his head, amused by Parker's dead serious voice and expression. 'Not to you three, which is coming through loud and clear and is, frankly, the freakiest part of this whole thing.' He pushed his chair back from the table. 'You have my sympathies, but I'm not interested in being a part of your whacked-out little club.'

'You already are a part of it,' Parker said. 'You just didn't know it. Hear us out. You've always wondered why you were different and where you got your special abilities. Are you really going to leave before you find out?'

Son of a bitch knew him too well. He'd pulled the trump card.

The professor leaned forward, expression earnest. 'If you choose not to join us, you walk away, no strings, no hard feelings.'

Zach hesitated. Yes, he longed for answers, but for the truth, not another fantastical work of fiction; he had spent his life conjuring those without any help from anyone.

'What do you have to lose, Zachary? A few minutes of your day, that's it.'

He held the man's gaze, then nodded and settled back into his chair. 'You've got five minutes.'

Truebell began. 'Zachary, you and I, Parker, Eli, we're all part of an ancient army. An army sent by the Creator to help humankind. To steer them toward the light and away from the dark and the destructive urges found there.' He paused. 'And to fight the beast.'

Zach almost laughed. Something in the man's eyes stopped him. 'The beast?'

'Do you doubt that evil exists, Zachary?'

Did he? Evil ran rampant in the world, acts of greed and avarice. But a beast? A creature to battle? He shook his head. 'Certainly not as a fiery red creature with horns, a tail, and pitchfork in hand.'

'Did I say anything about any of that?' He leaned forward. 'Evil, Zachary. As a force. One that can destroy, that can enter the body and devour the capacity for good.'

Zach inclined his head. 'I concede there is evil in the world and those who appear to be wholly evil.'

Eli spoke up. 'It's a great irony, Zach. We were sent to be guardians of the light. To protect all that is good and holy. Instead, many of us bowed to evil ourselves.'

Truebell went on. 'We started as beings of pure light. But enrobed in human flesh, we became susceptible to the same temptations as humans, those most deadly that wreak havoc on human will.'

Eli nodded. 'The sins that all ugliness in this world springs from. Envy and pride. Gluttony. Lust. Anger. Greed and sloth.'

Parker leaned forward. 'Seven of them, Zach.'

Seven. The divine number of completion.

The completion of an unholy circle.

'So we,' Truebell went on, 'sent to protect humankind from darkness, actually succumbed to it ourselves. With every transgression, our light diminishes. Weakened, bankrupt of light, we can become wholly dark.'

The last Saturday, a new Dark Bearer will be born.

'The transformation Parker told me about.'

'Yes.'

Zach frowned. 'So our perpetrator, the one who abducted Miller and Putnam, is a Light Keeper?'

'Was,' Lester corrected. 'He has been completely corrupted by the Beast, all but the last of his light force extinguished.'

Zach looked at Parker. 'And you believe all this Creator and Guardian crap?'

'I do. It's real, Zach.'

He shook his head, pulse pounding in his temples, quickly becoming a headache. 'No.'

'Why is it so hard to believe *this* is the truth? You've accepted there's a dark entity with the ability to kill. That it killed our sister Brite, that it tried to kill you. That it's behind the abduction of Gwen Miller and Patricia Putnam. Why do you doubt this?'

He flexed his fingers. 'Because I can *feel* his energy and I *saw* him murder Knight.'

'You asked me,' Parker murmured, 'how the Dark Bearer killed her. It stole her light. Sucked it out, fed on it. And her heart stopped.'

The wound on her shoulder, Zach thought, picturing it. And then it had gone.

He shook his head. 'This is crazy.'

'Is there night without the day, dark without the light?' He folded his hands on the table in front of him. Zach noticed how small and soft they looked. 'Good and evil are just two sides of the same coin. All beings of intelligence and free will have the capacity for both. You, me. Parker, Eli.'

Zach held his gaze. 'Suspending disbelief for a moment, what does this have to do with me or Sixers?'

'We created Sixers to help us find and train powerful Half Lights. Like you, Zachary.'

'Why?' He moved his gaze between them. 'What do you need me for?'

'Our numbers have been decimated. Half Lights like you are our last hope.'

Half Lights. Like me.

Several things they'd said clicked into place: That they were Light Keepers, but somehow he wasn't. He was a Half Light. Less than. Powerful for what he was, but still less than. Even so, they thought he could be of use to them.

'A Half Light,' he asked, 'what exactly is that . . . compared to you, Professor? And, I'm guessing, Eli and Brite Knight and,' – he looked at Parker – 'even my good buddy here?'

'You're correct, we are fully Light Keeper. Brite was also. You, and many others, are the product of a Light Keeper mating with a human.'

'A big no-no, I presume?' He saw by their expressions that "no-no" didn't quite cover it. 'I see. But hey, maybe they loved each other.'

He heard the edge in his voice and it was obvious they did, too.

'Try to understand, Zachary. We were sent to live among humans but remain separate from them, recognizable by our light. Messengers, protectors, and witnesses. Not to mingle our species and become human.'

'Mingle our species,' he repeated. 'So, I'm neither a human nor Light Keeper, but some by-product of cross breeding?'

'I'm not trying to offend you.'

316

'But you're doing such a good job of it.' Zach narrowed his gaze, moving it between the three men. 'You're saying, your pure race has been decimated. But not from war with the bad guys. By losing the battle with your libido. Brilliant.'

'The battle with our *humanity*,' Eli said. 'We're mortal angels, Zach. With a capital M.'

'Dark Bearers remain our biggest threat,' Parker said. 'They hunt us. They turn us. They spread fear, distrust, and hatred across the globe.'

Truebell continued. 'The products of Light Keeper and human unions have weakened light. With each generation, their light grows dimmer. Our gifts are mutated. They become unpredictable, volatile. All but useless against Dark Bearers.'

'Oh, even better.' Zach folded his arms across his chest. 'From a half-breed to a mutation?'

'There are thousands upon thousands of you, all with varying degrees of abilities. Ones we were certain could be cultivated and honed.'

'Enter Sixers.'

'Yes. We needed a way to facilitate the large scale, coordinated training of Half Lights. The FBI seemed the perfect choice; Parker was already an agent and had access. He designed the Sixer program as you know it, presented and implemented it.'

'So you're telling me the Bureau, the congressional oversight committees, Attorney General and Director of National Security are all on board with your whole angels and demons thing?'

Parker snorted. 'I've got a big picture of that. And

317

being locked up in a psych ward would be the least of our problems. No, as far as the powers that be are concerned, Sixers is just what I proposed: a program that utilizes the special abilities of a handful of individuals, *human beings*, in the fight against crime.'

'What I signed up for was a sham.'

'Not a sham, Zachary. A test. An introduction. To something so much bigger. So much more important.'

'Screw you.' He stood, sending his chair skidding backward. 'You've done nothing but manipulate and lie to me. From the beginning and at every turn. I'm not your partner in any of this, I'm your pawn. Your *half-breed* pawn at that.' He started toward the door. 'I'm out.'

Parker stood. 'We need you, Zach. You're special, first generation.'

Zach froze in the doorway, then turned. Looked at Parker. 'How do you know that?'

'I knew your mother. She was one of us, pure Light Keeper. That makes you special. Your abilities, your light, more powerful.'

Zach felt the words like a blow. They reverberated through him. Parker had known his mother. A Light Keeper, he said. One of them.

Had known.

Had been.

Past tense.

'Where is she?' he asked, voice thick.

Parker didn't blink. 'Dead.'

Zach laid a hand on the door casing to steady himself. 'How? When?'

'Does it really matter?'

'Yes, dammit!'

'Shortly after you were born. A Dark Bearer.'

It cut. Deeply, shredding. A jagged blade. 'Her name . . . what was it?'

'Arianna.'

That was it, then. He would never know her. 'Your five minutes are up.'

'Have you heard the term "the tipping point"?' Truebell called after him.

He looked over his shoulder. 'What about it?'

'The level at which momentum for change is unstoppable. *Unstoppable*, Zachary.'

'Which means?'

'The tipping point is near; the battle for the world has begun. Will destruction and chaos win the day? Or life and hope?'

Parker stood. Held out a hand. 'You wanted to be a hero. Here's your chance. Are you in, Zach? Or out?'

The static in his brain spiked. Fury took his breath. *Duped. Manipulated. Lied to.*

'I'm out,' he said flatly. 'But thanks for the memories, assholes.'

50

Parker caught up with him at the front gate. 'Zach, wait. We need to talk.'

He stopped, furious. 'No, you want me to listen. I think I've heard enough of your bullshit.'

'I need you to reconsider.'

'Seriously? It's all I can do to keep from decking you right now.'

'Maybe you should. You might feel better.'

'Don't tempt me. I'm out.'

He started off again. Parker called after him. 'You walk away from this, you walk away from Sixers as well.'

He called back. 'It doesn't even exist.'

'Tell that to Dare.'

Mick. Another life screwed with. 'Another one of your pawns.'

320

'She'll be fine. She's stronger than you are, Zach. You're weak. That's why you're quitting.'

He stopped, swung back to face him. 'You son of a bitch! I had a good life before this. I had everything I wanted, living was easy.'

'You were empty. That's why you said yes.'

He clenched his fists. Disgusted. 'Whatever you need to tell yourself, man.'

'No, it's whatever *you* need to tell yourself. Fact is, you're going to let those girls die, sit back and let other people step up to try and save—'

'The world? Right. The world's going to be just fine without my special little powers.'

'Of course. Take the easy way! You're good at that. Your mother would be ashamed.'

In a flash, Zach was in the other man's face. He shook with fury. 'Don't you fucking dare, you son of a bitch! You knew her—'

'She was strong and good. She—'

'You kept her from me. You kept it all from me.'

'You weren't ready! Obviously, you still aren't.'

Zach shoved him, hard. He stumbled backward.

Zach advanced, the urge to do violence – to pound Parker's smug puss to a bloody pulp – roaring through him.

He shoved again; Parker went down. But he didn't shut up.

'I should have known better than to think you could ever be a hero. You're a selfish, spoiled little boy. Keeping all your gifts to yourself, using them in whatever egocentric, self-serving way you can come up with.'

Zach snatched him up by his shirt, dragging him to his feet. Rearing back with his fist.

'I'm your uncle, Zach.'

Zach froze. 'What did you say?'

'Arianna, your mother, was my sister. My only sibling.'

'That's a lie.'

'You know it's true. You wondered why we can communicate the way we do, the way you can transfer energy to me? That's why.'

Zach released him. 'You son of a bitch.'

'Arianna and I could do the same thing.'

His uncle. Everything he had always wondered about his mother, Parker had known. Betrayal burned like acid in his chest. 'Go to hell, P.'

Parker grabbed his arm. 'Why do you think you have those gifts, Zach? What are they for? Is it all an accident, or part of a bigger plan?'

Zach shook off his hand. 'Spare me *your* attempt at philosophical BS; you're poaching on the good professor's area. I'm out.'

Parker called after him. 'Where are you going to go? You think you can outrun what you are? Now that you know the truth, where are you going to hide? The person you were before Sixers doesn't exist anymore!'

Zach didn't pause, didn't glance back. Maybe he couldn't escape what he was, but he as sure as hell could put as much distance between himself and Parker as possible.

51

The traffic light ahead turned red. Micki slowed to a stop, snatched up her phone and checked for a message from Zach. Nothing.

Where the hell was he?

The task force meeting had ended without him making an appearance. That hadn't surprised her. That she hadn't heard a word from him did. She had expected a message – something funny about her and a room full of suits. Or for him to be waiting for her at the Eighth, mouth curving into one those disarming, shit-eating grins of his when he saw her.

So she'd called him, left a message. Asked him to call.

Over an hour ago. Still nothing.

And she'd been unable to reach Angel. Anxiety

churned in the pit of her gut. Stupid. She should have instructed the girl to answer the landline if it rang.

The light changed; Micki gunned it. The task force had made a plan for tomorrow night. Undercover female agents, one for every club Miller and Putnam had visited the night they'd gone missing. Each celebrating her 'birthday'.

Their objective was twofold: play the part while paying close attention to everyone who interacted with her, befriend any other women in the club celebrating their birthday, and insinuate into their party, ever watchful.

Each 'birthday girl' would have three undercover agents covering her. One would be the buddy she'd come with. It was a good plan.

Micki had volunteered. Requested Club Kudzu. Requested Zach be her buddy. Which stacked the deck in her favor, big time.

She hadn't shared that there was a great possibility Zach had already located their perp and that maybe, just maybe, tomorrow night's operation wouldn't even be necessary.

Or that Friday really was her birthday. That little nugget wasn't any of their damn business.

Micki reached her street. Turned onto it. She saw that Zach's vehicle was parked in front of her house.

Relief shuddered through her. Followed by irritation. She'd been stewing her ass off, and he'd been happily doing his own thing. Typical Harris.

They were going to have a discussion about his communication skills.

She turned into her drive, parked, and hurried inside.

'Hollywood!' she called, snapping the door shut behind her. 'What the hell, dude, you can't bother to pick up your phone?'

Angel appeared in the hallway. She yawned and pushed the hair out of her face. 'What's up?'

'Where's Zach?'

'I don't know.' She yawned and stretched. 'He left. I took a nap.'

'He left?' She frowned. 'But his car's out front.'

She yawned again. 'He left with some guy.'

'Some guy?'

'Yeah.' She nodded. 'He got into a car with him. A black SUV. It was waiting at the curb.'

'Got in of his own volition?'

'What does that mean?'

'Nobody forced him.'

'Right. He talked to the guy, then got into the car.'

'What did the driver look like?'

'Dark hair was all I saw.'

Parker, Micki thought. It had to be. No doubt up to more of their super-secret FBI games.

'Don't be mad,' Angel said.

'I'm not mad.'

The girl rolled her eyes and Micki had to admit denying it had been lame. 'Okay, yeah, I'm pissed. Zach and I are partners; we've got stuff we need to discuss. Plans to set in place. At the very least, he needs to keep me posted on where he is.'

Angel shook her head. 'You know that's not the way Zach rolls.'

I do know that. Smart ass. Micki cocked an eyebrow. 'But how do *you* know it?'

She shrugged. 'I just do. What are we going to eat?'

'I don't know. How about we order pizza?'

Her phone sounded. Harris, she saw.

She picked up. 'Hollywood, finally. Where are you?'

'My apartment.'

She frowned. Something in his voice sounded wrong. 'What the hell for? You're supposed to be here.'

'I'm done, Mick. I quit.'

It took her a moment to comprehend what he was saying. She shook her head. 'Not funny, Hollywood. Why don't you get your ass over—'

'This isn't a joke. You should get out, too.'

She glanced at Angel. She had the strangest look on her face. Could she hear Zach? Or was she tuning into some other, gifted-only channel?

Micki turned her back to the girl, put some distance between them. 'Get out? What are you talking about?'

'They've been manipulating both of us. Lying and—'

'You were with Parker this afternoon. What did he say to you?'

'Parker's a douche, Sixers is a sham. I'm going home.'

'That's crazy, Zach. You can't do this.'

'Not leaving is what would be crazy. Get out now. Come with me.'

'Come with you? What for? What would I do?'

'We're partners, we'd figure it out.'

'You made a commitment. To Sixers. To Miller and Putnam.' She lowered her voice. 'To Angel.'

'I know things now, Mick. They can't be beaten.'

326

'Who can't?'

'Dark Bearers. Game's already over.'

His words affected her like a punch to the gut. She struggled a moment to find her breath.

'So you *give up*? That's why the game's over, why—'

'You don't understand.'

'You're right, you son of a bitch, I don't. And here I actually started believing in you and your hocus-pocus bullshit. You're just as shallow and self-absorbed as I thought.'

'There's nothing wrong with wanting my life back. You don't need me. You're the ace on this team, I'm the joke. You've got this, Mick.'

She didn't have it. Not this time. Not without him.

She closed her eyes, struggling to muster the courage to tell him. To expose herself, make herself vulnerable.

Admit weakness.

Mad Dog Dare was scared shitless.

'Mick?'

She opened her eyes. She couldn't do it. 'I made a commitment. To protect and serve. Serve even when the very ones I try to help curse me. When it's not glamorous and there's no applause. You made that commitment, too.'

'Angel is safe with you now,' he said. 'But not for long. That's what Parker said. Stash her with someone you trust, someone who's never met me.'

'I was right about you. You're a quitter. The going got tough and you—'

'Parker will replace me. You'll be fine.'

But she wouldn't. And she couldn't tell him that.

'I'm sorry, Mick.'

'Don't you hang up. Don't you—'

But it was too late. He already had. Quit on her. Left. Another letdown in a long line of letdowns by men.

Her cell, still in her hand, vibrated. 'Harris,' she answered, 'you son of a bitch, don't you ever—'

'Micki? It's me, Jacqui.'

Disappointment so bitter it stung. Her legs felt weak and she crossed to the couch and sat. 'Jax, hey. What's up?'

'I'm calling about your birthday. What was *that* all about?'

'My partner's an asshole. I thought he was calling to apologize.'

'Gotcha. So, Zander and I want to take you out for your special day. He made you something, but don't let him know I told you.'

'I can't, not tomorrow or Saturday. This investiga-tion—'

She stopped, remembering what Zach had said, about moving Angel. 'I need a favor, Jax.'

'Anything, Micki. You know that.'

'I need someone to stay with you for awhile, for safekeeping. She's in some trouble. There's a – I really need your help.'

'Sure. Of course. When?'

'Tomorrow, early. Say seven.'

She ended the call, and turned to find Angel sitting on the floor, pressed into a corner, knees drawn to her chest.

She lifted her gaze to Micki's. 'I heard what you said. You're sending me somewhere else.'

'Yes.'

'I like it here.'

'You're not safe. Not long term.'

'Why?'

'I don't know.'

'He's coming back.'

'Zach?' She shook her head. 'No. He's not.'

'He promised me he would.'

'Promises don't mean much to some people, Angel. Zach's one of those people.'

'No.' She jutted out her chin, though Micki saw that it trembled. 'He'll be back. I know he will.'

Micki felt for the girl. She understood. She'd been disappointed by every man in her life – except one. And he'd left her too, though through no fault of his own.

After awhile, you just have to harden yourself. But she wasn't about to say that to Angel. Instead, she crossed to her and held out a hand to help her up. 'Maybe you're right. Come on, let's order that pizza.'

Angel took her hand and stood. 'I am. You'll see.'

52

Friday, July 19
7:02 A.M.

The next morning, Alexander greeted them at the door. Jacqui hovered behind him, looking anxious.

He launched himself at her. 'Happy birfday, Auntie Mouse!'

She scooped him up, spun him around. 'Thank you, sweetheart!'

He squirmed for her to let him go. 'I made you a cawd. It has lots of glitter 'n a picture of Thomas! I glued it myself.'

'Why don't you get it for her?' Jacqui suggested.

He nodded and darted in that direction, stopped and turned back. 'Made a cake, too! 'nila with sprinkles. Lots of sprinkles.'

'Yummy,' she said. 'I can't wait to try it.'

''Kay. I'll get it,' he said. 'You wait.'

'No,' Jacqui said quickly, 'not the cake! Just the card for now, okay?' She smiled at Angel. 'Hi. I'm Jax.'

Angel returned her smile. Micki finished the introductions. In the next moment, Alexander was back with the card, then dragging Angel off to see his Thomas train set.

Micki watched them go, then turned to her friend. 'Thanks for doing this, Jax. I really appreciate it.'

'She seems like a nice kid.' Jax lowered her voice. 'Is everything okay? You look . . . stressed.'

She forced a smile. 'I'm okay. The new partner I told you about, he up and quit last night. Just as this investigation is really heating up.'

She squeezed her hand. 'Sorry, Micki. Did he say why?'

She shook her head, surprised by the bitterness she felt. 'Couldn't hack it.'

'It's been all over the news. No sign of those girls yet?'

'I really can't talk about it.'

'What's her story?' She motioned in the direction of the other room and Alexander's excited babbling.

'A good kid. Hasn't had it easy.'

'I get it.'

She looked at her. 'I knew you would.'

'You said . . . there were people after her. I just want to make sure, we're not in any danger keeping her here. Because of Alexander,' she added quickly. 'I'd help no matter what. You know that.'

'I do. And no, you, Alexander – and Angel – will be

completely safe.' Micki paused. 'I'd never knowingly do anything to put you two in danger.'

Jax hugged her. 'I wish you could stay. At least for a piece of cake.'

'Save me one for later. I need to go.'

Jacqui nodded and opened the door. Stepped outside with her. 'Be careful, okay?'

'You know I will.' She stopped, glanced back. 'Angel is special, Jax. She's different.'

She frowned. 'What do you mean?'

'Not ordinary, that's all. Just in case she— She just looks at things differently, that's all.'

'I think I can deal with that.'

'Call me if anything—' She shook her head. 'Listen to me being overprotective. It's a good thing I'm not a mom, I'd never let my kid leave the house.'

Jax laughed, they said their goodbyes, and minutes later she was on the road, heading to the Eighth.

Her phone went off. She answered. 'Detective Dare.'

'It's Parker.'

'We don't work together anymore, Agent. I have nothing to say to you.'

'He called you.'

'Of course he called me.'

'Because you were partners.'

The smug edge in his voice rankled. 'What do you want, Parker?'

'I thought you'd appreciate the official story before you walked into it this morning.'

'Damn decent of you. And here I thought you were a complete dick.'

'He's the one who quit, Detective. He couldn't handle the truth.'

'Which is?'

'Sometimes neither appropriate nor appetizing.'

'And that's all you're going to say?'

'Need-to-know, Detective.'

'You really are a piece of work.'

He went on, unperturbed. 'Harris's dad suffered a heart attack last night; he caught the first available flight back to California. Major Nichols has been informed. Time will pass. He will decide not to return.'

'Is it true the Dark Bearers can't be beaten?'

'You'll be assigned another Sixer when one becomes available.'

'What are you hiding from everyone?'

'Unless, of course, you want to quit as well.'

'I'm not a quitter.'

'Of course you're not. One of the reasons we selected you.'

'What about tonight? Will you be there?'

'Not I, but others.'

'Sixers?'

'Good luck, Detective.'

'Wait! Don't you even care? Did you even try to convince him to stay? Did you tell him we needed him?'

'Did you, Detective?'

A lump settled in her throat. 'This isn't about what I did or didn't do, Agent.'

For a moment, he said nothing. When he spoke, she

heard fatigue in his voice. 'I've got a war to fight, Detective Dare. I can't worry about one lost soldier.'

'One soldier? That's slightly dramatic, don't you—'

But he had hung up on her.

53

Angel sat on the couch with Alexander snuggled up beside her. From the kitchen came the clicking of computer keys as Jacqui worked on the paper she was writing for school. She was attending college online, studying to get a teaching degree. Angel wondered if she could get an art degree online, then scoffed at the thought. That would call for a computer, internet service, and a place to use them both. She'd never have that.

The TV flickered. Angel blinked. Focused on it. A series of buildings. Still abandoned after Katrina.

Crazy, she thought. After so many years, just left to crumble.

Her side tingled and she shifted uncomfortably. It had been doing that on and off all day. Not pain. This strange . . . awareness. As if it, her tattoo, wanted her attention.

She closed her eyes. Something was shifting inside her, a kind of movement. This feeling of . . . completion.

It didn't frighten her, though she wondered if it should. She'd seen this horror movie where the heroine had been inhabited by an alien. If she remembered it right, the character had felt the same way.

Eyes closed, Angel trailed her fingers through the boy's soft curls. The first time her side had hurt was on her birthday. At that horrible frat party. It had twinged, on and off, ever since. But this other thing, whatever was growing inside her, her first glimmer of it had occurred while talking to Zach yesterday, then ramped up this morning, when Zander had taken her hand.

A clarity, she realized. The reason she wasn't afraid. She was meant to be here now. With these people. All of them.

In a way she had never been meant to be anywhere. As if everything, all eighteen years of her life, had been leading to this moment.

'He's sound asleep.'

She opened her eyes. Jacqui stood in the kitchen doorway, eyes on her son, smile soft with love. A mom's love.

What she had never known. What she never would. It hurt.

'He likes you, Angel.'

'I like him.' She looked at Jacqui. 'He's really special.'

She smiled. 'I think so, too. But I would, I'm his mom.'

She doesn't know.

'Shame, isn't it?' Jacqui motioned toward the television. 'Beautiful old school.'

Angel turned her gaze to the screen. Sacred Heart church and school. Boarded and abandoned. Black and white graffiti scrawled across red brick. The playground with broken, lonely swings and toppled slides. Chain link fence, signs warning KEEP OUT.

'Where is that?' she asked.

'Lower ninth ward.'

'How come nobody's fixed it back up?'

'It's complicated. Cost. Location. Can't fill a school if there aren't enough children.' She clucked her tongue. 'I'm sure the archdiocese still owns it. Looks like they've been mowing.'

Angel stared at the TV. Her side burned and she winced.

'What's wrong?'

'My side. It hurts sometimes. It's not a big deal.'

Jacqui crossed to her, laid a hand on her forehead. 'You don't have a temperature.'

'I never do.' She tried not to moan as the pain spiked again. With it, the image of Micki popped into her head.

She looked hopefully up at Jacqui. 'Do you think Micki's all right?'

'I do,' she smiled gently, the same way Angel had seen her smile at Alexander. 'She's really tough, Angel. She'll be okay.'

'But what if—' She stopped, pressed her lips together a moment, then went on 'this time, she's not tough enough?'

Jacqui's smile wavered. 'Why are you asking me this?'

'I like her,' she said simply. 'I don't want anything to happen to her.'

'She'll be fine. Don't worry.'

'Jax?'

She stopped, looked back.

'How come you guys are friends?'

'She took me in when I had nobody.'

'Kind of like me.'

'I suppose so. Though I was robbing her neighbor's house. Or trying to.' She paused. 'I was pregnant with Alexander.'

Angel frowned. 'What happened to his dad?'

'That's a story for another time.' She cleared her throat. 'Anyway, Micki could have busted me – instead, she helped me. I owe her everything.'

Angel's side tweaked again. 'I'm going to go lie down.'

'Let me get Alexander first, I'll put him to bed.'

Angel waited, watching as Jacqui scooped the boy up. He whimpered and melted into her, as limp as a rag doll.

'I wish I had a mom.'

'You don't?'

'I'm an orphan. I was left on the steps of a church.' Angel saw Jacqui blink against tears. She looked quickly back at the television, afraid she might cry too. 'Who knows, maybe it was that one.'

Angel awakened with a start, heart thundering. The bedside light cast a soft glow, beating back the dark as best it could. She lay on top of the covers; the apartment was silent. She sat up and her sketch tablet slid off her chest.

In her dream. Someone. Calling her for help. Needing her.

Quickly, she grabbed her pencil and pad, began to draw. Focusing inward on the images from her dream. Gripping the pencil, her hand flew across the page. A curved line, a straight one. Hatch marks and smudges, light and shadow.

A figure began to take shape. One howling in pain. A female. Reaching out.

Angel brought her own hand to her mouth. Micki. The person in her dream was Micki.

54

Saturday, July 20
1:15 A.M.

Zach sat alone on the Moonwalk bench, gazing at the Mississippi, visible only by the lights it reflected – a tugboat, a barge, French Quarter businesses along this stretch of the riverside. Most reflective of all was the moon, big and bright.

He'd booked an early flight out. Back to California. Home. His family. All that was familiar.

He linked his fingers. Truth was, he didn't want to go. Didn't want to leave this place or the dream he'd held close for so long.

To discover who he was. And why his mother had given him up.

Instead, he'd found out *what* he was. A half-breed freak. His special abilities a mutation.

A mutation. Of course they were. Hadn't he known

340

that, deep down, always? Instead, he called them gifts. Special abilities.

Parker and his offer of superhero status had played right into that. The man had known exactly what card to turn at every juncture. Of course he had.

His mother's brother. *Uncle Parker.* Prick. Lying to him. Manipulating him. His own blood? His only sibling's offspring? Who did that?

The tipping point: the level at which momentum for change is unstoppable.

Change to what? A world filled with darkness and fear? It was already that. No, Parker and his little band of freaks were just trying to save their own butts. Using him and others like him to save *their* race from extinction.

Not his race. Not his battle.

Zach swore. He couldn't chase Mick's voice out of his head. Her accusations. That he was a quitter. A selfish, self-absorbed child.

A loser.

She hadn't used that word. But it had been implied. And no doubt, by her thinking, deserved.

Let her think whatever she chose, none of this was about him. A strategy. A war game.

He shook his head. Screw that.

His cell went off. 'This is Zach,' he answered.

Not Detective Harris or Agent Harris. Not anymore.

'Zach, it's me. Angel.'

'Angel? Are you all right?'

'You promised, Zach. You promised you were coming back.'

341

'I'm sorry, kiddo. There are things . . . going on that you can't understand.'

'That's what adults always say when they don't really care.'

Her words cut deeper than he could have imagined. 'I'm sorry you feel that way.'

'I do feel that way. And now you're one of them for saying it.'

She had been let down by everybody. Including him.

'You can't quit.'

'You don't understand.'

'Micki needs you.'

'She's strong, Angel. Stronger than I am.'

'You're stronger than you think.'

'I'm sorry.'

'She's in trouble. I dreamed it.' Her voice quivered. 'It's bad.'

He sat up straighter. 'What's bad? What do you mean?'

'It's all coming down tonight. She's at the center.'

'She has lots of protection, How do you know—'

'I saw it. Something weird's been happening to me. Things that were never clear are now. Pieces, popping into place.'

'Where are you?'

'With her friend, Jacqui.'

He didn't know Jacqui. Mick had never mentioned any friend, let alone one by that name.

'She has a little boy. He's really cute. He's special, too. But she doesn't know.'

'Angel, you stay safe, okay? Do just what Micki tells you, she'll—'

'It's her birthday, Zach. It's Micki's birthday.'

He felt as if he'd been punched in the gut. He looked right, toward the brewery complex.

'And she's there. With him, Zach. The one.'

He got to his feet, heart pounding. 'Where is she? What club?'

'I don't know.'

The lights of Kudzu's seemed to wink at him.

Micki would be there, at Kudzu's. She would have made certain of it. Undercover or not. Because of what he'd told her.

Without him. Without the special abilities he brought to the party.

'I'm five minutes from her, Angel. I'll make certain she's safe.'

'Don't leave her, Zach.' She sounded fierce. 'It's your job to protect her.'

'Sit tight. And be very, very careful.'

Seven minutes later Zach stepped into the club. A sea of young people. All of them moving with the throbbing music. Flashing lights. The smell of sweat. And sex.

And yet his eyes went straight to Mick. At the center of the dance floor. Arms up, hips undulating. She looked five years younger and outrageously sexy. A form-fitting, low cut top. Jeans so snug, they could've been sprayed on, tucked into a pair of badass cowboy boots.

Boots which no doubt served as the one place to conceal her weapon. No way Mad Dog wasn't packing heat.

As he watched, she tilted her head back, neck arching, hands in her hair. To attract. Entice.

It was working. A number of men were dancing with and around her. Hoping to get lucky. Zach shifted his gaze to the bar. Kenny was serving drinks, leaning on the bar, flirting with a blond. But every so often, slyly shifting his attention. To Mick. Watching her with those strange, liquid eyes.

Making his plans.

Zach started her way, winding through the partiers. Her back was to him as she moved. She spun around, saw him, and stopped. Her expression registered surprise, then cleared.

Zach fell into step with her, mirroring her movement. Moving closer. He felt the heat emanating from her. The scent of her perfume filled his nostrils.

Hands at her waist, he caught her, pulled her against him, matching her undulations, bodies brushing. It was damn erotic. Or would have been if he wasn't focused on saving her life.

He leaned closer still, lips to her ear. 'Surprise.'

'What are you doing here?'

She was angry; the emotion trembled there on her words. 'I'm staying. At least for tonight.' He paused. 'You need me.'

'Don't flatter yourself.'

He tightened his fingers on her waist. 'Happy birthday, Mick.'

'How did you know?'

'Angel. She called me.' He released her, then retreated. To her credit, she never broke character. Sliding sinuously up to another admirer, then laughing and flirting with yet another.

Zach's turn again. Drawing her close. Drinking in her perfume. 'Mr Twitchy's been watching you.'

'Kenny?'

He breathed deeply, his nostrils filling with the scent. 'Mmm hmm . . .'

'We had a moment earlier. Maybe it's time for another.'

She spun away from him, made her way to the bar. He watched, noting the Eighth was well represented. Her friend, Detective Stacy Killian, scooting over to join her. Laughing. Girlfriends out for a wild night. McConnell, alone at the bar. Brooding over his beer, missing nothing.

He moved his gaze over the room. No Parker, Truebell, or Eli. Bastards. Throwing her to the wolves.

Wolf, he amended. One of them. With weird eyes and a twitch.

At his hip, his cell phone vibrated. The same number as earlier, he saw and answered, voice low. 'Angel?'

A moment of silence, then, 'Who is this?'

A woman's voice. Not Angel's. Desperate-sounding. 'Zach Harris. Who are—'

Then he realized. 'Jacqui?' he said. 'Micki's friend?'

'Yes, but how—'

'Hold a moment, please. I need to find someplace quiet.' He headed out to the balcony, found a corner. 'Sorry about that. I'm Micki's partner.'

'Partner? But I thought— I saw this number and thought the worst.'

'Is Angel all right?'

'She's gone. I woke up. Thought I heard Angel rummaging about. I listened a few moments, then went looking. She left a note.'

'Read it to me.'

'"I know where they are".' Her voice trembled. '"I have to help them. Please don't be mad".'

'That's it?'

'Yes. I—'

'Where do you live?'

'Excuse me?'

'What area of the city?'

'Gentilly Terrace, but why—'

'She may be on her way here.'

'But how would she know where you and Micki are?'

'I can't explain other than to say she called earlier, worried about Mick. How far are you from the French Quarter?'

'On foot, a long way. By bus . . .' She paused, as if mentally working out a route. 'It's the middle of the night, not all buses are running and she's not even familiar with the nearby stops!'

The woman's voice rose, an edge of hysteria in it. He worked to calm her. Not easy to do when panic was knocking against his door as well. 'Do you have a car, Jacqui?'

'Yes, I— Oh my God. Wait.' Her phone clattered as she dropped it; he heard her rummaging for something. A moment later she was back. 'My keys are gone!'

His stomach sank. Angel out in the city. Unprotected. Tonight, Saturday, the seventh day of the week.

'What should I do? I have Alexander, I can't—'

'Stay put,' he said firmly. 'I'm coming to you.' She didn't question why and he asked for her address. She gave it to him and a moment later he reentered the club.

Micki, back on the dance floor. As if she sensed his presence, she turned, met his eyes. She smiled, completely in character. A temptress, teasing, seductive.

But he saw the question in her eyes. She had seen him on the phone, exit to the balcony, probably saw the strain around his eyes.

He started deliberately forward, also in character. The part of rejected lover teased to the breaking point. He pulled her forcefully against him.

She stood on tiptoe, wound her arms around his neck, found his ear. 'The phone, who?'

He responded in kind, nipping her earlobe. 'Not here.'

He caught her hand, laced their fingers and led her to the back hallway that led to the restrooms. There, he backed her up to the wall, arms on either side of her head, pressed fully against her.

'Jacqui,' he murmured.

She stiffened. 'What's wrong?'

'Now, none of that . . .' He trailed kisses along the side of her neck, smiling at the goosebumps that followed his mouth. 'Wouldn't want folks to see through our little act.' More kisses and nibbles, then back up to her ear. 'Angel took Jacqui's car and—'

From the corners of his eyes, he saw Amanda, the bartender from the other night, emerge from the ladies' room. He reacted, pressing his mouth to Mick's. He made it a long, deep, penetrating kiss.

At first, he felt her surprise and resistance, then her response. Melting into him, playing the game.

He drew back. 'She left a note. She may be on her way here.'

'Here? But—'

More people passing; another drugging kiss. 'The note wasn't explicit. I'm going to Jacqui's.'

She dropped her hands to his chest, curled her fingers into his shirt. 'I'll go. She's my—'

'No.' Her rubbed his mouth softly against hers. 'I'll . . . see . . . if I can pick . . . up . . .'

Two obviously inebriated young women stumbled into the hall, then stopped and stared.

Micki flattened her hands against his chest and pushed him away. 'Get off me, you creep! We're done.'

He stepped back, hands up as if to ward off an attack. 'You're crazy, you know that?'

'Whatever. Just stay away from me.'

'With pleasure, psycho.' He started toward the door, feigning disgust.

'Don't call me!' she shouted after him. 'Don't come see me. Not ever!'

In other words, call me the minute you know something. Or else.

Zach paused, looked over his shoulder at her. 'No worries, babe. This is so over.'

55

Micki splashed cold water on her cheeks. Her hands shook. Her legs felt weak. She had to snap out of it. Angel had left Jacqui's, putting herself in harm's way.

Zach would find her. He had to.

But letting him go without her went against her every instinct.

She had a job to do. Here. Zach didn't. Technically, Zach wasn't even part of this investigation anymore. And officially, neither was Angel.

Micki splashed more water, then ripped off a paper towel. Zach was no longer her responsibility to protect. Not her partner. Not anything but a major pain in—

Liar. Micki looked at herself in the mirror, cringing at the honesty in her reflection. She was still quaking inside. Still on fire. The effect of his mouth on hers, his lips trailing across her neck, chill bumps following, her nipples hardening.

She had to get a frickin' grip, like, right now. This instant. It'd been part of the job. They'd both been playing a part. He had mad skills.

She remembered calling him the magic man. Turned out he really was.

I am. Good in bed.

Hadn't even crossed my mind.

It will.

Son of a bitch was right about everything.

She met her own gaze in the bathroom mirror once more. This time with determination. Sinking into character. Time to convince Kenny-the-Dark-Bearer-morphing-bartender that she was his next victim.

Moments later, Micki learned that wasn't going to happen.

'Gone?' she said to the woman bartender, pouting. 'Where?'

'His shift ended.'

'But he promised he wouldn't leave without me.' Again with the pout. The slight slurring of her words. 'It's my birthday.'

'How about some friendly advice?' The woman cocked an eyebrow, but didn't wait. 'I'd stay away from that one. Kenny takes no prisoners.'

Micki looked at her, feigning confusion. 'What do you mean?'

'You'll fall hard and he'll break your heart.'

'But I really like him. And it's my birthday. He's my present.'

The woman laughed and shook her head. 'Tell you what, sweetie. Sometimes he grabs breakfast on his way home. The Who Dat Cafe. Maybe you can catch him there.'

Micki didn't waste any time. She found Stacy. 'I'm going after Kenny,' she said. 'The other bartender thought he might have gone to breakfast.'

'Hell no, you're not. Mac followed him.'

'Even better. I'll have back up if I need it.'

'We stick with the plan, finish the night here.'

'Can't do it, Stacy. Sorry.'

'Shit, Micki,' She lowered her voice. 'You're vulnerable.'

'I'm good. Got my badge, gun, and Mac.' She paused. 'He's our guy. I can't say why I'm certain of that, but I am. I find him, I call you and the rest of the cavalry.'

Two minutes later, Micki was out on the French Quarter street. She was familiar with the Who Dat, a late night hole-in-the-wall breakfast joint, favorite of locals, cops included. On Dauphine near Conti, off the beaten track.

She hauled ass. Anyone watching would know she was not only stone cold sober, but on a mission.

A half-block from the cafe, she slowed, caught her breath. Fluffed her hair, straightened her top. And prayed he was there and he bought her empty-headed, hungry for sex act.

Her prayers were answered. He sat at the counter, staring at his plate of bacon and eggs. She scanned for Mac, but didn't see him. She should play it smart.

Notify Stacy and the rest of the team. But she had this. She could take him if she had to.

She sidled up and slipped onto the stool next to him. 'Hey.'

He glanced her way, gaze sharp. 'What're you doing here?'

'You left me.' She laid a hand on his thigh, curving her fingers intimately around it. She felt him shudder slightly. 'I thought we had something special going tonight.'

'Did you?'

'Mmm hmm.' She moved her fingers in slow circles. 'Where's your friend?'

'Ditched her.' Micki smiled drunkenly. 'She wasn't any fun.'

'I noticed that.' He paused a moment, then smiled. 'I'm going to a party. Want to come along?'

'Sure.'

She stood and swayed. He caught her elbow, steadying her. 'Not too drunk?'

She giggled. 'Not if you'll hold me up.'

'I think I can manage that.'

'Maybe I better use the little girls' room before we go.'

'I'll take you.'

'I can do it, silly.'

'Wouldn't want you to fall down.'

''Kay.' She giggled again, resisting the urge to roll her eyes at the silliness of it. 'If you insist.'

'I do.' He wrapped an arm around her waist and she leaned into him, letting him support her. The more helpless she appeared, the more overconfident he would be. And the greater her element of surprise.

A single stall bathroom, Micki saw. She had hoped for several stalls to muffle a call to Stacy.

She playfully pushed away. 'You stay.'

He grinned. 'I'm not going anywhere.'

She shut the door and turned the bolt, then retrieved her cell, tucked into her bra.

Got him, she typed. Asked me to a party. No Mac.

Stay put I'm on my way

I'll try to stall him. No promises.

He tapped on the door. 'You okay, babe?'

'One minute,' she called back, quickly flushing the toilet. She ran the water, then the hand dryer.

When she emerged from the bathroom, she found him right outside the door.

'Sorry,' she said. 'I texted my friend.'

'How come?'

'She's freaking out.' He led her to his car, a sporty little number. Black. 'Nice wheels.'

'Thanks.'

He opened the passenger side door. She slid in, conscious of her weapon, tucked into her boot. Positioning her feet to afford her the easiest access to it. Wondering when he would make his move. What it would be.

He went around the car, climbed in. 'Why's your friend freaking out?'

"Cause of those other girls.'

He started the car, but didn't pull away from the curb. 'The ones who went missing?'

She nodded. 'They were out celebrating their birthdays, too.'

He smiled, the curving of his lips snakelike. 'And you're not scared?'

'Should I be?'

He reached over, caught her chin, turned her face to his. She met his gaze and realized her mistake. His dark, liquid gaze sucked her in. Lethargy stole over her, creeping up her limbs, leaving her fingers tingling, her head foggy.

'Of course not, sweetheart. Nobody else is grabbing you. I've got you now.'

Micki told herself to blink, look away, break the connection. But couldn't. His gaze was hypnotic. The way Zach's had been, when he'd broken his promise and used his mojo powers on hers.

But this was different from Zach's as well. Darker. Suffocating. Strangling her free will.

This was how he did it, she realized. How he'd gotten Miller and Putnam out of their apartments and into his car without a struggle.

'Baby?'

'Yes?' She heard her response as if from a great distance.

'You're really tired. Why don't you lay your head back and rest. I'll wake you up when we get to the party.'

She wanted to argue. Fight it, him. But found herself obediently laying her head back against the rest, closing her eyes.

'That's a good girl,' he murmured. 'Sweet dreams.'

56

Jacqui lived in a small apartment complex sitting square in the middle of a mixed residential area. Zach parked in front of the building and climbed out. The glow of the streetlights revealed a neighborhood that had seen better days.

He found her apartment number and knocked. She opened the door as far as the chain allowed.

'I'm Zach,' he said. 'Jacqui?'

She nodded and a moment later allowed him in. A small boy clung to her leg. He looked as worried as she did.

'This is Alexander.'

'Hey, Alexander,' he said.

The boy looked up at him, expression serious. 'You gonna fin' Angel?'

'I am, buddy.' He returned his gaze to Jacqui's. 'Can I see the note?'

She led him into the small kitchen. 'It's there,' she said, indicating the open tablet on the table.

Angel's sketch pad. He crossed to it. She had jotted the note on the page with the drawing of her tattoo.

Heart with inner flames. A winged creature. Constellations. Seven of them.

Seven.

It looked so familiar. Not because he'd seen the drawing before. Someplace else. Some—

The Putnam scene. The chaos of foodstuffs on the floor – mayo, pickles, peanut butter, jelly, milk and eggs. Ketchup at the center, exploded. Crude but similar enough to have tweaked his memory.

He read the note: *I know where they are. I have to help them. Please don't be mad.*

'What do you make of it?'

'It sounds like Angel.'

He reached down but didn't touch the paper. Just in case Angel hadn't written this. Hadn't left of her own volition.

He hovered his hand over it. Her energy clung to it. Emanating up, hand tingling, wrist, forearm. He closed his eyes. Angel's emotions panicked. Excited. Determined.

Save the girls.

Girls, plural.

Not Mick. Miller and Putnam.

Angel had somehow figured out where they were. Zach turned the page. His knees went weak. A drawing. Of Mick. Horrible, howling in pain. A darkness around her, overcoming her.

The reason Angel had called him.

He laid his hand on it. Angel, sitting up in bed. Terrified. For Micki's safety. Her decision to call him. Nothing new.

Beside him Jacqui made a sound of distress. 'Oh my God, is that Micki?'

He turned the page back to the note, not wanting to upset the woman more. 'That's why Angel called me earlier. She dreamed Micki was in danger.'

'Is she?'

'I just left her, she's fine.' He wished he felt as confident of that as he sounded. 'She has plenty of backup.'

Jacqui rubbed her arms as if to chase away a chill. 'That drawing . . . it's so horrible. Why would she dream that?'

Zach didn't answer; instead, he turned the conversation back to Angel. 'I need you to focus. The coeds who went missing, I think Angel figured out where they're being kept.'

'But how could . . . I don't understand.'

'Let me worry about that, okay? Let's talk about Angel. When did you last see her?'

'Seven-thirty, eight o'clock, something like that. Her side was hurting.'

Her tattoo. His gaze shifted to the image. 'Go on.'

'I was worried, but she said it did that sometimes.'

'Where was she?'

'On the couch. She and Zander. He was asleep and she was watching TV. I was here, in the kitchen.'

'What was she watching?'

'A PBS show. On Katrina.'

He frowned. 'Hurricane Katrina?'

'Yes.' She nervously chewed her bottom lip. 'Places that flooded in the storm but are still abandoned.'

Abandoned places. Of course. What better location to stash two women the entire city was looking for. 'What places?'

'I don't know, I was in here and—'

'Deep breath,' he said softly, meeting her eyes. 'You've got this.'

She did as he suggested, breathing deeply, in and out, then nodded. 'I don't know about the entire show, but she and I talked about one of the places. An abandoned church and school.'

'Where?'

'Lower ninth.'

'Name of the church?'

'I don't remember!'

'Think, Jacqui. It's important.'

'It was Catholic because I remember saying the archdiocese probably still owned the property.'

Her tattoo. A heart with a flame burning in it.

'Sacred Heart,' he said.

'Yes! That's it. How did you—'

'I think that's where she's gone. Do you have a computer?'

'Yes. Right here.'

She retrieved the laptop from her computer bag, opened it and made a sound of surprise. 'The church, it's right here. She must have looked it up.'

Zach turned the device his way. Angel's energy was all over it. 'This is definitely where she went. I'm going after her.'

'What should I do?'

'Just wait here. If Mick calls, fill her in.'

'Maybe I should call her?'

He laid his hands on her shoulders, looked her in the eyes. 'Answering could compromise her. This may be nothing. It probably is nothing.'

'You're right,' Jacqui agreed. 'Angel got an idea in her head and acted on it.'

'Good.' He dropped his hands. 'Stay calm. I'll call you the moment we're on our way back. Until then, you and Zander get some sleep.'

'I don't think there's much of a chance of that for either of—' She stopped, looked around. 'Zander, where'd he go?'

'He was right here,' Zach said. 'Just a moment ago.'

'Zander, where are you? Mommy needs you to answer.'

Nothing. Total quiet. Zach frowned. 'He could have curled up somewhere and gone to sleep. Kids do that, right?'

'Alexander!' she called again, voice rising as she hurried into the other room. 'Answer me right now!'

He didn't answer and they looked under beds and in closets, anywhere the three-year-old could hide.

Jacqui was growing hysterical. 'It's the middle of the night. We were standing right here!'

'Exactly,' Zach said. 'He couldn't have left without our—'

'Oh my God.'

He followed the direction of her gaze. The pet door. His heart stopped. 'Has he ever—'

'Yes. But I made him promise never to do it . . .' Her voice trailed off, as if realizing how silly that sounded. 'I keep it latched, just to be safe.'

But it wasn't latched, they found a moment later. A cry slipped past her lips. 'It's pitch black out . . . and he's just a little boy!' She was trembling, near tears. 'Anything could happen.'

'Do you have a flashlight?'

'Yes.'

'Get it. I have one in my car. I'll help you look.'

'But Angel—'

'Will have to wait,' Zach said, the passage of time settling like weight on his shoulders. 'He can't have gone far.'

57

Angel stood on the steps of the abandoned church, a monstrous hulk in the blackness. No glimmer of light from anywhere, as if all that was good had left this place long ago.

A force had led her here. Navigated for her, like an internal GPS. The padlocked gate had simply fallen open at her touch.

But the force had also led her to this moment. All her life she had felt its call. And she had searched for that something. The why to her life. Her purpose.

This was it. What she had been created for. Why she was different from other kids. Why she dreamed in symbols; why she had dreamed the image of the heart and felt compelled to permanently mark her body with it.

Her side began to ache. The tattoo started to thrum, mimicking the beat of her heart. She turned her face to the sour breeze and shuddered. Something foul lived here.

The missing two were here: Gwen Miller and Patricia Putnam. She sensed their despair. Their fear rippled along her nerve endings. Weirdly, instead of frightening her, the twin emotions seemed to bring her to life.

Her destiny, she thought. Get in, free them, and get out.

Angel moved her gaze over the path ahead to the church's facade, then the sprawling school to the right. She closed her eyes. Focused. Like lifting, the way opened up to her.

She bypassed the church and followed what had been a breezeway to the school. The door stood open. Waiting for her.

She stepped through; it slammed shut behind her.

She jerked at the sound and glanced over her shoulder, then turned back to the hallway before her. It curved into a semicircle and had what appeared to be doorways to classrooms at various intervals. She brought a hand to her tattoo, picturing it. The church was the heart, literally the Sacred Heart. The classrooms the constellations.

She picked her way forward. Chaos frozen in time. Desks and chairs upended, books tossed. All manner of debris, covered with mold and other decay.

What once was a place of learning was now a landscape of judgment, of human trial.

'Hello,' she called out. 'Is anyone here?' *Nothing.* 'Gwen? Patricia?'

Then came a whimper. It seemed to emerge from nowhere and mingle with the roar of blood in her head. 'Where are you?' she called. 'I'm here to free you.'

'Here!' Another voice had joined the first. 'We're here!'

She started in the direction the voices had come, moving as quickly as she could through the destruction. *'Hello, little one.'*

She stopped, heart thundering. The voice was in her head, but also resounding off the walls.

'I've been waiting for you.'

She turned in a slow circle, searching the darkness. 'Who are you?'

'You know me.'

The voice curled over and around her, somehow familiar, reassuring, and magnetic. 'No,' she said defiantly. 'I don't know you.'

'Angel,' the voice chided, *'you can't deny me.'*

'How do you know my name?'

'Because I created you.'

Created her? Like she was the result of a lab experiment. A sort of Frankenstein. 'If I know you, show yourself.'

Angel waited. Nothing shifted in the dark; the silence grew heavy. She pressed forward. 'Gwen, Patricia! Where are you?'

'Here,' they cried, sobbing. 'Please help us! He's coming!'

Angel found the classroom, the locked door. She peered through the window and saw the two. Huddled together, chained to the wall. Terrified, but alive.

She hadn't been wrong.

This was her destiny.

The door was metal, its hinges rusty, the frame crumbling. She threw herself against it once, then again. Pain shot through her side, her shoulder – sharp, white hot. She realized she was crying. She tackled it a third time. It groaned, began to give.

Thank God, she thought. Thank—

Suddenly, she wasn't alone. A presence. Circling, caressing her. As she imagined a lover would. Gooseflesh raced up her arms, over her torso; the hair on her head seemed to stand up. A part of her awakened.

'I'm your destiny, Angel.'

'Get out of my head.'

'You can't deny me.'

And then she realized. The thing that had terrorized her, that had killed Brite and tried to kill Zach. The thing Eli and the others had whispered about, that they had been so afraid of.

Fear exploded inside her, with it the instinct for self-preservation. What had she been thinking? She wasn't strong enough to do this. Not near strong enough.

It laughed. *'It's right for you to be afraid, dearest Angel.'*

Closer, stronger. Enveloping her.

'You wondered why you never fit in? I'm why.'

'No.'

'*You're a part of me.*'

She reared back and kicked the door with all her might; searing pain shot up her leg like a bolt of electricity. She kicked it again and again until it collapsed inward.

'*Breathe me in, my sweet child. I'm all around you.*'

It was. Swirling energy. Limitless. Dark. Roiling with power.

'*Do you not feel a part of yourself awakening? Coming to vibrant life? That's me. In you, Angel.*'

'What do you want from me?'

'*So easy. Just turn and go. Leave this place.*'

'I can't!' she cried.

'*Save yourself. Walk away.*'

Angel looked at the two sobbing women. Leave them to die and she lived. 'Why?' she whispered.

'*You can't help them anyway. I'm too strong. You know that.*'

She did know it. She didn't know either of these women. She couldn't fight this thing; it was too strong.

She began to tremble, so forcefully her teeth chattered. Tremors from the inside, as if her very marrow was at war with itself.

Resistance rose up in her. 'No.'

Pain ripped through her. She doubled over, fell to her knees. 'No,' she said again. 'I won't—'

Her gut twisted. With a soul-shaking cry, she threw up. Once, then again. Tears streamed down her cheeks. Her skin crawled, like millions of spiders were attacking, attempting to pick the flesh from her bones.

'Please,' she begged. 'Stop . . . Please. . .'

'*Just say the word.*'

No more pain. He would release her and she could run. Leave him and this place far behind.

Yes.

The word whispered across her brain. Sweet, refreshing. Like a summer rain. Say it. Take the offer, walk away.

No . . . more . . . pain.

She opened her mouth to say it aloud. Instead, a name tumbled out. 'Eli,' she whispered. Then again, stronger this time, 'Eli . . . Zach . . . help me.'

The building groaned, the floor shook. The monster took her then. Gathered her into its darkness. Snakelike, surrounding her, squeezing. Tighter and tighter. Her chest hurt. She fought for breath.

'*Stupid girl. Do you really think they can beat me?*'

Her chest hurt. She fought for breath. And against hopelessness.

'*They're coming for you. They will die with the other two.*'

The image of Eli filled her head. Bathed in light as he emerged from his car. The image warmed and she held tightly to it. Her thoughts turned to Zach. His smile, his kindness. Micki's, too. Jacqui and little Zander. They didn't know her, yet they had taken her in. Cared for her.

Anger burst from her very core. If he hurt them, she would find a way, somehow, to make him pay.

The monster laughed at her unspoken threat. '*You thought you would stay with her. That she would care for you. She will be dead. And it will be your choice.*'

The anger turned white hot. Spiked into hatred.

'*That art museum he promised? How? He will be dead as well.*'

With the hatred came strength. A strength she had never known before. Like a lion coming to life inside her.

The monster's grip on her loosened.

'*Did you endure all the taunts, the teasing and rejection for this? To die here, give yourself for these women you don't even know? Is that your destiny?*'

Her friends were coming for her. Micki. Her brothers, Eli and Zach.

'*Choose to save yourself and your friends. Walk away, let these girls die.*'

It was manipulating her, she realized. Using her emotions to control her. To get what it wanted.

Why? What did it want from her?

'*Do it, Angel. Walk away.*'

'Never,' she managed, her voice a defiant croak.

'*We wait then. Seeing their pain may change your mind.*'

58

Zach and Jacqui scoured the neighborhood without a sign of Alexander. Jacqui seemed about one shallow breath away from totally losing it.

'Let's go back to your place,' Zach said, keeping his tone as reassuring as he could. 'He might have gone home. He might be waiting there for you.'

'Do you think so?' she asked, voice quivering. Hopeful.

'I think it's a strong possibility.'

So they did, Jacqui at a pace just shy of an all-out run. As her unit came into view, she cried out in relief. Alexander was there on the porch, sitting next to a tall man with blond hair.

Eli.

'Alexander!'

'Mommy!' He trotted down the porch steps and launched himself into her arms.

'Thank God!' Jacqui hugged him hard, then held him at arm's length. 'Don't you ever do that again!' She shook him lightly. 'Anything could have happened. Someone could have stolen or hurt you!'

He started to sob. 'Wanted to fin' Angel. She's my friend.'

She scooped him up, cuddled him tightly to her. 'You scared me, baby.'

Zach looked from her to Eli. The man's bright blue gaze met his. He smiled slightly.

'I came to help you.'

'I don't need your help.' Zach narrowed his eyes. *'Get out of my head.'*

Jacqui interrupted their silent exchange. 'I don't know how to thank you.'

'No thanks necessary,' Eli said, standing. 'Glad I happened along.'

'Where was he?'

'The bus stop.'

'My God.' She tightened her grip, so much that Zander squirmed. 'Do you live in the neighborhood?'

'Up the way.' He motioned vaguely. 'I've seen you two around; and when I saw him alone, I knew something was wrong. He didn't want to come with me, but I convinced him.'

Eli shifted his gaze to Alexander. 'Remember what I said, Zander. Listen to your mom. The street's no place for a little guy like you to be.'

Zander nodded, squared his shoulders, though his chin wobbled. 'Cross my heart.'

Jacqui frowned slightly. 'I'm going to get him to bed. Thank you, Mr—'

'Just call me Eli.'

'Eli,' she repeated, then looked at Zach. 'Thanks, both of you.'

She held his gaze. He nodded slightly. 'I'll be in touch.'

The moment the door snapped shut behind them, Zach faced the other man. 'Get the hell out of my life. I don't need you, Uncle Parker, the professor, or any of the rest of you.'

'You do need us, whether you want to or not. That is, if you plan to save Angel and Micki.'

Zach's heart sped up. 'What do you know?'

'Everything but where they are. I'll explain while you're driving.'

Zach hesitated a moment, then headed to the Taurus, parked by the curb. He unlocked it and they both climbed in. He started the engine, but made no move to shift into Drive.

He looked at Eli. 'You know what's going down, but not where. How is that?'

'You don't get it, Zach. You take for granted that others can do what you do. We can't.'

'Picking up thoughts, memories, feelings; influencing others to buy drinks or spill them; getting girls to say yes – these are all nifty tricks. But if not for Angel, I wouldn't know where they were either.'

'Her dreams and premonitions, that's what she does.

That ability makes her special. It's why we need her.' He looked at him. 'And we need you, Zach.'

'Right,' he muttered. 'For what? My parlor tricks? To be your trained monkey?'

'Like I said, you underestimate and undervalue yourself. Yes, Angel's a prophet. But you're a tracker. That's unique. Even among Full Lights.'

'A tracker?' he repeated. 'What the hell is that?'

'Just what it sounds like.' He paused a moment, as if giving Zach a moment to connect the dots, then went on, 'You possess the ability to track Dark Bearers. And not just the mini-me-minions, but the original: The Ancient One.'

'Whoa, back up, brother. The Ancient One?'

'The original. Everything starts somewhere.'

He snorted. 'Like the snake in the garden.'

'A rather brilliant metaphor, yes. The snake, Lucifer, Satan, the dragon, destroyer. He appears in some form in every culture and belief system across the globe and throughout history.'

Evil in the world. He'd already accepted it existed, he wasn't about to quibble over who came first, at least not now. 'I followed the energy trail, big deal.'

'Actually yes, a big deal. A very big deal. You feel its energy, have a physical response to its presence. You saw it attacking Brite. I can't do that. Lester can't. It's a very special gift, Zach.'

Zach flexed his fingers on the steering wheel, processing. He looked back at Eli. 'If you don't pick up the Dark Bearer's energy, why the fear of touching Angel after her brush with it?'

'You saw what happened when you transmitted to Parker. That's a best-case scenario. Worst case, the Dark Bearer uses her to get to us.'

'That night I went into Kudzu's, I felt nothing. No energy at all.'

Eli's lips lifted slightly. 'Yeah, you did. You felt the absence of it. Loudly, I'll bet. They can't hide from you, Zach. Which brings us to tonight. Without you, we wouldn't be here. We wouldn't have the opportunity to stop the final conversion. That's why Parker recruited you; he hoped you inherited it from your mother.' He paused. 'It's why we need you.'

'She was a tracker, too.'

'Yes. And fiercely loyal to our cause.'

'But not your kind,' he shot back. 'Considering she committed the ultimate "sin" of mating with a human.'

'She fell in love, Zach. How can I stand in judgment of that?' He laid a hand on his arm. 'You have questions, I get that. And I'll answer every one of them. But now we need to go. Time's running out.'

Angel. Mick. They needed him.

It burned to swallow his questions – like bile in his throat – but he nodded and shifted the sedan into Drive.

59

'Wake up, baby. We're here.'

Micki's eyelids lifted to darkness. Her thoughts left the world of dreams to the nightmare of the moment. To what had happened, where she was. Who she was with.

That he had a gun. Aimed at her head.

She reached for her own, found that it was gone. He laughed. 'Game changer, baby.'

She worked to stay in character, despite his strangely liquid eyes and the smell of decay gagging her. 'I don't know what you mean.'

'You're a cop,' he said. 'A detective. Michaela Dare.'

Great. 'You helped yourself to my shield?'

'And your phone. Nice tits, by the way.'

'Fuck you.'

He laughed and pressed the gun's barrel to her temple. 'Get out of the car. Now.'

Micki stalled. 'Where are we?'

'You'll know soon enough.' She hesitated and he smiled, the stretching of his mouth over his teeth grotesque. 'Everyone else is here. Including someone you care about.'

'Who?'

'Last chance to get out of the car. Or you and your chambered bullet will become intimately acquainted.'

Her only chance to take him down was to do as he ordered. She opened the car door, climbed out.

An abandoned church, she saw. A Katrina leftover. Which narrowed the possibilities. Micki moved her gaze over the landscape. Its size and scope. Her money was on Lower Ninth.

He nudged her with the gun. 'Time to party. You lead.'

Micki picked her way slowly, waiting for her eyes to adjust to the darkness. He followed her, matching her steps, gun pressed between her shoulder blades.

'Pretty smart, figuring us out.'

'Us?'

'The teacher and me.'

Teacher? For a moment she was confused, then she realized he meant the Dark Bearer. 'That's what you call it? Not beast or monster?'

'Shut up.'

'That's what it is, a monster. It's killing you.'

He jabbed her with the gun, so hard she stumbled. She silently swore at the sign of weakness. 'Back up's on the way.'

'No, it's not. I read your text messages. Answered your cop friend. Let her know you were wrong about me and safely home.'

'That won't hold. They'll follow my phone's pings—'

'Your cell is long gone. Besides, it'll all be over by then.'

'We'll all be dead?'

'Yes.' A violent shudder rolled over him. 'I have to get this out of me.'

She recalled what Parker had shared – about the process of becoming a Dark Bearer, that the final extinguishing of light was nearly unbearable.

She took a stab. 'It's not the last Saturday. It can't happen.'

'I have four now. The teacher promised.'

Four? With Miller, Putnam, she made three, Unless . . .

Angel.

The realization took her breath. Her thoughts raced. Which meant Zach, if not here, was on his way. But what could he do? No weapon. No backup.

She had to get her gun back.

The closer they got to the church, the more ragged Kenny's breathing became. His steps became uneven, the gun barrel jerked against her back.

'You don't have to do this,' she said. 'It's not too late.' He didn't respond. They climbed the church steps, reached the door.

'Open it.'

She heard the screaming the moment she entered

the church. The scream of terrified women. Women in pain. As if being tortured.

'You son of a bitch! Where are they?'

Micki whirled around. The bartender was no longer handsome. Pain contorted his classic features, his pupils had expanded to become dark, empty pools.

The moment of horror passed. 'Give me the gun,' she said. 'I'll make the pain stop.'

A violent shudder racked him. 'Shut up.'

'You don't have to hurt anyone, not anymore. I know you were once good, Kenny. Before the Dark Bearer's lies. Try to remember.'

He looked at her with those strange eyes and in them she saw something, a flicker of the person he once had been. It gave her hope.

She held out a hand, beseeching him. 'Don't do this. Help me save them.'

He convulsed in reaction to her plea. 'It's too late.'

'It's never too late! You have good in you. I see it still.'

'Rip it out, Teacher! I beg you!'

At his agonized howl the hair on her arms and back of her neck stood up. She pressed on, eyes on his face but acutely aware of the gun in his grip.

'There's good left in you, Kenny. Please don't do this—'

He jerked. His flesh began to undulate. As if a creature inhabited his skin and was fighting to get out. His eyes rolled back in his head, then forward. He went stock-still.

In complete control, he met her eyes. 'The light can't

win. Look at this place, this world. Corruption at every corner of the globe.'

His voice had changed. His entire demeanor. As if he had been inhabited by another.

The Dark Bearer.

'There is good,' she said, voice shaking. 'There is love. And kindness and—'

'And uncles who like to sit their little nieces on their lap, and mothers and grandmothers who look the other way.'

The sickly sweet smell of tobacco and whiskey filled her nostrils. Her thoughts tumbled back; memories of sweaty hands and hot, quickening breath against her ear. Whimpering for him to stop.

Micki couldn't breathe. She struggled to fill her lungs. To expel the memories.

'You don't believe in a good world, Michaela.'

'That's . . . not . . . true.'

'Oh, that's right, Hank came along. Your precious savior.'

She flinched – the sound of Hank's name on his lips was like a curse. 'What do you know about him?'

'That he died of a heart attack.' That mouth twisting into an obscene grin. 'Isn't that what they told you? And him, with no previous indications of heart disease.'

'You killed Hank?' She took an involuntary step back. 'Is that what you're saying?'

'How could that happen in a good world?'

'You son of a bitch! You—'

'Why are the innocent judged harshly while corrupt

378

run free?' His voice morphed into Hank's. 'Beheadings, pollution, greed . . .'

He hadn't moved, yet it felt as if he was coming at her from every direction. His voice an assault.

'. . . children starving, disease rampant.' His voice changed again. Uncle Beau's, straight from her nightmares, slurred from drink and husky with perverted desire. 'Don't forget, Michaela, this is our little secret.'

'Stop it!' she screamed, curving her hands into fists. 'You bastard! You killed him!'

'What do you want to do about it?'

'I'm going to kill you. Somehow, someway I'm going to see you destroyed!'

He laughed. The sound echoed strangely through the abandoned sanctuary. 'You see, Michaela, you believe in the darkness. The power of evil. Violence and brute force. You live it every day.'

'Mick!'

'Stay back,' she shouted. 'He's got my—'

Kenny convulsed and swung toward Zach. Micki seized the opportunity and lunged for the gun. The shot rang out. Micki felt the bullet enter her chest. Explode. Reverberating clear to her marrow.

She collided with the bartender. They went down together. A second explosion sounded. In her head. As if she was being blown wide open, shattering into a million sparkling pieces.

'No! Mick!'

Zach's panicked shout mingled with the sound of blood gushing. A gurgling with her every breath. The bartender-being rolled off her.

'Mick, no . . . hold on, sweetheart—'

Floating. Above herself. Gazing down at him, his hand pressed to her chest, red seeping through.

'Help!' he shouted on a sob. 'Someone . . . help!'

The bartender, she saw, bleeding out. No longer contorted with pain, handsome again.

No help for him.

No help for her.

'Come back, Mick. You can't die. You can't! You're too damn stubborn.'

She opened her eyes. Saw his face. Tears on his cheeks. Tried to smile, to tell him he'd be okay without her . . .

The sound of her pumping blood slowed.

Cold. She was so cold.

'Leave her, Zach.'

The voice was rich and deep. So very calm.

'I can't.'

'Go get Angel and the others.'

'No. My fault—' His voice caught. 'I think she's . . . is she—'

'I've got her. The others are coming.'

Light bloomed behind her eyes. Blindingly brilliant and warm. Like a brilliant cocoon, beckoning her in. To be comforted and cradled, reborn.

Zach left her. She followed, calling out. No, she realized. No voice. No mouth, vocal cords or lungs. Just energy.

She hovered above the scene. The sobbing women; Angel on the floor, writhing in pain, screaming for Zach to go, save himself. Zach battling an invisible foe, being mangled like a rag doll.

And she could do nothing.

'*Micki, come back.*'

No! Zach needed her. Angel needed her.

Ribbons of light, curling around her, drawing her away. She fought them. How could she leave them? Her job . . . to protect and serve. Without her—

'*You're needed here, Michaela. We chose you.*'

Below, Zach got to Angel, covered her. A human shield, light emanating from him. Bright for the briefest moment, quickly dimming, the darkness becoming complete.

The ribbons of love and acceptance found her once more, cradling her, sapping her resistance. Drawing her gently back to her broken body.

One last glance back. A final goodbye.

Figures surrounding Zach and Angel. Many of them. Pulsing with light so bright it blinded; waves of it filling every crack and corner.

Home, she thought. Hank waiting for her.

Her eyes cracked open. A figure over her. Beautiful. Iridescent.

Are you an angel?

Something like that. I'm Eli.

60

Monday, July 22
Noon

Zach stood in the doorway of the hospital room. Sunlight tumbled through the window, bathing Mick in light. It softened her features, making her look more like an angel than the ass-kicking cop she was.

She sat up in the bed, gaze fixed on the TV and the News at Noon.

'*In a daring rescue early this morning, NOPD Detective Zachary Harris—*'

As if sensing his presence, she looked his way.

He smiled. 'Hey.'

'Hey to you too.'

He crossed to the bed. 'We did it.'

She cocked an eyebrow. 'You sure did. You're a bona fide hero.'

He pulled over the chair and sat. 'Can't believe everything you see on TV.'

As if on cue, they both turned to the screen.

'—*the other detective involved was shot during the operation and is hospitalized but expected to recover.*'

Zach blinked. In that fraction of a second, the events of that night played through his mind: the sound of shots, Mick's body jerking at the impact, holding her while her blood drained out, helpless to stop it.

He looked at her, smile gone. 'Thought I'd lost you, Mick.'

For a long moment, she was silent. When she spoke, her tone was low but fierce. 'I was dying, Zach. In fact . . . I died.'

He shifted his gaze slightly. She couldn't know the whole truth. Maybe ever. 'I'm sure it felt that way, but—'

'No.' She shook her head. 'I felt my blood run out, my heart slow to a stop.'

'You lost a lot of blood, Mick. Lost consciousness.'

'The doctors can't believe how I've healed. Where the bullet entered, its trajectory . . . I shouldn't be here, let alone be sitting up talking. A miracle, they said.'

Her voice thickened and he reached across and caught her hand, recalling those moments. Eli, drawing her limp body to his; wrapping himself around her, cocooning her in the most beautiful light he had ever seen.

Mick squeezed his hand tighter. 'I don't think . . . I didn't deserve a miracle.'

A lump formed in his throat. 'You did, Mick. And you'd deserve a dozen more.'

Her eyes grew bright and she looked quickly away. 'A dozen?' she quipped. 'If you hang around, I'm going to need a hell of a lot more than that.'

'It's okay to cry, Mick.'

'I'm not crying.' She looked at him with manufactured bravado. 'Mad Dog doesn't cry. Mad Dog crushes skulls.'

He tightened his fingers around hers. 'Sorry I got you shot.'

'There's not a YouTube video, is there?'

'Not that I know of.'

'Lucky me,' she said, her attempted sarcasm coming across tremulous.

'Kenny's dead. You know that, right? He shot you, then turned the gun on himself.'

She shook her head, turning her gaze to the window, the sun shining through. 'Why'd he do that, Hollywood?'

'Who knows? Maybe he realized there was no way out?'

She looked back at him. 'I think he wanted to do the right thing. He still had good in him.'

'Listen to cynical, badass Michaela Dare, seeing the best in someone.'

'When I was dying, I had this vision. An angel. He wrapped me in his wings.'

Zach held his breath. She wasn't supposed to remember Eli's presence, nor that of the other Light Keepers or Dark Bearer. Just as Miller and Putnam didn't. They remembered Kenny, being abducted and tortured, their fear, the chaos. Passing in and out of consciousness. And finally, being saved.

Angel, on the other hand, was special. In the circle. 'It was . . . beautiful,' she went on. 'The most beautiful thing I'd ever seen. That's all I remember.' She searched his gaze. 'What did I miss?'

For a moment, his memory flooded with the image of Angel in the grip of the Dark Bearer. He felt its terrible, suffocating presence. Remembered his fear as it turned on him when he tried to free her.

'Zach?'

He blinked, shooting her his trademark shit-eating grin, hating himself for what he was about to say. 'Just me saving the day. Freed Miller, Putnam, and Angel. Called for backup and medical assistance.'

She lowered her voice. 'And the Dark Bearer?'

'Took off.' That much was true. Lester and his assembled army had driven it off with their lightforce. He recalled Truebell's words after: 'Darkness, Zach, cannot exist in the light.'

But it would be back, as strong as ever. Until then, they waited. And trained.

She was looking at him strangely, eyebrows drawn together in thought. He smiled. 'I guess he knew he was licked. I'm pretty damn scary.'

She shook her head. 'It was there. I felt it and . . . it took over Kenny's body. And—'

She bit the last back and massaged the bridge of her nose.

'What, Mick?'

'It knew things. About me. My past.' She paused. 'How could that be?'

'Don't know, Mick.'

'You're certain there was nothing else? I have this feeling . . .'

He squeezed her hand again then released it. 'I brought you something.'

'You did?' She eyed him suspiciously. 'I don't see anything.'

'Wait there.' He went to the door, poked his head out, and gave the nurse's aide a thumbs-up. 'It's time,' he said.

A moment later, Mick was scowling up at them. 'What the hell, Hollywood?'

He crossed to the window and raised the blind. The nurse rearranged bags, tubes and monitors and rolled her bed to the window, positioned so she could see out.

'For you, Mick.'

'A view of the parking lot?'

'There, in the valet's spot.'

Zach knew the moment she saw them because she caught her breath. Jacqui, holding a bouquet of flowers. Alexander with balloons, bobbling like crazy as he jumped up and down with excitement. Angel with them, waving a handmade GET WELL SOON sign.

And with them, almost as good as new and ready to roll . . .

'The Nova?' she said, turning her gaze to him. 'How did you . . . it wasn't supposed to be ready for—'

She bit the words back. Shook her head, a smile

386

tugging at her mouth. 'It's always going to be like this, isn't it? You the hero, me the zero? That is, if you're staying.'

'I'm staying, partner. It looks like you're stuck with me.'

Now read the beginning
of the second
Micki and Zach novel,

If You Dare

Prologue

LOST ANGEL MINISTRIES. Zach Harris stood at the wrought-iron gate, gazing at the sign as it swayed in the breeze. The iron fence circled the property, a Victorian home from days gone by, repurposed into a center that helped lost and disenfranchised youth. Youth who were . . . unique.

The front door opened and a teenager darted out, calling 'Bye' over her shoulder. She was small with a spiky, pixie haircut, the spikes dyed Irish green. She met his eyes as she reached the gate. Beautiful eyes. A brilliant green that matched her hair.

Like him, was she a Half Light? A product of the co-mingling of the human and Light Keeper races? Or could she be Full Light, one of the rapidly dwindling number that remained?

'Hey,' she said, slipping past him.

'Hey,' he responded, and headed through the gate and up the walk. It felt weird, thinking of himself as not completely human. Part light, enrobed in human flesh, sent to guide the human race? Part mortal angel, locked in a life-or-death battle with an ancient evil?

It felt like total bullshit. It pissed him off. He might not want to buy in, but at this point, he didn't have a choice. Like it or not, his eyes had been opened.

From the neutral ground behind him came the rumble of the streetcar. He glanced over his shoulder at it, bright, shiny red, windows shut tight to keep the heat out. He reached the door, looked directly at the security camera and was buzzed in.

Eli met him in the foyer. He looked totally unfazed, as if saving lives and battling the forces of darkness had the rejuvenating properties of a spa day.

'Zach, buddy—' he clapped him on the back '—great to see you. Come, they're in the conference room.'

They started in that direction. Eli turned his extraordinary gaze on him. 'You've been to the hospital and seen Michaela?'

'Left just a little bit ago.'

'How is she?'

'Healing quickly. Very.'

'I do good work.'

The cockiness annoyed the crap out of him. 'She says she remembers being surrounded by a beautiful, healing light. Like being wrapped in an angel's wings.'

Eli stopped and cocked his head. 'Did she? That's curious. And what did you tell her?'

'That she had lost a lot of blood, was in shock or hallucinating.'

'Good. Here we are.'

'Wait.' Zach laid a hand on his arm, stopping him. 'I thought you said she wouldn't remember anything.'

'That's why it's curious.' He smiled. 'I don't think it's anything you need to worry about.'

Famous last words, Zach thought as he stepped into the conference room. Only two at the table: His Sixer point man, Parker, and Professor Lester Truebell.

'Zachary.' Truebell stood and held out his hand, smiling.

Zach took it. 'Professor.'

'No worse for wear, I see.'

'Tell that to every muscle, joint and bone in my body.' He indicated the four of them. 'We're it?'

'For today, yes.'

'No Angel?'

'She's not ready.'

The comment rankled. More secrets. More need-to-know bullshit. 'I see nothing's changed since the last time I sat across this table from you.'

The elfin Truebell shook his head. 'Everything's changed, Zachary. Sit. Please.'

He did. Parker spoke up. 'No hello for me, Zach?'

Zach looked at him, not masking his anger. 'I may have to work with you, Special Agent Parker, but I don't have to like you. And I sure as hell don't have to respect you.'

Parker leaned back in his chair and folded his arms across his chest. 'You don't think that's a little harsh? And formal, considering we're family?'

'From our first meeting, everything out of your mouth has been either a lie or a manipulation. Or both.' He arched his eyebrows. 'So, no. Not too harsh.'

'Sixers wasn't a lie. There was just more to the story.'

'There always is, and that's the problem.' He shifted his attention back to Truebell. 'Why am I here today?'

'You know why.'

'Do I?'

'Are you in,' Truebell asked, 'or out?'

Zach wished he could say he was out, shake this whole experience off, and go back to the life he had known before. But that life was gone forever. 'Saturday made a believer out of me.'

Truebell nodded. 'You know its destructive power now. You understand our urgency.'

Zach's head filled with the memory of the power turned on him, his helplessness against it. 'Yes.'

'And now you know our power as well.'

The joining of the Light Keepers. The explosion of light. The howl of rage as the Dark Bearer had been forced out.

Darkness cannot exist in the light, Zach.

But it could put up a hell of a fight.

'How many of us were there that night?' Zach asked. 'A dozen?'

'More. Fourteen.'

'Fourteen to overcome one? I suppose you've noticed those odds suck for us.'

'They do, indeed. So, Zachary, now that you're a believer and you know the odds, are you with us?'

He held the professor's gaze. 'I'm in. For now.'

Professor Truebell smiled slightly. 'Not quite the gung-ho response I'd hoped for, but it'll do for now. One last thing—' He folded his hands on the table and leaned toward Zach. '—I have to have your word. You'll do what you need to do, concerning Michaela?'

He hated this. She was his partner. Secrets put her in harm's way.

'*No, Zach. They make her safer.*'

He looked at Eli. '*Get out of my head.*'

'*You have to trust us.*'

'*I trust her.*'

'Zachary? Your answer.'

'Yes. I'll tell her nothing of the Light Keepers and nothing of the true nature of the events of that night.'

'You won't regret it.'

He regretted it already. 'What's next?'

'We wait.'

'For what?'

'A Dark Bearer to strike.'

1

New Orleans, Louisiana
Friday, October 16
11:25 P.M.

'You're sure it's cool if I go?'

Angel Gomez smiled at her fellow barista and waved her toward the door. 'Girl, go. Have fun.'

Ginger hesitated. 'Micki'll tear me apart if she finds out I left without you.'

'I won't tell her, so she'll never know. And you've got to admit, Micki's a little over the top when it comes to her rules. It's kinda stupid, considering that before moving in with her, I'd been living on my own for years.'

'Still—' Ginger glanced at the clock '—it's only a half hour—'

'And only five blocks home for me. I've got my phone, my mace and a set of loud-ass lungs. Go. And tell Bryan I said to be good.'

Ginger laughed and snatched up her backpack. 'He always is.'

'*That's* not the kind of good I'm talking about.'

A moment later, Ginger was gone. And Angel was alone. She made herself busy completing the last of the day's clean-up and the next day's set-up. Ironically, Friday night was the quietest night of the week at Sacred Grounds. During the week, nestled as it was within biking distances of both Tulane and Loyola universities, it was packed with students either caffeinating to cram for tests or caffeinating to not crash after cramming for them. Friday, by this time, everyone was decompressing. Parties, dates, movies, gaming. Study hall was over. Let the good times roll.

Angel smiled to herself. So much had changed since that terrible night three months ago. So much that was good. She was happy in a way she'd never been before.

She could almost forget what it had been like to have that Dark Bearer in her head, to be at his mercy.

No, she thought. The nightmare was over. Eli, the professor and the other Light Keepers had sent it packing.

Angel hadn't told anyone about him being in her head, not Micki, or Zach or even Eli. She didn't want them to know. She was afraid they'd look at her differently, like she wasn't *really* one of them. Like they couldn't trust her. But she'd promised herself she would, if he ever came back.

'You still open?'

She looked over her shoulder. She hadn't heard the

door open, hadn't heard the chime that announced the arrival of a customer.

Gorgeous. The guy in the doorway was simply gorgeous. Dark, wavy hair. Bright white smile. Beautiful hazel eyes she could see from across the cafe. He took her breath away.

'I surprised you,' he said, 'Sorry about that.'

'No, I—' She cleared her throat. 'I was just closing up. What can I get you?'

Was that hopefulness in her voice? Geez, she was pathetic.

'Whatever's easy.'

'I could do a pour over if you want hot? I've already emptied and cleaned the machines—'

'How about cold?'

'Iced tea? Iced coffee? A bottle of water or juice?'

'A bottle of water's fine.'

She retrieved it from the cooler behind her. 'I haven't seen you in here before.'

'It's my first time.'

She handed him the bottle. 'You a student?'

He shook his head and took a long swallow of the water. Angel found herself staring at his neck, the way the tendons stretched with the movement.

'Finished with all that,' he said. 'Out in the working world.'

'What do you do?'

'I'm in sales.'

'What do you sell?'

He laughed. 'You're a very curious girl, aren't you?'

She flushed. 'Sorry. I guess I'm being rude.'

'How old are you?' he asked.

At the question, her heart skipped a beat. She wanted to say 'old enough' but that would have been *really* rude. 'Almost nineteen.'

'I'm twenty-two.' He reached for his wallet. 'What do I owe you?'

'It's on me.'

'You already closed out your register, didn't you?'

'I did, but that's my bad. Don't worry about it.'

He took a five-dollar bill from his wallet and stuck it in the tip jar. 'I've got to go. Thanks – what's your name?'

'Angel.'

'Angel,' he said. 'I'm Seth.'

That smile again. For a split second she couldn't breathe. When the second passed, she returned the smile. 'Hi, Seth.'

'See you around, Angel.'

She watched him leave the coffeehouse, a strange sense of loss rolling over her, and bringing with it the urge to run after him, ask him out.

She got her cell phone and texted Ginger.

u missed the cutest guy ever. he just left.

u get his #

got his name. Seth.

u should have asked him to party

Angel tried to picture that and laughed. Right. That wasn't happening. Ever.

gonna finish closing talk 2 u tomorrow

She pocketed her phone and quickly finished doing just that. Five minutes later, she flipped off the neon OPEN sign and locked up.

The cool, damp night settled around her like a cloud. She shivered and started home, thoughts turning to Seth. Ask him to party? Ask him for his number? Odd, unwanted Angel Gomez with a guy like him? Never gonna happen.

What was it about him, she wondered? She'd never been super-interested in guys, not that she was gay or anything, but she'd been able to take them or leave them. Until him. Tonight. His smile. Something about his eyes. Looking into them, she'd felt like the two of them were . . . connected somehow.

She suddenly became aware of another person coming up behind her. She glanced back. A kid in a hoodie, head down, hands in the jacket's pockets. She stepped to the right so he could pass her.

But instead of breezing by, he slowed down, fell into step with her. 'You want to party?'

A kid. Maybe sixteen. She thought of what Ginger had texted and almost laughed. This kid clearly had no trouble doing what her friend suggested. 'With you?'

'Why not?'

'You're too young, kid.'

'How about some weed?'

'Not interested. Get lost.'

He followed her. 'Pharmies? A little crank or coke?'

She stopped and turned toward him. 'I don't do drugs and I don't like people who push them. Take a—'

In that instant, he grabbed her purse and yanked hard. The strap snapped; he turned and ran.

'No!' she cried and took off after him. Her phone was in there. Her ID. Today's tips.

The mace.

She never saw the other kid. He leapt out from behind a pick-up truck and knocked her sideways, into the bushes. Angel went down, her head snapping back, hitting the ground with a thud.

Seeing stars didn't stop her from fighting him. She kicked and clawed. 'Get off me, creep!'

The first kid had doubled back. Her purse landed on the ground near her head.

'Gimme a hand,' the guy holding her said.

'What's the problem? You can't handle a *girl*?'

'She's stronger than she looks, okay? Lemme have your jacket.'

'What for—'

'I'm gonna shut her up!'

In the next instant, the sweatshirt was pressed over her face. Angel fought. Squirming. Kicking out. When the jacket slipped, the guys came into focus. Both so young. Why were they doing this to her?

She sucked in a lungful of air and screamed. Once, then again.

'Shit!' The one on top of her howled. 'Shut her up!'

'Dammit Pong, how am I—'

'Idiot, hold the jacket over her head!'

The first one smashed the hoodie over her face again, this time so tightly she couldn't breathe. The smell of sweat, stale tobacco, and something cloyingly sweet filled her head. She thought she heard her name being called. '*Eli? she answered. Is that you? I need you!*'

'Get the fuck off her!'

In the next instant, the kid was dragged aside. She heard the sound of a blow, then a grunt of pain and footfalls on pavement.

'That's right, you'd better run!'

She clawed free of the hoodie, gasping for breath. Seth, she realized. It had been his voice she'd heard.

He knelt beside her. 'Are you okay?'

Angel blinked. 'Your nose is bleeding.'

He laughed softly. 'And yours is running.'

She wiped it with the back of her hand. It was a mess. 'I guess it is,' she said and burst into tears.

He gathered her against his chest and just held her, letting her cry. Every once in a while he awkwardly patted her back.

After a minute, she pulled herself together and wiped her tears with the heels of her hands. 'Sorry for being such a cry-baby.'

'Are you serious? Those creeps attacked you. If you didn't cry, I'd be a little freaked out.'

She tried to laugh but it came out as cross between a whimper and a hiccup. 'What're you doing here?'

'I heard you scream.'

'But how, where—'

'I'd gone back to Sacred Grounds, hoping you were still there. To get your number.'

'You did?'

He laughed. 'Why do you sound so surprised?'

'Are you serious?'

He looked confused by the question. 'Think you can stand?'

She nodded and he helped her to her feet.

'We better call the cops.'

'No.' She shook her head. 'No cops.'

'Those guys—'

'My roommate's a cop. I'll tell her.' He didn't look convinced. 'Please. I just want to go home.'

'Where do you live?'

'A few blocks up. On Dante.'

'You think you can walk it?'

She nodded, though her legs felt rubbery. 'I'm fine. Thanks for your help.'

His eyebrows shot up. 'You don't seriously think I'm just going to leave you to walk home alone?' He must have read her expression, because he frowned. 'No, Angel, I'm not.'

He put an arm around her. 'Let's take it slow to start.'

She nodded. They went a few steps before she remembered and suddenly stopped. 'Wait, my purse! The first guy snatched it—'

'And you ran after him.'

'Yes.'

'And the other guy was waiting and jumped you. Classic move.'

It was. And pretty stupid of her, falling for it. She was smarter than that.

'There it is,' he said, pointing toward a cluster of azalea bushes. 'I'll get it.'

When he handed it to her, she looked quickly through and let out a sigh of relief. 'They didn't take anything.'

'They must not have had time.' He put his arm around her again. 'Come on, let me get you home.'

Despite the ten-year age gap and the differences in their backgrounds, Bailey was meant to be with Logan – she's sure of it. It's natural that they should marry as soon as they can.

But when Logan brings Bailey home to his magnificent estate on ninety wooded acres, her dreams of happily-ever-after begin to unravel. She can't ignore the rumours about what happened to Logan's first wife and then when a local woman goes missing, all signs point to her husband.

Has Bailey made a terrible mistake trusting Logan? What happened to his first wife? Suddenly Bailey is facing an impossible decision: should she believe what everyone is saying, or should she bet her life on the man she loves, but hardly knows?

Complex, compulsively readable and utterly thrilling, *The First Wife* is a sensational novel from internationally bestselling author Erica Spindler.